After th

Susan E Jones

First published in 2023 by Blossom Spring Publishing
After the Rain Copyright © 2023
ISBN 978-1-7392326-7-2
E: admin@blossomspringpublishing.com
W: www.blossomspringpublishing.com
Published in the United Kingdom. All rights reserved under
International Copyright Law.

For Jan

"I chose you because of your education and love of reading." These were the lofty words Mrs Grist wrote in her letter informing me that I was her selected candidate for the position of 'lady's companion' – a role that I still think I'm unfit to fulfil.

The news of my success came as such a surprise that I had to read the letter several times before I could believe what I was being told. How can I describe my feelings once it had finally sunk in? No sense of pride or satisfaction, certainly, but relief perhaps that the struggle to keep a roof over my head was over, at least for the time being. But since the news meant that I was to begin a brand new life in London, far from my village in the West Country, it's fair to say that my strongest emotion on receiving the letter was one of fear.

I'd been in service for many years at Farringdale House, the home of Lord and Lady Radcliffe and their family; work which, despite the drudgery, always gave me a sense of accomplishment. It was a pleasure to see the beds well made – the sheets perfectly smoothed down and tightly tucked in – the furniture dusted and polished to a shine, and a blazing fire taking the chill off the rooms that were in use. Now, as Mrs Grist's companion, I do little more than sit with her, make polite conversation, fetch her spectacles or writing paper, compliment her on her piano playing, or read aloud when she complains of tired eyes. I don't particularly enjoy that last task, even though I do love reading and appreciate her taste in novels. She frequently interrupts or sighs when I mispronounce or stumble over a word, which makes me wonder if she's already beginning to regret choosing me as her companion.

It's true what I told her though – I have had an education, though not for as many years as I would have liked. I went to the local school in my village until I was fourteen. Father thought I was clever enough to become a teacher, and although Mother insisted that such a profession would make me too 'high and mighty', he urged me to do well in my lessons. Mother would scoff at his pride in me and point out that if I did become a teacher, I wouldn't be able to marry and what kind of a life would I lead then? I suppose that was true; even if her remarks were a little unkind, she surely had my best interests at heart. Still, I was prepared to give teaching a try, just for a few years at least. But then Father died – he'd suffered from a weak heart since returning from the Crimean War back in the fifties – and Mother took me out of school. My elder brother Edward had already left school and was an apprentice carpenter – a good, solid occupation, according to Mother – while Harold, my younger brother, was permitted to stay on in school until he was fifteen, even though he'd never had a head for academic learning.

Edward, being the eldest, was Mother's favourite, though Harold was almost as close to her heart. My dear sister Ethel, who died in childbirth at the age of twenty-three, was Father's darling, but he always maintained that while she was the beauty of the family, I was the brains. Unfortunately, my brains didn't get me very far after he left us. Mother had good connections with Farringdale House, where she'd worked for the Radcliffes as a housemaid until she married Father, and she recommended me for a position there. She said it would tide me over until I got myself married. After a year or two I didn't mind too much. My head by that time was full of dreams; I'd forgotten about becoming a teacher and all I desired in life was to marry my sweetheart

Arthur and start a family. Sadly, those dreams never came to pass; they were destined to remain illusions of what might have been.

Enough about the past. I'm now a lady's companion and must be thankful that Mrs Grist chose me. Since I wasn't living in London, having never travelled further than twenty miles from my village, she selected me based on an exchange of letters. Later on, she said that she'd been impressed by my letter writing skills and the fact that I'd listed some of the books I'd read, having confessed that reading fiction was one of my favourite pastimes. She told me in her first letter that her husband, Mr Frank Grist, had passed away two years ago and, since her youngest son was no longer living at home, she needed someone with similar interests to converse with at intervals during the day. I worry that once she comes to the conclusion that I'm not a talkative person at all and that my interests, besides reading, are few and far between, she'll have serious misgivings about her decision to employ me.

I hope and pray that my fears are unfounded. I must look on the bright side. After all, here I am, living in London! Who would have thought it possible that Bessie Hardwicke, a spinster of thirty-nine, would have the courage not only to change her residence, but her profession as well? It was actually my best friend Patty who suggested that I apply for the position. Patty lives in London too – though, unlike me, she has a husband. Dear Patty! For years she's been keeping a close eye on me, in the same way that I kept an eye on her when we were at school together and she was bullied because of her limp. As soon as she heard that Farringdale was cutting its household staff and that I could soon be out of a job, she began to search for positions I might be suitable for.

I was so sad to leave Farringdale House, even though

it was no longer as grand as it had been in Mother's time. There was a rumour that once the eldest daughter, Lady Sophia Radcliffe, left for the continent – she was to marry an Italian nobleman of substantial means – some servants would have to be dismissed. I didn't think that would include me as I'd worked there for so long and was well thought of, but I decided to follow Patty's advice, mainly because I was in desperate need of some kind of change in my life. But I'll always be indebted to the Radcliffes for their kindnesses and their interest in me. I'd been a favourite of Lady Marguerite Radcliffe ever since I rescued her youngest son Alexander when he fell into the river. Oh, I wasn't such a heroine – he would never have drowned. But he was stuck in some reeds and I managed to pull him out, along with his brother Cecil's brand new bicycle. If it had been left to Cecil, the bicycle would have been rescued before little Alexander! It was Lady Radcliffe who taught me social etiquette and how to speak correctly – competences I then passed on to my nephew Walter – and she was more than happy to give me a glowing recommendation when I told her of my application. She said she envied me and that if she were ten years younger, she'd move to London herself. I think she was just trying to cheer me up; I hated having to say goodbye to those familiar faces I'd grown to love.

There I go again, talking about the past! It's just that I can't stop thinking about everyone I've left behind, especially the Radcliffes and my dear nephew Walter. But let me now try again to speak about present and not dwell so much on the past.

The first week I was here, Mrs Grist took me on a tour of the city. We sat on the top deck of a red motorbus. It was quite an experience for me as I'd never been on a motorbus before. But I found being up so high quite frightening, especially when the driver turned corners, much too quickly in my opinion. I was terrified the bus would topple over! Mrs Grist pointed out some historic sights, such as Buckingham Palace, the Houses of Parliament, Big Ben, Westminster Abbey, and so on. These were places I'd heard mention of, but never thought I'd see with my own eyes. It was thoughtful of my new employer to show me London in this way, but I was so overwhelmed by the size of the city and its traffic – horse-drawn carts and carriages, motorcabs and buses, bicycles, not to mention the hundreds of pedestrians all moving with a sense of purpose that you just don't see in the village – that I don't think I showed my appreciation in a way that pleased her. To be honest, it was the little things that stuck in my mind, like the girl selling flowers in Trafalgar Square – such an explosion of colour in the baskets that surrounded her! – and the fact that, in residential streets, one could see right into rooms on the first floor of folk's houses. How are the occupants able to bear so many probing eyes?

Mrs Grist hasn't taken me out since then, but I've done a lot of walking on my days off and managed to get a feel for the borough of Wandsworth where we live. The Church of Holy Trinity is not far away and I usually attend the morning service on a Sunday. When I asked Mrs Grist which church she attended, she said she didn't feel the need to worship in public; she had her own ways of communicating with her maker. I must have looked surprised because she then told me, in quite a sharp tone, to fetch her Bible from the bookshelf and to make sure I replaced any books that I borrowed in alphabetical order. She said she'd been shocked to find a Collins next to a Thoreau. I didn't tell her that I haven't as yet borrowed any books at all, or that those I'd removed on *her* instructions were still in a pile on the table next to her easy chair.

"I'd like you to go to the pharmacy, Elizabeth," Mrs Grist says, giving me a shilling. "I need another bottle of my special tonic. I haven't slept for two nights in a row."

She insists on calling me Elizabeth, even though I've told her that I've always been known as Bessie. I can't remember a time when I was called Elizabeth. But Mrs Grist says Elizabeth is a more refined name, and that's how she intends to address me. "Well, don't be surprised if I don't answer to it," I said, without thinking. She looked at me critically and said, "You will answer to whatever I choose to call you." I shall have to be more careful in my responses in future. I don't want to lose this position, as I'd also lose my room and board and, for the first time in my life, would be well and truly destitute.

I've noticed, however, that Mrs Grist often appears to reflect on some of her more cutting remarks and later gives not exactly an apology, but an explanation of sorts. After a few minutes she tells me that the reason she prefers to call me Elizabeth is because she knows how demeaning it can be when people use a diminutive of one's proper name.

"My own Christian name is Frances," she says. "But people insist on calling me Fanny, no matter how many times I correct them. The only person who addressed me as Frances was my husband, and I think kindly of him for that."

Well, all I can say is that I hope there are other reasons for her to think kindly of her late husband aside from his addressing her by a name she prefers!

"In fact," she continues, "funnily enough, his name was Francis. But everyone called him Frank. Fortunately, he never insisted that I call him Francis, or our life together would have become quite confusing!"

She gives a high-pitched laugh that makes me jump.

I have no objection to going to the pharmacy; it's good

to have a reason to go outside for a walk. I've no idea what Mr Fielding, the pharmacist, puts in Mrs Grist's tonic, but she doesn't seem to be able to live without it. I've been sent on the same errand so many times in the last few weeks that Mr Fielding knows me by name. "Bessie," he says, "I know what you're here for," and he produces the tonic without my having to ask for it. For the first week or so he called me Miss Hardwicke, but then asked me what my given name was. I told him it was Elizabeth, but added that everyone called me Bessie. "Then I shall call you Bessie," he said, "that is, of course, if you don't mind." I shook my head and said, "Of course not," and he smiled in a way that made me blush.

I must admit that it took no small amount of courage for me to step inside the pharmacy for the first time. The shop looked so daunting with its many shelves lined with glass bottles of varying size and colour, and the set of apothecaries' scales and pestle and mortar on the gleaming mahogany counter. But Mr Fielding has always made me feel welcome and never fails to put a smile on my face. In fact, I think he's the only person who has greeted me warmly since I arrived in London, other than Mrs Grist of course, but her friendliness on the day of my arrival has been waning ever since.

It's hard to get used to this lack of warmth in those I've met so far. As I've said, I come from a small country village where everyone knows one another and, while that may be a nuisance at times, it does mean that the locals always greet one another cordially and exchange a few words about the weather or their respective families, or any other topic that takes their fancy. Here, it seems, there's none of that. At church, a few of the older – probably widowed – ladies have begun to acknowledge me, but I haven't had a proper conversation with any of them. The younger ones are all with their husbands and children, and the sight of such close-knit families makes me feel so alone. Perhaps it's up to me to speak first, but I feel so shy and out of place. It's obvious that I'm a newcomer and a spinster. I don't want their pity, but I'm desperate for friendship. The only thing that's keeping me going at the moment is the thought that on Sunday week I'll be going to Patty's for tea. I'm counting the days until then.

Patty is married to a Londoner who works as a groundsman at a boys' school in Clapham. His name is Robert Cartwright and he's a kind, worthy man. She met him on the train when she was travelling up to London to visit a distant relative. It was the first time she'd made that journey alone and, as she told me afterwards, she was a bag of nerves. Patty isn't the type of person who would normally talk to strangers – and I don't think Robert is either – but an obstacle on the tracks meant they were both stuck in the same compartment for several hours. It was must have been quite frightening for Patty, and I don't doubt that Robert's kindly presence helped to calm her down. After that, they corresponded for a year or more until finally he made her a marriage proposal by letter. Imagine that! Patty didn't know how to respond – she had never so much as walked out with a man before and was now being proposed to by someone she'd met on the train!

I wish Mother had been alive to witness Patty's marriage. She always scolded me for filling the head of 'that poor girl Patty' with my highfaluting ideas. "You mark my words – she'll never find a husband," she used to say. Well, Mother, Patty's married now, despite my bad influence, which may well have been to her advantage in the end. I was so thrilled to attend Patty's wedding as her maid of honour, though I suppose Mother would have been ashamed that I was still a maid and not a matron.

Before her marriage, Patty was living at home with her mother, Celia Harris, a skilled seamstress, who was beginning to find her work difficult because of arthritis in her hands. Mr Harris had passed away suddenly the previous year and mother and daughter were struggling financially. They had to resort to taking in laundry to help make ends meet. In his letter, Robert said that he would not dream of separating mother and daughter, and that if Patty were to make him the happiest man in the world by accepting his proposal, then Celia should move to London as well. That may have been why Patty cast aside all doubts and consented, as she could never have left her mother alone. My friend's disability – a consequence of polio as a young child – means that too much exertion leaves her feeling exhausted; hence her options for employment – domestic service for instance – are limited. Robert has turned out to be heaven sent. He adores Patty and treats Celia like his own mother. I'm happy to say that the feeling is now mutual. Sadly, they are unable to have children. I know Patty would have loved a child of her own, but Robert says he doesn't mind. He's around youngsters all day long and claims that all he needs at home is peace and quiet.

I feel a bit more cheerful today. I've just received a postcard from Walter, my nephew, who's like a son to me. He's my late sister's only child and has just turned nineteen. When Ethel was taken from us, Walter was just five years old. My stillborn niece Catherine was put to rest with her mother in a grave alongside those of our parents. Frederick Blanch, Ethel's husband, loved her dearly and we all thought he'd never leave little Walter, but he wasn't able to cope without his wife. He returned to his hometown in Lancashire to live with his brother, who found him a job at one of the cotton mills. Walter was left with my older brother Edward and his wife Mabel, with the understanding that Fred would be back for him as soon as he was settled. But he never returned.

Edward and Mabel's two sons were already nine and ten years old at the time of Ethel's death and, although Edward didn't mind taking Walter in, Mabel was none too pleased about having to care for a younger child. I suppose she did her best, but her temper had always been short and, as a result, Walter didn't have the happiest of childhoods. Some years later, we heard that Frederick had remarried and was a father to two more children, but they are all strangers to Walter. I'd always had a soft spot for my little nephew and on Sunday afternoons, when the weather was fine, I'd take him for walks in the woods or along the riverbank where we'd feed the ducks, look for water voles, or catch tiddlers in the shallows. We'd then have a picnic and I'd read him stories from the children's books I'd borrowed from the Farringdale House nursery. I loved those afternoons with Walter and I like to think that he enjoyed them just as much as I did.

The Great Globe in Swanage is pictured on the front of the card. Walter writes:

'Dear Aunt, I hope this finds you well, as it leaves me. We are presently camping at Swanage. We arrived here on Thursday and are having splendid weather so far. Shall be stopping here for a fortnight. Sadly, Joseph was unable to come to camp this time due to illness. We all hope he will get better soon. Don't you think the Great Globe is a wondrous sight? It stands some ten feet in diameter, weighs 40 tons, and is situated near Durlston Castle. I hope to be able to see it for myself before returning home. With much love, Walter'

The enormous globe is indeed a marvellous sight to behold and I do hope Walter has some free time to visit it before leaving Swanage. He's a member of the Territorial Force, which is made up of volunteer infantry battalions and is considered an alternative to conscription. He's been enrolled in the Territorials for two years now and this is his second time away at camp. Going to camp is like a holiday for Walter. Not only does he learn the basics of musketry and skills required for armed combat, but he also makes new friends and plays lots of sports. It's such a pity that his cousin Joseph – brother Harold's eldest son – is unable to go with him this time. I know he was looking forward to the training just as much as Walter was.

Walter has always been close to Harold's children – Joseph, Margaret and Richard. In fact, he would have been much happier living with them, as Harold's wife Dorothy is a kind, sweet woman and would have loved Walter as one of her own. But, being the eldest, Edward felt responsible for him when Ethel died and Frederick left the village. Not only that, but he was earning good money as a skilled carpenter and in a better financial position than Harold to support an additional child.

"Is your nephew William an educated boy?" Mrs Grist asks me when I show her the postcard. "How does he earn his living?"

"His name is Walter, not William," I say, "and, yes, he's had an education. He's a stonemason and is never without work. He completed his parish apprenticeship last year and is now taking on jobs independently."

"Well, I suppose one trade is as good as another," she says dismissively.

I feel like pointing out to Mrs Grist how capable Walter is in his job, which requires both creative talent and physical strength, but I say nothing. It also annoys me that she insists on misremembering his name. This is the third or fourth time she's called him something other than Walter. It's as if she does it on purpose. Being a lady's companion is much harder than I thought it would be! There's no physical activity to tire me out, like at Farringdale House, but there's more than enough mental aggravation! I'm finding it difficult to sleep at night – my mind keeps going over and over Mrs Grist's remarks as I try to find some words of kindness or encouragement. But I've found few so far; instead, my employer seems determined to make me feel inadequate and homesick.

It's a muggy afternoon in late August and we're sitting in the drawing room, me on the settee and Mrs Grist in her easy chair. It's a large room with wide bay windows and sturdy wooden floors, covered by two exquisitely patterned Turkey carpets. The settee, two easy chairs and an ottoman are situated around the fireplace; no fire has been lit for several days because of the warm weather. A round mahogany table – covered with writing and sewing materials – several upright chairs, a sideboard, a console with drawers and a piano fill the other half of the room. At that end, double doors lead through to the dining room, where Mrs Grist takes her meals. The dining room, in turn, has a door that opens onto the stairs leading down to the kitchen.

My own room is in the attic and is furnished with a single bed, a narrow wardrobe and a small chest of drawers. I don't need more; my possessions are few and far between. The best thing about the room is that it looks out onto a garden at the back of the house. I am so glad to have a small window, which I keep open most of the time. In the early mornings, listening to the dawn chorus, I can almost imagine I'm back in the countryside. In fact, I sometimes think that there are more birds nesting here in London than back home. Why they choose to stay in the city, I cannot imagine, though Mrs Grist believes it's because there are fewer predators here than in rural areas.

The garden was probably well cared for when Mr Grist was alive, but it's now overgrown and unkempt. But I don't mind. I love to see the grass with its carpet of daisies and buttercups, the honeysuckle vine, and the pink and white hydrangeas that are now at their peak. And there's an alder tree at the far end of the lawn, which provides some shade on sunny days.

One Sunday, shortly after I arrived here, I took a chair outside and sat reading my book. Mrs Grist came back unexpectedly in the middle of the afternoon and asked me what on earth did I think I was doing. I just said I was just enjoying the fine weather and did she mind if I made use of the garden once in a while? She said she didn't mind, but to make sure that I brought the chair inside in case it rained later on. As if I would leave it outside! But I think she must have been embarrassed by the state of the garden, as the next day she gave a young lad sixpence to tidy it up. He didn't know what he was doing, but went to work – or, I should say, ran amok – with a pair of shears and then spent an hour or so pulling up what he thought were weeds, but were in fact wildflowers. To be honest, I think the garden looked much better before he'd ever set foot in it.

My employer is busy with her sampler – making slow progress in my humble opinion – and I'm knitting a pullover for brother Edward, though my hands are so clammy that I keep dropping stitches. I have Walter's postcard next to me and from time to time I re-read his message, admiring his neat cursive handwriting.

"Does Wilbur have a young lady?" Mrs Grist asks, observing me still looking at the card.

"Do you mean Walter?" I say, finding it hard to

hide my irritation.

"Your nephew," she says.

"Yes, Walter does have a young lady he's presently stepping out with. She's a lovely girl, both pretty and intelligent. Her name is Edie. But neither one is in a hurry to settle down. They're prepared to let time takes its course."

"And this Edie, is she in domestic service?"

"No, she's training to be a nurse. She attends lectures at the hospital in town and is starting to help with patient care."

"So she's from a middle class family?"

"She's from a farming family. But she's always wanted to be a nurse and, fortunately, her parents support her choice of career and are paying for her studies. Her two older brothers both work on the farm."

"Hmm, I see. If she's as lovely as you say she is, unless he acts quickly, Wilbur may lose her to one of the doctors. They often choose their sweethearts from among the nursing staff."

"If you mean Walter, I don't think he has any fear of that happening."

"Mark my words, Elizabeth – a stonemason's wife may not be so appealing to her once she starts mixing with those in the medical profession. Besides, she'll have to give up being a nurse if she intends to marry. Has your nephew considered that?"

"I'm sure he has, but they're both still young and I don't think marriage has entered into either of their heads just yet."

"Well, if he wants to keep her, he'll need to make his intentions clear, and I would advise him to do that sooner rather than later."

I try to think of a response that will put Mrs Grist in her place, but there's nothing I can say without causing offence. My employer, it seems, always has to have the last word.

2

Patty and Robert live in the borough of Lambeth, close to Clapham Common. Robert has written to me, providing detailed directions on how to get there tomorrow. It's about two miles from Mrs Grist's house so shouldn't take me too long on foot. I'm hoping that the rain will hold off. It's rained constantly for the last few days, which hasn't helped in lifting my spirits, though I am buoyed by the thought of seeing my dear friends once again. I'm not saying it doesn't rain just as much in the West Country – it does. But in the countryside a rain shower makes everything look fresh and clean – the grass is greener and the flowers are more colourful and vibrant. Mr Blake, the gardener at Farringdale House, used to say with a chuckle that the flowers had washed their faces and were ready to greet the public, while the trees, shaking raindrops from their leaves, were telling us to steer clear unless we wanted *our* faces washed. In the city, in comparison, the rain just makes the streets muddier and more slippery, and the humidity following a shower causes the ever-present smell of sewage and refuse to become even more pungent.

Mrs Grist looks surprised when I tell her I'm going to Clapham on Sunday to visit my friend from the village.

"Oh, your friend Patricia?" she says. "The one you were at school with?"

"Yes," I say. "Patty. She's my oldest and dearest friend."

"How fortunate that she married into a good family," she says, methodically sealing the letters she wants me to post and affixing a penny stamp to each of them.

"Oh, I don't think Robert's family is any better off than Patty's. His father was a chimney sweep who was born and raised in a London workhouse. But Robert was more fortunate. He had a good singing voice and was spotted by his church chorister, who then went on to support his education."

I have said more than I intended, but hope that by drawing attention to Robert's humble origins, she will understand that Patty has not married above her station. I think she believes Robert to be a teacher at the school, whereas in fact he's a groundsman. Since I know that this knowledge will cause my friends to fall considerably in Mrs Grist's estimation, I shall not be the one to enlighten her on such a detail. In fact, although his daily occupation is not equal to his hard-earned qualifications, he does tutor some of the younger boys in reading and arithmetic in the evenings, a task which supplements the meagre wage he receives each week for taking care of the grounds. So I am not being entirely dishonest in letting Mrs Grist continue to believe that he is one of the teaching staff.

"I see," she says. "Well, he's certainly done well for himself if his background is as lowly as you say."

"He has, but he's worked hard for his gains. There are those who have the advantage of a good education, but don't do well because they are too lazy to study. Robert is not like that at all. He didn't want to let his benefactor down, so he studied day and night to make sure he did well in school."

I suddenly recall overhearing a conversation between Mrs Evans, the housekeeper, and Mrs Hopper, the cook, during which Mrs Evans said that Mrs Grist's youngest son Phillip was an idle boy in his youth and loath to study. In the end, his uncle found him a job with an insurance broker. Mind you, the housekeeper and the cook are always gossiping – I don't think they have a good word to say about anyone – so what Mrs Evans said may not be true. In any case, Mrs Grist doesn't seem the least bit put out by my last remark; perhaps she's always believed that Phillip, her favourite child by all accounts, is just as diligent as his two brothers.

Talking about Mrs Evans and Mrs Hopper, I should mention that they are both quite hostile towards me. I've tried to be friendly with them, but to no avail. I think they regard my position as being above theirs – which I suppose it is – but I do wish they'd treat me as an equal. The fact is, I still think of myself as a servant rather than a lady's companion. I haven't told them anything about my background, as I haven't had a proper conversation with either of them – they both seem intent on ignoring me. But I've heard them making fun of my accent. It's true that my West Country accent is quite different from theirs, which I believe to be Cockney. Mrs Hopper, according to Mrs Grist, was born within earshot of Bow Bells – that is, the bells of the Church of Mary-le-Bow in Cheapside – which apparently makes her a true Cockney. Sometimes I'm unable to understand what they're saying to each other, as they often talk in what's called 'rhyming slang'. I think they do it on purpose to confuse me. We have many odd expressions in the West Country, which are probably quite foreign to a Londoner, but to say 'apples and pears' instead of 'stairs' seems to me to be a very strange way of talking. Something else I need to get used to, I suppose.

Yesterday, when I went to the kitchen to make myself a cup of tea – it was quite late in the evening and Mrs Grist had gone to bed – they were sitting together at the kitchen table enjoying a glass of sherry. I knew it was Mrs Evans' birthday, as I'd heard Mrs Hopper wishing her many happy returns earlier in the day. I greeted them both in a friendly manner – sometimes I think I overdo it – but they just said, "Evening" and carried on with their conversation in hushed tones. I hurriedly made my tea, as it was clear that my presence was unwelcome. Well, from now on, I won't make any effort to be friendly. I'm desperate for friendship, but I'm certainly not going to beg for it.

Come to think of it, it was a bit strange to find them in the kitchen at that hour. Neither one lives in the house. Mrs Evans usually leaves at about five o'clock and Mrs Hopper at about seven after serving Mrs Grist her supper. She often leaves the washing up until the next morning. On my first evening in the house, I did it for her. Since I have my own supper in the kitchen, I didn't think twice about washing all the dirty dishes afterwards. Never again. Mrs Hopper was furious. I thought it was a kindness, but she obviously thought I was poaching on her turf. Now I just wash my own plate and leave the rest. It goes against the grain, but I don't want another confrontation. At Farringdale House we used to share the chores. There was no pecking order amongst the servants and everyone was treated equally. I would always be grateful if Amelia or one of the other girls changed the bed linen in Lady Radcliffe's room, and they would thank me if I took it upon myself to scrub the kitchen floor. Still, there's no point in reminiscing about those times. I'm a lady's companion now and must start acting like one.

Anyway, the fact that Mrs Evans and Mrs Hopper were sipping sherry together in the kitchen so late in the evening made me wonder. Why were they not at home with their families? After all, they are both married with several children. Wouldn't Mrs Evans want to celebrate her birthday with her family rather than in the company of Mrs Hopper with whom she gossips all day long? And while I wouldn't dream of saying anything to Mrs Grist, I'm pretty sure that the sherry comes from one of bottles she keeps in the pantry for special occasions. I just hope she doesn't suspect me of pilfering!

Finally it's Sunday, after a week when time seemed to drag endlessly. Fortunately, the rainclouds gave way to clear blue skies yesterday evening and today is sunny and warm. I usually rise at seven so as to have my breakfast in the kitchen before Mrs Hopper arrives at eight o'clock. But on Sundays I have a bit of a lie in, since neither she nor Mrs Evans comes to work and it is, after all, my day of rest. The church service doesn't start until ten o'clock, so there's no need for me to hurry. Mrs Grist usually visits the home of one of her sons or her sister-in-law on Sundays, so is absent for most of the day. It's such a pleasure to return to an empty house after church and to be free to read or write letters in my room and take my meals in the kitchen without fear of disturbing Mrs Hopper.

Although Patty and Robert aren't expecting me until three o'clock, I decide to leave early and spend some time on Clapham Common before making my way to their house. Mrs Grist says there's a motorbus that will take me there, but I tell her I prefer to walk. She also asks me if I've been on the underground railway since arriving in London. I shake my head and tell her that I find the thought of travelling underground rather frightening and certainly wouldn't attempt it alone. She gives me one of her scornful looks. Perhaps when Walter visits me, I might suggest a journey on the underground railway, which Londoners call 'the Tube'. I won't be the least bit afraid if he's with me. He said he would try to fit in a trip before the end of year and I'm keeping my fingers crossed that he's able to do so.

For once, it's quiet in the streets. A few children are out playing with their hoops or enjoying a game of tag, and one or two couples are taking a leisurely stroll in their Sunday best, the ladies looking most elegant in their fine silks and matching parasols. My walk takes me past the hosier and draper, the confectioners and my favourite, the jeweller and watchmaker. I spend a minute or two looking at the beautiful pocket watches in the shop window and wish I had the money to buy a brand new one for Walter. Mrs Grist pays me a small wage, in addition to my room and board, but it barely covers my personal needs, minimal though they are. Still, I'm putting away a few pennies a week and will make sure I have enough saved to show Walter around the city if and when he visits.

I stop for a few minutes on the bridge over the River Wandle and observe a group of six or seven swans. Their shapely white bodies are too beautiful for the muddy brown water through which they move with such grace. The sight of these regal birds makes me nostalgic for the River Frome near my old family home in the West Country. Patty, Ethel and I used to play on its banks when we were children and we'd often see a family of swans gliding past. We'd pause in our game of make-believe and gaze at them in awe. I remember that before going home, we'd collect bunches of wild watercress and give them to Mother for sandwiches and salad. Or in the early autumn, we'd pick blackberries and rose hips and return home with stained hands and clothes. Those simple pleasures seem a lifetime ago. It's been fourteen years since Ethel left us. Father and Mother were already in their graves, and so was my Arthur. No, I mustn't think about Arthur now. Even after all this time, the thought of losing him is still so painful.

Once I reach Clapham Common, I sit down on the grass near one of the ponds where some small boys are floating their model boats. From here I can see the bandstand with its distinctive cupola and elegant columns. Mrs Grist told me that it's the largest one in London. Not having seen any others, I cannot dispute that claim. Families and couples are spreading out blankets close to the platform, which suggests that there may be a concert later this afternoon. Patty and Robert are indeed fortunate to live so close to such a wide expanse of greenery and to be able to take advantage of free entertainment on a Sunday afternoon or evening. It's so pleasant sitting here, watching folk relaxing and having fun as if they haven't a care in the world, though I expect they have their worries like the rest of us. I'd like to stay longer, but of course, Patty is waiting for me and I'm longing to see her – it's been more than a year since we were last together.

My friends live close to the south boundary of the common. Robert says the Roman Catholic school for boys, where he works, is less than a quarter of a mile from their house. Did I mention that Robert is a Roman Catholic? Patty said right from the start that it didn't bother her one little bit, but I think her mother Celia was a bit wary at first. But she's now come to appreciate what a fine person Robert is, and says that if anyone dares to denounce his faith in her presence, she'll give them a piece of her mind! A bishop's consent was needed for the marriage, which was quite an ordeal at the time, but Patty now believes it makes their union more sacrosanct. She and her mother usually attend the local Anglican church on Sunday mornings, but Robert is not a regular churchgoer, despite being a devout Catholic. He says there's enough religion at the school to make up for his frequent absence from church on a Sunday, so he's sure he will be forgiven. But Patty says he regularly goes to confession to admit his guilt, just in case!

Their two-up two-down terraced house is like all the

others in the street and has no yard or garden in the front. It must have taken Patty and her mother some time to get used to living in a house where the front doorstep meets the pavement, especially since their West Country cottage had an exquisite rose garden in the front and a large vegetable patch at the back. But after Mr Harris died, Celia found it difficult to manage the garden and Patty couldn't help much because of her disability. So perhaps it was a blessing that they had a good reason to give up their village home, difficult though it must have been.

I can see Patty peeping through the net curtains as I approach her front door. She opens it before I have a chance to knock.

"Bessie, my dearest friend!" she cries, hugging me tightly. "I can't tell you how pleased I am to see you! It's been such a long time! Come on in."

I'm quite overcome with emotion as I follow Patty into her front room. My eyes fill with tears as I relish this longed-for moment. And there is her mother Celia, looking just the same, despite her change in circumstance. She gets up from her window seat and also gives me a hug. It's wonderful to be amongst friends once again.

"Robert will be back very soon," Patty says. "He just had to pop over to the school to talk to one of the boarders. He tries to involve himself in the boys' lives, even though he's only a groundsman. I think the Catholic brothers are a bit strict, so for the younger ones, he's a friendly face. Sit yourself down, Bessie. You must be tired from your walk."

"Oh, Patty, don't fuss," I say. "I'm not tired at all. I sat on the common for almost an hour before coming here. It's such a lovely day and there was so much to see. How elegant some of the ladies look in the latest fashions! You'd never see styles like that in the West Country, would you? Apart from the young ladies at Farringdale House, of course. But I still haven't got used to all the hustle and bustle of the city. You know how slow life was in the village. How long did it take you to feel at home in London?"

"I still don't feel at home, Bessie. I yearn for the countryside – the green meadows, the shady woods, the rippling brooks… I'm sounding quite poetic, but I could go on and on. Still, I'm not complaining. We have everything we need here, and Robert is so good to both of us. And we do have a small garden at the back of the house – you'll see it later. The soil is chalky, so it's hard to grow anything, but it's better than nothing. Robert says that when he gets a break, he'll take us to the country for a few days. We can stay on his brother's farm in Surrey. The fresh air will do us all good."

I'm glad to hear that I'm not the only one who misses the village. But then Patty points out that the one thing she doesn't miss is the village gossip! And for that matter, neither do I. I remember that when it became known that Patty had a sweetheart, it was the number one gossip item. It was always assumed that because of her disability, she'd be unable to find a husband. She believed that too – despite my strongly disputing it – and nobody could have been more surprised than Patty herself when the gossipmongers were proved wrong. How pleased that made me!

"And you, Aunt Celia?" I say, turning to her mother. "Do you miss the village?"

"Oh no, not at all," Celia says to my surprise. "I like it here much more than Patty does. Sitting by the window and watching the world go by is one of my favourite pastimes. We couldn't do that back home. We didn't have the time and, besides, hardly anyone passed by our house. And if a soul did walk by and you were looking out, they'd be staring in at you!"

"Oh, Mother!" Patty exclaims. "Who wants to look at people? We used to watch the birds and the squirrels, and remember the little hedgehog that visited us every day? I miss him so much!"

"But Patty, it's so much more interesting to observe people," Celia counters. "Why, this morning I saw the lady who wears that preposterous red hat with a feather in it, and she was with yet another gentleman! That's three different suitors in one week!"

"Really, Mother. He may have been her brother or a relative. You do talk nonsense sometimes."

Patty and Celia are so different, not just in character but in their looks too. Patty takes after her father. She's taller than Celia, has soulful brown eyes and a pale complexion. She always wears her dark hair in a bun at the nape of her neck, but I've seen her with it loose and it's thick and wavy. Celia, on the other hand, has blue eyes, a rosy complexion and flaxen hair, though it's mostly silvery grey now. They disagree all the time, but neither one could live without the other. When Patty contracted polio as a child, Celia really thought she was going to lose her only child. She has never forgotten the devastation she felt at that time and thanks the Lord every single day for letting her daughter live.

"Now, Bessie," Patty says. "You must tell us all about your new position. Is the formidable Mrs Grist really as awful as you've made out in your letters?"

"She's not really that bad," I say, feeling a bit guilty. "I think I may have exaggerated. But she does sometimes make unkind remarks without realising it. I'm sure if she thought twice before blurting things out, she'd realise that some of the things she says are quite hurtful. She has some good qualities though – she's generous and doesn't make too much of a fuss when things go wrong. For instance, yesterday, the housekeeper broke a vase and I think it was of some value. Mrs Grist just told her not to worry about it, that she'd never liked it anyway. Not many employers would be that understanding."

"That's true. How are *your* relations with the housekeeper, Bessie? Any better?"

"No, Patty, not at all. Mrs Evans isn't the least bit friendly towards me, and neither is Mrs Hopper, the cook. Believe me, I've tried my best to get along with them. I'm not a very sociable person, as you know, but I've really made an effort. Still, they seem determined to dislike me, however friendly I try to be. Nothing I do or say will melt their icy looks. I'm not going to try anymore."

Tears fill my eyes for a second time as I speak about my troubles, and Patty hands me a hankie as I search for mine. I don't want to spoil our time together by being miserable, but I really do feel hurt by the treatment I've had to put up with, which is so unjustified.

"Don't get upset, dear Bessie," Patty says, putting her arm around me. "Once they understand that you're not a threat to them, they'll be more friendly – I'm sure of that. When we first moved here, I found it so difficult to talk to people. I always thought they despised me because I wasn't from around here and talked with a strange accent. But now I realise that it was all in my head. They didn't despise me at all – they neither liked nor disliked me. When you think about it, it's no different back home – it's just that we'd known the local people all our lives and knew where we stood with them. Any strangers in the village would be looked at with suspicion until folk knew what their intentions were. The first time Robert visited, he was treated with such wariness, you'd have thought he'd committed some kind of a crime!"

"Yes, of course, you're right," I say, though I'm not at

all convinced that things will improve in the Grist household. "I'm sorry, Patty. Let's not talk about those women any more. I hear a key in the door. Is that Robert coming in?"

The front door opens and Robert steps into the parlour. He's a short man – possibly an inch or two shorter than Patty – and slight in build, with receding dark hair and spectacles. He could never be described as handsome, but what he lacks in appearance, he more than makes up for in character. And Patty says he's much stronger than he looks; she's seen him pull up the roots of a tree stump with his own two hands.

Patty immediately gets up to put the kettle on and Robert sits down in the easy chair next to Celia's window seat.

"You look well, Bessie," he says. "I hope London's living up to your expectations. How are you settling in? Do you like your new job?"

"Oh, I like it well enough," I say, not wanting to repeat my complaints to Robert. "Of course, changes are not easy for someone of my age, so it's probably taking me longer to get used to my new situation than it would were I ten years younger."

"Listen to yourself, Bessie! At your age! Come on now, you're still a young woman. You don't look a day over thirty."

"Well, thank you for the compliment, Robert, but I'm in my fortieth year, as you well know. Patty and I are the exact same age. But don't think I'm complaining – I'm not. I was ready for a change and I couldn't wish for a better position. I'm practically a lady of leisure now."

"You deserve nothing less. There's not a day that goes by when Patty doesn't speak about what a good friend you've been to her."

I feel myself reddening. I'm not used to receiving

compliments. Fortunately, Patty comes in with a tray of cups and saucers, which she places on a side table. I get up from my seat and go into the kitchen to help her. She's prepared an appetising spread of dainty sandwiches, slices of home-baked Madeira cake, and scones with strawberry jam and Devonshire cream.

"We usually have our meals in the kitchen," Patty says, "but you're our special guest and it's much nicer in the parlour. You take the teapot and plates through and I'll bring the sandwiches and cakes."

"It all looks delicious, Patty. You shouldn't have gone to so much trouble."

"What trouble? We have to have tea, Bessie. Robert is always starving when he comes in from work. And it's no different on a Sunday – he's just as hungry. For a small man, he eats enough for someone twice his size!"

Patty is really spoiling me. I can see that she's brought out her best tea service; it's of fine bone china, prettily decorated with violets. The scones and slices of cake are carefully arranged on a three-tiered stand, and she's made a pyramid of the sandwiches. It's nice to be fussed over, but I wish I were able to reciprocate in some way.

"Now, milk and one sugar, isn't it Bessie?" Patty says. "Help yourself to sandwiches. There's egg and cress, tongue and mustard, and salmon paste. Take a few before Robert devours the lot."

"There's a boy at the school," Robert says as we begin to fill our plates, "who's having difficulty settling in. He's younger than most of the lads, and he's a boarder. His parents died in a tragic accident and an uncle – a bachelor, whom he barely knows – is now his guardian. The man clearly doesn't want to bother himself with raising the boy, so has sent him to board at the school. It's a good school and the fees are not insignificant, so I suppose he does have the child's best interests at heart.

But Brother Luke tells me that his reading skills are poor and he's falling behind in class. I'd like to tutor him myself, but Patty will never forgive me if I stay at the school a moment later than I already do. So I was wondering, Bessie, if you'd be interested in reading with the boy, perhaps for an hour or two every other Sunday afternoon? Patty told me what a wonderful job you did with your nephew. You're obviously a natural teacher. What do you say to helping this poor lad?"

I say nothing for a few moments. Robert's request has caught me off guard. It's true that I helped Walter improve his reading skills, but do I want to do the same with an unknown boy, who is obviously still distraught from the loss of his parents? But how can I possible refuse given his present circumstances? Even if he makes no progress at all in reading, he'll come to know that he can turn to me for solace as he tries to find his place in the frightening world of older boys and male teachers.

"Yes, of course," I say finally. "I'll be happy to help him, but please don't expect miracles. Walter was keen to learn and trusted me. I was his aunt after all, and we were close. This boy may not be so accepting of my efforts."

"I think he will, Bessie. He's a good boy, though terribly shy. Why don't you give it a try next Sunday? If the weather's fine you can take him to the park or the common, or if it's raining, you're welcome to use the school library. His name is Michael Turnbull and he's eleven years old. I can give you a couple of books from the school library to start off with if you like. *Tom Brown's Schooldays* might be a good choice. Hughes' classic would give the boy some tips about boarding school life – not much has changed in the last seventy years – and what he has to say about bullying may be of consolation. It's my belief he's being bullied, which is not helping him get over his sorrow."

"My goodness, the poor lad. Don't the other boys have any idea what he's going through?"

"Probably not. And, to be honest, most of them have their own personal misfortunes, which are often just as bad as Michael's. For now, he just needs to understand that to be the victim is practically a rite of passage for new boys at boarding school. Anyhow, see how it goes, Bessie. And if you have other books in mind, then feel free to use them too."

"Walter used to enjoy *David Copperfield* when he was about the same age. I still have a copy that I can bring along. Dickens also wrote about bullying – how David suffered when he was sent away to school – but there's a lot of joy in the novel too."

"That sounds perfect. Shall we plan to meet next Sunday? You'll be doing the boy a huge favour, believe me. Thank you, Bessie."

The more I think about it, the more I question what I'm getting myself into. I know nothing about this boy and he may well object to having reading lessons on his day of rest. Robert has proposed that I 'give it a try', as if our first meeting is to be a trial. But I know full well that even if Michael is difficult, I won't want to admit failure and will persevere, not just to gain Robert's approval, but also to prove to myself that my success with Walter can indeed be replicated.

Still, I'm half inclined to write to Robert and tell him I've changed my mind – that I'm not up to the challenge – but then I receive another postcard from Walter, which makes me determined to keep my promise. He writes so beautifully, with no spelling or grammatical mistakes, and I know it's thanks to my efforts that he's become more literate than many who've received a far better education than that provided by our village school.

The postcard shows a picture of Christ Church College, Oxford University. It reads:

'Dear Aunt, You will see from this card that I arrived here safely, just after five o'clock. I came through Reading, which is a longer route, making it about 65 miles. I had a puncture two miles out of Oxford, so had to walk that. Oxford looks like a splendid place – I can see why they call it the city of spires. The ancient university buildings are a source of inspiration for a stonemason like myself. I hope you will like this card. Christ Church is one of the most impressive colleges and was founded in 1546. Thank you for your kind letter. Your affectionate nephew, Walter.'

He cycled sixty-five miles! And knowing Walter, he probably did it all in one go without even stopping for a break. He doesn't say what he's doing in Oxford, but I imagine that it's building restoration work of one kind or another. The centuries-old colleges must be in constant need of repair by skilled stonemasons like Walter. But as much as he enjoys his work, I'm sure that being in a university town is going to make him wish he'd had a college education himself. I know he'd have succeeded in whatever profession he elected to study. If only I'd had the funds to support him!

So I *will* meet with Michael next Sunday. If I can pass on to him the lifelong love of books that I've instilled in Walter, then I'll have done him a good turn. After all, my position here with Mrs Grist provides me with little fulfilment. Perhaps the task of befriending Michael and teaching him to appreciate the works of our great authors will give me a new sense of purpose. However much I try to ignore the fact, becoming a lady's companion has created a hole in my life that I've so far been unable to fill with anything meaningful. Hopefully, that's about to change.

3

Mrs Grist is unwell and has taken to her bed. Insisting that it's a bout of influenza, she asks me to go to the pharmacy to pick up another bottle of her tonic, as well as some eucalyptus oil that she intends to inhale. Mr Fielding raises his eyebrows when I request the latter of these items.

"What exactly is wrong with her?" he asks, retrieving a bottle of the famous tonic from underneath the counter.

"She just says she has the flu," I say. "She does seem a bit feverish and complains of a headache, but other than that..."

"Mrs Grist regularly *says* she has the flu, Bessie. A distant relative of hers died from the Russian pandemic in Ireland some twenty years ago and, since then, every time she feels the slightest bit unwell, she thinks she's caught the same sickness. She's probably just under the weather, but if you notice her condition deteriorating, then you should tell her to send for the doctor. She probably won't want to do that; not because of the expense, but because she knows full well that she's exaggerating. Still, you need to insist on it. As I've told her a thousand times, *I* am not a doctor."

The thought of insisting on anything with Mrs Grist fills me with dread. Mr Fielding notices my glum expression.

"What's the matter, Bessie?" he says.

"I don't think she'll listen to me," I say hesitantly, "but I'll give it a try."

"Don't worry. I'm sure her sickness won't last for more than a day or two. Here is the eucalyptus oil. She should just add two or three drops to boiling water and then inhale. Make sure she takes plenty of hot drinks – a beef tea diet will do her good. Tell her I said so."

"All right. Thank you. Goodbye Mr Fielding."

As I turn to leave, a young woman enters the shop, smiling familiarly at the pharmacist.

"Ah, Bessie," Mr Fielding says. "Before you go, let me introduce you to my daughter Mathilda. Mathilda, this is one of my best customers, Miss Bessie Hardwicke."

"Oh, I'm pleased to meet you, Miss Hardwicke," Mathilda says warmly. "How is it that I haven't seen you around before now?"

"I've only been living in the neighbourhood for a couple of months," I say. "I live in the next street but one, with Mrs Grist. I'm pleased to make your acquaintance too."

"Mrs Grist? Really? Now that's someone I *do* know." She steals a look at her father. "She's also a frequent customer, isn't she, Papa?"

"She used to be, but Bessie runs her errands now," Mr Fielding says. "She's Fanny's companion and a most pleasant one I must say." He turns to me and adds, "Mathilda was my assistant-cum-housekeeper before she became Mrs Ronald Cavendish earlier in the year. Now she's left me all alone, fending for myself."

"Oh come off it, Papa. I'm here almost every day to bring you your dinner and to tidy up after you. Ronald says I look after you more than I do him."

I've always imagined Mr Fielding to be a family man with a wife and several children. But Mathilda's last remark implies that her mother is no longer living. I don't know why, but I feel a bit embarrassed to witness such banter between father and daughter. For a second time I turn to leave the shop.

"My wife succumbed to tuberculosis some five years ago," Mr Fielding says, as if reading my mind. "She'd been ill for a long time. Mathilda looked after me – and

34

her mother – for years before she became a married woman."

"I'm so sorry to hear that Mrs Fielding is deceased," I say. "But it must be a blessing for you both to have each other. I'm happy to have met you, Mrs Cavendish. I do hope we meet again."

"Please call me Mathilda, Miss Hardwicke," she says before adding, "and the pleasure is entirely mine."

"Then you must call me Bessie. Goodbye and thank you."

As I walk back to the house, my mind is preoccupied by this unexpected introduction, which has given me a glimpse into Mr Fielding's personal life. Mathilda is an attractive and well-dressed young lady. Beneath her wide-brimmed hat, I noticed that her chestnut hair was carefully styled and soft curls framed her youthful face. Over her high-collared, white silk blouse, she wore a short, dark green velvet jacket that matched her straight, ankle-length skirt. On my regular walks, I've noticed some young ladies with skirts above the ankles, but it seems Mathilda has not yet adopted this new fashion, though I think it would suit her well. I'm no follower of fashion myself, but I like to observe the way the ladies dress here in London and compare them with the Radcliffes, especially Lady Sophia, who frequents some of the most celebrated fashion houses in London and abroad. In my humblest of opinions, Mathilda compares very favourably!

Mrs Grist is annoyed when I tell her Mr Fielding's advice – that she should stick to a beef tea diet, along with plenty of hot drinks, and that the doctor should be sent for if she's no better by the morning.

"Did you really need to tell him so many details, Elizabeth?" she says. "All I asked you to do was to collect my tonic and buy some eucalyptus oil. Why did you need to have a conversation about my health?"

"I'm sorry, Mrs Grist, but he was concerned about you. He wanted to know what your symptoms were when I asked for the eucalyptus oil. I couldn't *not* tell him."

"Does he think he's a qualified doctor? He may be a substitute physician for those who can't afford a proper medic, but *I* am not in that category. You've probably heard him expounding his so-called curative therapies to all and sundry. Beef tea diet indeed! He may think he's doing his customers a kindness, but – mark my words – one day his… his quackery will come back to haunt him!

"In any case, Elizabeth, I'm feeling much better now. Mrs Hopper made me a cup of Horlicks and added a drop of brandy. I fell asleep for an hour or so and when I awoke, I was no longer feverish. So please let Mrs Hopper know that the Horlicks did the trick and that for lunch I'll have a bowl of the oxtail soup she recommended, to be brought to my room. I'm beginning to believe that her remedies are more effective than those of our pharmacist. And I would warn you against fraternising with the man, Elizabeth. He's a widower, as you're no doubt aware, and tongues around here are desperate for a bit of gossip."

My goodness, what on earth can have occurred between Mrs Grist and Mr Fielding to make her so strongly opposed to his harmless suggestions? And to caution me against fraternising! I didn't even know he was a widower until this morning and I certainly wouldn't take advantage of such information. What kind of a person does she take me for? Even more inexplicable is her sudden high regard for Mrs Hopper. After all, it's common knowledge that a cup of Horlicks and a drop of brandy can help to relieve the symptoms of a cold.

The cook doesn't even stop what she's doing to listen

to me as I convey Mrs Grist's message. She refuses to acknowledge my presence the first time I address her, which means I have to repeat the instruction. That doesn't go down too well, but at least she looks up from her task of chopping onions and mutters, "I heard you the first time." Needless to say, I leave the kitchen as quickly as possible.

What do I do now? There are so many hours in the day when I feel completely useless. I can't relax because I'm at Mrs Grist's beck and call. She has a little bell on the table next to her easy chair and another one alongside her bed, which she'll ring when she needs me, so I have to make sure I'm within earshot. Usually she's happy for me to sit with her in the drawing room, reading or sewing, but there are other times when I sense that she prefers to be alone. I'll then excuse myself and escape to my attic room. To be honest, I like it best when she sends me on errands, so I can at least get away from the house and all its tensions for half an hour or so, though I have to be careful not to stray too far, since my absences are usually timed.

Since it looks like she'll be staying in her bedroom for the rest of the day, I begin to search for my battered copy of *David Copperfield*. I couldn't bear to part with the book – its pages brought back so many happy memories. I know that Walter also reminisces about those pleasant afternoons we spent on the riverbank, or in the warm kitchen of Farringdale House when the cold or wet weather kept us inside. I preferred to be out of doors if at all possible, so I could have Walter all to myself. In the kitchen, there would always be someone who'd interrupt our reading or conversation to make a fuss of him and give him treats – a chunk of freshly baked bread slathered with butter, or a jam tart straight from the oven. But I was selfish, I didn't want to share him with anyone.

I know this sounds silly, but I've often drawn parallels between Walter and David Copperfield. There are definitely some similarities. Like David, Walter suffered personal loss at an early age and had to enter the adult world with very little guidance from loved ones. The only person who truly cared for his wellbeing was his aunt – in other words, me. I've taken him under my wing, just as David's Aunt Betsey took him under her wing. Even our names are similar – I'm Aunt Bessie, she's Aunt Betsey. What a strange coincidence!

Walter's Aunt Mabel, Edward's wife, was only too pleased to let me take him out for an afternoon. Not that he caused her any trouble at all – he was a quiet boy and was never rowdy like some of the lads in the village. He loved animals and yearned for a dog, but Mabel was having none of 'that nonsense' as she called it. Edward wouldn't have minded a dog – we'd always had dogs growing up – but Mabel said she had enough bodies to take care of without a dog as well. Later on, when her sons were no longer living at home – one is married and lives in the next village, and the other is an able seaman in the Royal Navy – she only had Walter and Edward to care for, and a dog would have been good company for Walter. Edward certainly didn't need much attention – from early morning until late in the evening, he'd be in his workshop, oblivious of the hour. It's my belief that Walter sensed that he never truly belonged to Edward's family and, to add to his misery, he was made fun of at the local school because of a slight stutter that began when his mother died and his father went away. Fortunately, he no longer has that affliction. I don't know if I can take credit for its disappearance, but I do know that reading aloud helped him gain vocal confidence.

Here I am again, reminiscing about when Walter was a boy, and now he's a grown man of nineteen. He and

Edward still live together. Four years ago, Mabel sadly passed away. Despite all her faults, she didn't deserve to die before her fortieth birthday. It was very sudden – a fatal heart attack, so I'm told, and I was truly sorry for Edward's loss. I think he and Walter continue to muddle along fairly well. A village girl comes once a week to clean and do laundry, but Walter does most of the cooking. Who would have guessed that he'd be such a dab hand in the kitchen? He says he used to watch his aunt preparing supper while he was sitting at the table with his books – it was, after all, the warmest room in the house. Edward actually admitted to me that he's a better cook than Mabel ever was, and I find that easy to believe. Mabel didn't enjoy cooking and looked upon it as a chore, whereas Walter sees it as an art and likes to experiment. Unusual for a young man of nineteen, but Walter has always been different from those his own age. He never fails to surprise us with new talents or innovative ideas that he keeps hidden up his sleeve, revealing them only when the right moment comes along.

Here it is, my treasured copy of *David Copperfield*, with the inscription, 'To my dear Walter, with much love, Aunt Bessie'. Walter insisted that I keep it when he left school and started his apprenticeship. He said he couldn't trust his uncle not to throw away items that he thought were no longer useful, and he didn't want to risk losing the book and all its memories. Edward got rid of all Mabel's possessions within a matter of days after she died, and hasn't kept any of his sons' things either. He's a good man, but wholly unsentimental. I'm quite the opposite – sentimental in the extreme – and I believe Walter takes after me. But no, he takes after his mother, of course. Ethel was sentimental, like me, and would never have discarded any of Walter's baby clothes or toys, and especially not books. She wasn't a great reader, but she had a certain reverence for books. I can still picture her holding one of the great classics and stroking its leather cover, as if it were a piece of expensive silk or velvet. I've seen Walter do the same thing. I suppose some people might think that such a gesture is unbecoming in a man, but I beg to differ. After all, our great poets and authors could never have produced their masterpieces were they not enthralled by the written word and the multitude of feelings it has the power to impart.

I'm daydreaming again – as I always do when I think of Walter, or of Arthur, though I must try not to think of him during my waking hours. The ringing of Mrs Grist's bell brings me back to the present. I close my suitcase, push it under the bed, and scurry away to her bedroom. She wants me to go on another errand and gives me directions to the house of a man called Hornby. I'm to buy a bottle of sherry from him. She believes that a drink of sweet sherry mixed with egg yolk will do wonders for her sore throat. One of Mrs Hopper's trusted remedies, no doubt. I have no idea what this Mr Hornby does for a living. He came to the door about a week ago with a package for my employer and appears to be an uneducated, unaccommodating sort of man, not the kind of person I would expect Mrs Grist to associate with.

"I noticed yesterday that the bottle of sherry I'd saved for such a time as this is almost empty," Mrs Grist says. "Have you any idea how that may have occurred, Elizabeth?"

"No, Mrs Grist," I say. "The last time I looked, the bottle in the pantry was full."

"Hmm, all right. Don't dawdle or spend too long chatting with Mr Hornby. As soon as you get back, ask Mrs Hopper to prepare the sherry and egg yolk right away and bring it up to me."

Is she accusing me of drinking her sherry? Of course, I

know what has occurred. Mrs Hopper and Mrs Evans consumed more than half a bottle the other evening. I wouldn't dream of telling tales, but I resent the fact that she suspects me. I hardly ever touch alcohol – I might have a glass of something or other at Christmas, but that's it. Even if Mrs Grist offered me a drink, I'd refuse it. Actually, I'm a bit concerned about *her* consumption of spirits. Only this morning she had brandy with her Horlicks and now she's asking for sherry. And most evenings she takes a drop of gin with lime cordial before supper. Is that excessive? To me, it is. But then, for all I know, London drinking habits may be entirely different from those back in the village where only the menfolk frequent the local public house and indulge in drinking spirits, often to excess. Anyway, that's Mrs Grist's business, not mine. But I do wish she hadn't asked to me to go to the house of that horrible man with his bad teeth and leering looks. And to imply that I might spend time chatting with such a character!

Anyway, without further ado, I set out to buy the sherry. What a thankless task this is for a good Christian woman like myself! I know I shouldn't be complaining. I need to keep telling myself how lucky I am to have this job. I repeat it over and over as I walk to Mr Hornby's house, which I find easily. The neighbouring houses look fairly respectable, with neat front gardens and clean doorsteps, but his house is an eyesore. The garden is overgrown with nettles and brambles, and the path to the front door is barely discernible. Does he have a wife, I wonder? I wouldn't think so. I mean, who would want to marry such an unpleasant man? Well, I suppose there are many desperate women who would, but I'd rather go to the workhouse than live in holy matrimony with a man like Mr Hornby.

I knock several times before he appears. He's wearing

a dirty white vest and a pair of loose grey trousers held up with braces. I feel embarrassed and insulted that he should confront me in such a state of undress. I quickly state Mrs Grist's request and look away. He says nothing, just goes back inside leaving the door wide open. Much to my embarrassment, I catch a glimpse of a woman not much younger than myself, wearing just a chemise and drawers, lazily climbing the stairs that face the front door. Well, the goings-on in Mr Hornby's house are no concern of mine, but I'd rather not be a witness to them. I don't consider myself a prude, but I do try to maintain a small degree of decorum. It's inconsiderate of Mrs Grist to send me here.

Mr Hornby returns, holding out a bottle. I quickly drop into his open hand the coins Mrs Grist has given me and turn to leave. "Wait a minute," he says, counting it greedily.

"Tell Fanny I now have the gin," he says finally, with a smirk. "She knows how much it costs. She can send you again. I like your innocent face."

My innocent face! What does he mean by that? And he called her Fanny! Are they on first name terms? What on earth is the connection between this uncouth man and a respectable lady like Mrs Grist?

I wrap the bottle of sherry in some brown paper I had the good sense to bring with me and make a hasty retreat. Now I have to face Mrs Hopper in the kitchen for a second time today. I'm beginning to feel quite sorry for myself despite my earlier resolve to concentrate solely on my good fortune.

I arrive back just in time. Mrs Hopper is about to leave, having prepared a cold supper for Mrs Grist, in case she feels like eating later on.

"Oh, sorry to bother you, Mrs Hopper," I say boldly, ignoring her accusing look. "Mrs Grist just sent me to buy sherry, as she noticed yesterday that the bottle in the pantry is almost empty. She'd like you to make her a drink with egg yolk."

The cook knows full well that I know who consumed the sherry, and I hope that this knowledge will discourage her from being rude to me.

"No bother," she says, taking the bottle. "Tell her it'll be ready shortly."

I think that must be the politest discourse I've ever had with Mrs Hopper, or with Mrs Evans for that matter.

I tell Mrs Grist that Mrs Hopper is preparing her drink and I relay Mr Hornby's message. She mumbles a thank you and closes her eyes. I take that as my cue to go back to my room where I'm content to carry on reliving my memories of reading and playing with Walter. The horridness of the last hour soon begins to dissipate. Life is not so bad, I tell myself. I have Sunday to look forward to, even though I'm a bit apprehensive about meeting Michael for the first time and even more so about my ability to help him read fluently. But after the unpleasantness I've experienced this afternoon, sitting on the grass with an innocent boy and reading *David Copperfield* will be a breath of fresh air in more ways than one.

4

Robert has written to me suggesting that we meet in a small park near the school. He thinks it best to keep the first meeting between Michael and myself brief. An hour or so should give us ample time to get to know one another and for me to test his reading ability. Should *David Copperfield* be too difficult for him, he'll provide more suitable material for our next meeting.

Now that it's finally Sunday, I'm feeling quite excited. It was always my ambition to teach, but my life took a different turn when I was compelled to go into service. I don't regard my afternoons with Walter as teaching, though we did spend a lot of time reading books. This is going to be quite different. But I mustn't make it too formal or Michael will surely resist my efforts, as most boys his age would. I'd like him to look upon me as a friend, an aunt even, rather than a tutor. Tutor sounds too scholarly and a little off-putting. Since there are only male teachers at his school – brothers of the Xaverian order, according to Robert – he may get teased if his classmates find out he's being 'tutored' by a woman.

Fortunately, the weather today is fine, so Robert's suggestion that we meet in the park is a good one. I'm sure Michael will be happy to be out of doors if he's been cooped up inside the school all week. Robert says the boys are not free to leave the school grounds without consent, though they do have outdoor games every day, weather permitting.

I arrive early in Clapham and take a stroll around the perimeter of the park. I've already located the large horse chestnut tree next to the entrance on the north side where I'm to meet Robert and Michael. I have in my bag my treasured book, a blanket and two cream buns, and I'm hoping Michael and I can find a quiet spot to sit down and have a pleasant chat.

After a few minutes, I spot Robert and a young boy approaching. Anyone would think they were father and son. Like Robert, Michael is slight, with straight dark hair and a narrow, pointed face. He's wearing what I understand to be the school uniform – a short brown jacket with matching waistcoat, a white shirt with a stiff collar, and a pair of long trousers tucked into ankle boots. The clothes seem to hang off his small frame. As they approach and Michael sees me, he hangs his head in embarrassment.

"Hello Bessie," Robert says cheerfully. "May I introduce Master Michael Turnbull?" He turns to Michael and says, "Turnbull, this is Miss Hardwicke. She loves reading and is adamant that you should find pleasure in it too."

"Hello Michael," I say, smiling. "I hope you don't mind me calling you Michael. I've been very much looking forward to meeting you. I'm sure we're going to become good friends in no time at all."

Michael raises his eyes slightly, but says nothing.

"Why don't I leave you two to get to know one another?" Robert says. "You're in good hands, Turnbull. Just relax. No one is going to make you do anything you don't want to do. I'll come to take you back to school in about an hour."

Michael murmurs his thanks and Robert, giving me a smile, turns and walks away.

"Shall we sit down on the grass, Michael?" I say. "What do you say to a cream bun before we get started?"

I spread the blanket on the grass and give the boy a bun. He manages another 'thank you', but it's clear that he still feels awkward. I feel so sorry for him. He is having to cope with such a lot of changes in his life at so young an age. I decide not to press him to talk if he doesn't want to; I need to give him time to get over his shyness.

We finish our buns and I pull *David Copperfield* out of my bag.

"Do you know this book, Michael?" I ask.

He shakes his head.

"Well, I'm sure you've heard of the author, Mr Charles Dickens. *David Copperfield* is one of my favourite books, and it's also a favourite of my nephew Walter. We used to read it together when he was about your age. He's grown up now, but still loves it."

I begin to read: "Whether I shall turn out to be the hero of my own life, or whether that station will be held by anybody else, these pages must show."

You see, Michael," I say, looking into the boy's sad brown eyes, "our hero, David Copperfield, is about to tell us the story of his life, which has plenty of ups and downs, like most people's. Some folk say that the book is a fictionalised autobiography of Mr Dickens' own life."

Michael looks puzzled, which I take as a sign to explain further.

"By that I mean that part of the story is true, in that it mirrors the author's life – that's called an autobiography – and part of it is made up – that's called fiction. Dickens had such a vivid imagination that it would have been quite easy for him to turn his life into a page-turning novel like this."

Michael nods, though I'm not sure he fully understands.

"Do *you* like writing stories, Michael?" I ask. "If you had to write a story about your life so far, who or what would you include?"

This is a risky question, given the boy's bereavement, but it might be good for him to talk about his family –

and even the tragedy – rather than continue to suppress his feelings of grief or anger.

Michael is silent for a few moments. He plucks a blade of grass and begins to twist it around his forefinger.

"I'd write about playing in the back garden with my sister," he says finally. "There was a broken-down shed that we called our den, and we used to go there to hide from Father when he was in a temper."

"You have a sister, Michael? What's her name?"

"Harriet."

"And where's Harriet now?"

Michael looks away, but not before I catch sight of a tear rolling down his cheek.

"I don't know where she is," he says, his voice quavering. "Uncle Gordon won't tell me. He says he doesn't know, but how can he not know? I just want to be able to write to her. I didn't even say goodbye to her."

"Oh, Michael," I say. "I'm so sorry to hear that. You do need to be able to stay in touch with her. Have you told Mr Cartwright that you don't know where your sister is?"

"No, I can't tell him things like that. What good will it do?"

"I don't know, but he might be able to help. But don't worry. Leave it with me. I'll try to find out where your sister is. It may take a while, but I'm sure we'll find her eventually."

"Thank you, Miss. Please try to find her. I just need to know she's all right. I miss her so much."

"Of course, I understand. Listen, Michael, why don't you call me Aunt Bessie? I think you and I are going to get along splendidly and we should start by doing away with formalities."

Am I being too familiar? I miss the time I used to spend with Walter so much that perhaps I'm trying to replicate it with this boy. Well, it looks like we need each other. He misses his sister Harriet and I miss my nephew Walter. Not only that, but we've both found ourselves in unfamiliar situations and in dire need of a comforting friend.

"How old is Harriet?" I ask. "Is she younger or older than you?"

"She's thirteen. Nearly two years older than me. She isn't just my sister – she's my best friend too. She always stood up for me when I was teased at school or when Father got angry."

"Did your father get angry a lot?"

"Yes, especially when he came home from drinking at the pub, which was almost every night."

"And your mother, did she not also take your side?"

"Mother was ill a lot of the time. She used to spend most days in bed. Harriet cared for her and kept house. But Father was never satisfied."

"I know it's hard for you to talk about it, Michael, but how did your parents perish?"

"They died in a fire. It started in their bedroom – we think one of them accidentally knocked over a candle. Harriet and me, we were at our neighbour's house. The fire brigade came but it was too late. Both Mother and Father were already dead."

"I'm so very sorry, Michael. It must have been such a terrible shock for you. Do you think Harriet might still be at your neighbour's house?"

"No, I don't think so. Mrs Radford said we could only stay until a relative came to take us away. If no one came, then we'd have to go to the orphanage. There's only Uncle Gordon – we don't know any other relatives – they live far away, in Ireland, I think. So no one would've come for Harriet. And I know she won't stay in an orphanage – she'd run away and try to find work. She told me as much."

"Did your Uncle Gordon give a reason as to why he couldn't take you both?"

"Not at first. He just said I was to come with him right away. I said I couldn't go without Harriet – she'd gone to look for our kitten Romeo in what remained of our house. She'd been told not to go there as it was dangerous, but she loved that kitten so much. Uncle Gordon said we'd come back for her later, but it was a lie. He told me afterwards that he couldn't take care of both of us and that since Harriet was almost a grown-up, she could look after herself."

Michael begins to weep again. I hand him my handkerchief to wipe his eyes and put an arm around him.

"Don't get upset, Michael. We'll find her. She can't be far away. Where did you used to live? Was it close by?"

"We lived in Hammersmith – Greyhound Road."

"And what did you say was the name of the neighbour you stayed with?"

"Mrs Radford. Her husband is away at sea, or so Rosamund says. Rosamund is her daughter and is Harriet's friend. She'd wave to me on my way to school."

"Did Harriet go to school, Michael?"

"No. She used to, but had to leave when she was eleven. Harriet was clever – she could read and do sums better than anyone in her class – but Father said that girls didn't need schooling and that she should stay home to take care of Mother and cook our meals."

"All right, Michael. That's enough about the past for now. Try not to think the worst. Harriet sounds like a sensible girl, and I'm sure she's safe and not in any trouble. Let's do a bit of reading now. Reading is good for taking our minds off thoughts that worry us."

I can't help wondering whether reading *David Copperfield* is such a good idea after all. The tale of orphaned David and all the trouble he encounters might upset Michael still more. But I decide to give it a try. I can always skip the distressing parts and, besides, the story might have the effect of giving Michael the courage to overcome his difficulties. Young David faced one challenge after another with fortitude and determination, and walked all the way from London to Dover to find his one remaining relative.

Michael's reading is not as bad as I thought it might be. Admittedly, I'm not a teacher so am unable to compare him with other eleven-year-olds, but in my opinion, he reads quite fluently. We take it in turns to read aloud. He actually gives a chuckle when Aunt Betsey meets the nurse Peggotty and, addressing David's mother, declares, 'Peggotty! Do you mean to say, child, that any human being has gone into a Christian church, and got herself named Peggotty!'

I am trying to remember Walter's reading level at the age of eleven, but those Sunday afternoons in the countryside seem so long ago. And perhaps children in private London schools are expected to learn more quickly than those in village schoolrooms, where the slower children always hold back the brighter ones. Certainly, Walter was near the top of his class in most subjects and would have been one of those obstructed from learning more. Still, despite the all the limitations of the village school, it saddened me when Edward made him leave at the age of twelve to begin an apprenticeship.

At the end of the first chapter, I close the book and suggest that we take a short walk. I don't want our first session to be too taxing on the boy, especially since he's still terribly upset about being separated from his sister.

"Do you miss your friends at your old school, Michael?" I ask, but regret the question when he says that he didn't really have any friends.

"The other boys used to make fun of me because I was the shortest in the class," he adds after a short pause. "It's the same in the school here – everyone teases me. They've nicknamed me 'Shortie'. I hate it."

"You should just ignore them, Michael," I say. "If you show that that you're upset by what they say, they'll continue to tease you. If you ignore them, they'll soon get tired. They want a reaction from you, and if you don't give them one, they'll stop doing it."

Michael looks dubious. Not mentioning that it's Patty, Mr Cartwright's wife, I tell him about a friend I had at school who used to get teased because of her limp, and that I helped her overcome the shame she felt every time someone imitated the way she walked.

"Sometimes children can be cruel," I say. "They don't really mean it, but they rarely think about the harm they might cause by saying something hurtful. If you can make one good friend – like that girl at my school became my best friend – you'll be a lot happier. Try to find someone with similar interests to your own. It could be a sport like football or cricket, a game of hopscotch, a love of adventure stories, playing make-believe, anything really. But in order to make a friend, you first need to start talking to the other boys and joining in their games. Just give it a try and tell me the next time we meet whether or not it worked."

Michael doesn't respond. I can understand how hard it's going to be for such a shy boy to strike up a conversation with a classmate, especially if he's likely to be overheard by the bullies who are intent on tormenting him.

We are about to embark on our third walk around the small park when we see Robert striding towards us waving his hand.

"Ah, that was well timed," he says. "How did you get

on, Turnbull? Did you enjoy reading with Miss Hardwicke?"

"Yes, sir," Michael mumbles.

"We got along wonderfully," I say. "Michael's a good reader. He just needs to have a bit more confidence in himself. We'll work on that. When do you think we can meet again?"

"In two weeks' time?" Robert suggests. "I believe there's an outing planned for boarders next Sunday, so the following week should suit Michael, if it suits you, Bessie. Would you like to come back to the house? I know Patty would love to see you."

"That's kind of you, Robert, but unfortunately, I don't have time today. Mrs Grist stayed home and asked me if I would help her with some sewing. But give my love to Patty and Aunt Celia and tell them I'll see them Sunday week."

"It was lovely meeting you, Michael," I say before leaving. "We'll continue with the tale of young David Copperfield the next time we see each other. Goodbye until then."

"Goodbye, Miss," Michael says. He gives me a look that implies that he doesn't want Robert to know that I've asked him to call me Aunt Bessie. It will be our little secret, as I don't want him to know either.

I hurry back to the house. I'd found it difficult to leave this afternoon, even though Sunday is supposed to be my free day. Mrs Grist, still feeling under the weather, hadn't gone to her son's house as planned, and told me she'd appreciate it if I could help her with a dress alteration. She said that if she was feeling better, she wanted to wear the dress to a luncheon the next day at the home of her sister-in-law.

I didn't want her to know about my reading sessions with Michael – I thought she might think I was getting a bit above myself – so I said I was meeting an old friend who was in London for the wedding of her niece, but that I'd help her as soon I got back. I don't know what came over me, why I felt the need to make up such a story when I could have just said I was going to Patty and Robert's. It's quite unlike me to tell such untruths. Of course, she then started asking a lot of questions about this imaginary friend, so the small white lie became a much bigger falsehood. I'm dreading her questions when I arrive back at the house, and shall have to try to change the subject as quickly as possible. Why is it that Mrs Grist always manages to bring out the worst in me?

5

I've been awake most of the night fretting about how I can possibly help Michael locate his sister Harriet. Clearly, I cannot do it alone. I realise, after much consideration, that I will need to enlist Robert's help. It's not that I don't trust Robert – he's like a brother to me – but I don't know how appropriate it is to involve him in the search, which could well lead nowhere. And how will Michael react when he finds out that I've confided in Robert, who's well known to pupils and teachers alike? Still, there's no reason why Michael should find out. I'll ask Robert not to mention anything unless we meet with success.

So as soon as I get up, I write a letter to Robert, telling him that I believe Michael's wellbeing at school is contingent on his finding out what has become of his sister. I ask him if he might be able to find some time the following Sunday to accompany me to Hammersmith to call on the neighbour with whom Michael and Harriet spent a couple of nights after their parents tragically lost their lives. I enclose a note to Patty, apologising for not coming to see her after my first session with Michael. I ask if she'll allow me to take Robert away from her for an hour or two on Sunday to help me locate Michael's sister, if he agrees of course. Naturally, if she wants to come along too, I'll be delighted to see her.

With the letter sealed and stamped, I rush out to the post box in the adjacent street, hoping to catch the next collection. On my return, I spot a postcard lying on the doormat. It's addressed to me and I know right away that it's from Walter, who never fails to keep me up to date on where he's presently working. He says he's in Lydbrook, which is not too far from home. At least when he works locally, he can spend more time with his sweetheart Edie at the weekends. On the front of the postcard is an image of the old village church. Walter writes:

'Dear Aunt, I hope this will find you well, as it leaves me. I am now assisting in the restoration of the church in Lydbrook, near the Forest of Dean. We bike here every day except Sunday, though it's a long, hard pull. Fortunately, when we arrive, we are able to quench our thirst at the Anchor Inn, where we receive a good welcome. The countryside is lovely in this area, though I haven't had a chance to explore it yet. I'm told the Forest is home to a great variety of woodland birds. I have my sketchpad with me, so I hope to have time to do a few drawings. If I succeed in producing a decent sketch, I will send it to you. Your affectionate nephew, Walter'

Well, it sounds as if Walter is still spending a lot of time on his bike. I do worry that Walter and Edie spend so little time together. Whenever Walter is free, between jobs, for instance – though that's rare these days – Edie is busy with her training at the hospital. But thankfully, they're both still young and have plenty of time ahead of them. I shouldn't be too concerned, though obviously Mrs Grist thinks otherwise. It's just that Walter is so smitten with Edie that if anything should go wrong in their courtship, I don't think he'd easily get over it. Listen to me, being so negative for no reason at all! I suppose it's because of the terrible way in which my courtship with Arthur ended – but that's a story it pains me to tell, even after all these years.

My pleasure in receiving a postcard from Walter is soon overshadowed by a sharp remark from Mrs Evans, who appears in the hallway as I'm about to go back upstairs to my room.

"Madam has been ringing for you," she says. "You know she needs to go out today. Why do you always disappear just when you're needed?"

I don't reply. There's nothing to say as we both know it's not true. I'm always around to attend to Mrs Grist's requests – this is the first time I've missed her ringing the bell. Not only that, but it's infuriating the way Mrs Evans never addresses me by my name. I don't care whether she calls me Bessie, Elizabeth, or Miss Hardwicke, but she should have the courtesy to give me a name on the few occasions she deigns to speak to me.

Somehow Mrs Evans and Mrs Hopper have found out that I used to work at Farringdale House. I overheard them talking about me the other evening. Mrs Evans said that I only got the job because Mrs Grist couldn't afford to pay a proper wage to a 'real companion' and took me solely because I was 'inexpensive'. I've always known that I wasn't proper companion material, but it's not such a difficult job – reading aloud, doing bits of sewing and running a few errands – so I think I get paid more than enough, considering that my board is free of charge. Besides, their remarks reflect more unfavourably on Mrs Grist than on me. I wonder how she would react if she could hear them! She thinks they're both so loyal, but neither one of them has a good word to say about her.

She doesn't appear to be in any hurry and doesn't even mention my lateness, though she probably wonders why I appear agitated and red in the face. In fact, she's been kind to me these last few days, despite feeling under the weather. I was quite late back yesterday, but she didn't comment on it at all and asked no probing questions about my afternoon with my fictional friend.

"Ah, Elizabeth," she says. "Just the person I need. The dress fits perfectly now, but I'd like you to sew another button on the bodice. I want it fastened right at the neck.

Don't worry, it's not going to choke me. There's just enough room for one more button if you'd kindly take care of it for me."

"Yes, of course, Mrs Grist," I say, taking the dress from her and carefully laying it on the sewing table. In front of me is a bowl full of buttons of every size and colour. I select one of mother-of-pearl that matches the others on the rust-coloured silk dress. It takes me just five minutes to add the button and fasten a loop to secure it. I'll say one thing for Mrs Grist – she certainly knows how to dress tastefully and in accordance with her age, which I'm guessing is about fifty. The garment really becomes her and its colour accentuates her rich auburn hair, which as yet shows hardly a strand of grey.

As if to dispel any disapproval on my part – although I have only compliments to offer – she tells me that she's worn black for long enough. "Believe it or not," she says, "it's now been more than two years since Frank passed away."

Mrs Grist's good dress sense reinforces the fact that I have none. But even if I were able to afford stylish attire and had the looks to go with it, I believe I'd still dress in the same plain, drab fashion. My employer tells me that I look as if I'm in perpetual mourning – always in black or grey. She says I make myself appear ten years older than I actually am. I think she's probably right, but I've been wearing dark colours since Ethel died. I'm not much to look at anyway with my dull brown hair, which flatly refuses to submit to any style, and my long pale face. Mrs Grist also told me that I make my face look longer because I rarely smile. I did manage a slight grin at that remark, though I felt like asking her what there was to be cheerful about. What with her changeable moods and the unpleasantness I experience daily in the kitchen, it's often a struggle to keep myself from weeping, let alone manage a smile. There I go again, complaining about my situation. I've obviously completely forgotten my resolve to keep reminding myself how fortunate I am.

"Thank you, Elizabeth," she says when I hand her back the dress. "I'll go and get dressed now. If I need you again before I leave the house, I'll ring for you. I should be back within three hours. We'll start reading my new copy of *Jane Eyre* as soon as I return."

A letter from Robert arrives in today's post. He says that if it's something I've set my heart on, then he'll willingly assist me in my attempt to find Harriet. But he also warns me not to be too disappointed if there's no happy outcome. If we do manage to locate the girl in an orphanage, he writes, then it's for her own good that she remains there, as clearly there's no one who is prepared to give her a home. At least she'll have a roof over her head, receive three square meals a day, and be taught skills that will be of use to her in the future. If she's already thirteen, he adds, then it won't be long before she's able to find work, perhaps in service, and be in a position to fend for herself. But we can of course put her in touch with Michael so that they're able to write to each other.

I'm grateful that Robert has agreed to help me, and I can understand his reticence. After all, he encounters youngsters every day – each with their own troublesome history – and cannot become overly concerned about one boy's personal suffering. He introduced me to Michael so that I can help him with his reading, not so that I can embark upon a quest to find his sister. Since I'm Patty's closest friend, he obviously feels obliged to assist me, even though he doubts that it will lead anywhere. I feel a bit guilty about involving him and will try not to make it a long drawn-out process. If we don't discover Harriet's whereabouts on Sunday, then we'll leave it at that. At least we'll have tried. I should never have made such a promise to Michael. He's going to be so disappointed if I have to tell him that, despite my best efforts, my mission has been unsuccessful.

Robert proposes that we meet at one o'clock on Sunday outside the St Thomas à Becket Catholic Church in Wandsworth and take a Hansom cab to Hammersmith. He says the parish priest there is a friend of his and on the few occasions he attends church on a Sunday, he chooses that particular place of worship. It's just up the road from my own church and I've passed the red brick building many times on my walks.

I was hoping that Patty could come too, but clearly, she won't be attending church with Robert. I feel a bit embarrassed about meeting Robert without Patty, but it's really no different from meeting one of my brothers. I'm not unhappy about being a single woman – or a spinster if you want to use that ugly word – except in situations like this. I feel people are staring at me and making judgements that are unfair and probably untrue. Robert will of course do everything possible to put me at ease – he's that kind of man, always alert to people's feelings – but the fact that he's able to sense my awkwardness will make me even more self-conscious.

Robert is already waiting for me outside the Catholic church, as arranged. He waves down a Hansom cab and we both climb in. I enjoy the bumpy ride through the narrow streets, which are much less busy and noisy than usual. Robert strikes up a conversation with the cab driver, an elderly man with long silver hair and an accent so pronounced that I can hardly understand a word he's saying. But from Robert's side of the conversation, I gather that they are talking about our Royal Family. The old king, Edward VII, eldest son of the late Queen and Empress, Victoria, died earlier this year, and George V succeeded to the throne. Robert mentions the timing of his coronation; it apparently won't take place until the middle of next year, as tradition dictates that such an extravagant and, in many ways, joyous event cannot be held until a sufficient period of mourning has passed following the death of the former monarch.

"I'm so happy you're now living in London, Bessie," Robert says to me. "You can come with Patty and me to see the coronation procession next year. It'll be a once in a lifetime occasion and we'll make sure we get to Westminster Abbey in plenty of time so as to catch a glimpse of His Majesty."

"Oh, thank you, Robert," I say. "I've been so preoccupied with the changes in my own small life that it hasn't even occurred to me that much bigger changes are taking place at the palace. The coronation is sure to be a wondrous event and I'll be delighted to spend the day with you and Patty."

It's true, I haven't given it much thought at all. Only now is it sinking in that living in London presents me with many wonderful opportunities that I would never have dreamt of being able to experience, living as I did in a small village in the West Country. I can't wait to let Walter know that I'll be going with Robert and Patty to see the coronation next year. I wonder if he and Edie could come up to London to join us. That would make the occasion even more special. But it would probably be too much to expect.

The cab driver drops us off on Greyhound Road – he didn't even need a map to locate it – and Robert hands him the fare. I have no idea how much a Hansom cab from Wandsworth to Hammersmith costs, but I offer to pay. As I expected, Robert refuses my coins.

"Well, that must be the Turnbulls' house," he says, pointing to a modest terraced house that is completely gutted on the upper floor. "I wonder who actually owns the property and if they're planning to rebuild. I suppose it depends on whether or not they have insurance. It's lucky that the fire didn't spread to any of the neighbouring homes – the walls between these eighteenth century houses don't always observe the minimum thickness standards and the construction materials are often inferior. But I've heard it said that after the Great Fire, a century earlier, timber and thatch were no longer commonly used in construction. We can be thankful for that, I suppose."

It distresses me to think that Michael's parents died in that house, and it's not surprising that the boy is still suffering from the trauma of such a tragedy. Robert notices that I'm finding it hard to look at that house without tears springing to my eyes.

"Come on, Bessie," he says, placing a hand on my arm. "Don't upset yourself. Let's go and find Mrs Radford. I'm sure she'll be able to help us."

It's eerily quiet, even for a Sunday. It's as if all the residents are staying indoors with their curtains drawn, so as not to have to look at the charred remains of the Turnbulls' house. Robert knocks on the front door of one of the neighbouring houses. An elderly man wearing a long nightgown underneath a thick woollen jacket – even though the day is unseasonably warm – answers after the second knock.

"Excuse me sir," Robert says. "We're looking for a Mrs Radford, who we believe lives in this street. Can you please tell us in which house she resides?"

"It's number ten," the old man says gruffly. "This is number eight. Eunice Radford usually goes out at this hour on a Sunday, but you might catch her if you're quick."

"Thank you, sir. Sorry to have disturbed you on your day of rest."

He nods and closes the door. We proceed to number ten, which is on the other side of the fire-damaged house. This time a pretty young girl in a spotless white dress answers the door. Robert asks her if we can speak with her mother. "Yes, just a moment sir," she says politely. She turns away and shouts up the stairs, "Ma! It's for you!"

A moment later Mrs Radford comes to the door. She is also good-looking and smartly dressed in a purple dress, gathered at the waist, with a pink and white patterned shawl around her shoulders.

"Good afternoon," she says. "What can I do for you?"

Robert makes the introductions and explains our mission. "All we want to do," he says, "is find Harriet so we can put her in touch with her brother, who misses her terribly."

"Look, Mr... Sorry, what did you say your name was?" Mrs Radford says, frowning.

"Cartwright. Robert Cartwright."

"Mr Cartwright. I did look after the two children when their parents perished in the fire. The boy was here for just two nights. Then an uncle, a Mr Gordon Turnbull, came and took him away. He said he couldn't take the girl – he claimed that she was older and could look after herself. Girls were trouble, he said, and he, being a bachelor, couldn't be dealing with the likes of a young woman. But, of course, she can't look after herself. She's only thirteen. So I contacted the Sisters of Gethsemane who run an orphanage right here in Hammersmith, and two of the sisters came and took her away. The family's Roman Catholic – I don't know if you know that – so it seemed the right thing to do. But the poor girl made such a scene – she didn't want to go – and my daughter Rosamund was upset with me for days afterwards. She and Harriet are good friends and she wanted to know why she couldn't live with us. But I can hardly make ends meet as it is – my husband Roy is away at sea for weeks at a time and there's no money coming in until he returns.

"You do understand, don't you? I would have liked to let her stay, but what would Roy say were he to come home and find another mouth to feed? Harriet's a good girl and a responsible one – she cared for her poor mother throughout her long illness – but she's also impulsive and sometimes leads Rosamund, who's younger, astray. I hated letting her go, but what could I do? I did what I thought was for the best. So she's with the Sisters of Gethsemane, a mile or so from here. You'll find her there."

Mrs Radford takes a handkerchief from her pocket and wipes her eyes. Talking about Harriet and the fact that she had to send her away is understandably upsetting for her.

"Thank you, Mrs Radford," Robert says. "You've been most helpful and you did the right thing. We'll get in touch with the sisters and take it from there. Good day to you and thank you again."

"Well," Robert says as we walk away, "it looks like we've learnt all we need to know. Harriet is with the Sisters of Gethsemane, right here in Hammersmith."

"Yes" I say. "Let's hope she's still there."

"What do you mean?"

"Well, Michael said that if she was put in an orphanage, then she'd surely run away."

"Oh, come on, Bessie. That's just a young boy's imagination. It might be what *he* would want to do, but his sister is older and hopefully more sensible."

"I do hope so, but he told me she said it herself. So

what do we do now, Robert? Visit the orphanage?"

"I think, Bessie, it would be best for me to write to the sisters first. They might not take kindly to our arriving on their doorstop asking to speak to Harriet. I'll let them know I work for the school where her brother is a student – that may give me some small degree of authority. And the fact that I'm of the Roman Catholic faith myself might also help our cause."

"Yes, you're right, of course. I'm sorry for being so impatient. I'd like to have something positive to tell Michael next Sunday, but there's no need to rush things. It's important that we're well received by the sisters if and when we go to the orphanage."

"It's possible that I may receive an answer by next week if I post a letter tomorrow. I'll certainly let you know if that's the case. In the meantime, don't worry. I think we're well on the way to reuniting brother and sister."

"Yes, it's been a successful afternoon. Thank you, Robert."

I'm trying to sound optimistic, but I'm not as confident as Robert is that Harriet will remain in the orphanage. Michael didn't sound as if he was imagining it when he said Harriet would run away rather than stay in such a place. And if she has made an escape, how on earth will we even begin to find her?

6

It's all doom and gloom in the house this morning. Mrs Grist is in one of her moods and is complaining about everything. She makes Mrs Hopper come and take away her breakfast egg, saying she should know by now that she likes her eggs *soft-boiled*. And she says the toast is burnt, though it looks perfectly fine to me. Mrs Hopper isn't at all happy about these criticisms and she scowls at me as she walks away, as if it's my fault! I'd love to hear what she's saying to Mrs Evans in the kitchen, but I intend to keep my distance from both of them for the rest of the day.

Fortunately, by mid-morning my employer has calmed down a bit. No doubt she's feeling some remorse for her harsh words. She says her nerves are bad as she's again run out of tonic, and asks me to go to the pharmacy for another bottle. I'd be interested in knowing what is actually in her tonic, but it would be too forward of me to ask Mr Fielding. Whatever it is, it seems to do her good, as she's always snappy and anxious when she runs out.

It's only a short walk to the pharmacy, but I'm glad to be out of doors, especially since the sun is shining and there's a fresh autumnal nip in the air. Mr Fielding gives me a smile as I walk through the open door of his shop. There are no other customers and he's holding a mop! He says he's just finished cleaning the floor and is about to start dusting the shelves. I don't think I've ever seen a man undertaking such tasks before. I compliment him on the splendid job he's doing.

"Mathilda wasn't well and couldn't come yesterday afternoon, and she may not come today either," he says. "There's a girl who drops in once a week to give the shop a thorough clean, but she won't be here until Friday and the floor was looking a bit grubby, so I decided to mop it myself. I can put my hand to any number of household chores, but if Mathilda's here, she won't let me lift a finger."

"Oh, I hope she's not too poorly," I say. "Quite a few people seem to be under the weather. I think it must be the change in temperature."

'Oh no, don't worry. She's not what I would call ill. Didn't I tell you? She's going to have a baby!"

"Really? That's wonderful news! Is the birth imminent?"

"No, not for many months. She's still at the morning sickness stage. But she'll be over that in a week or so and I'm sure she'll be as right as rain for the remainder of her term."

"Well, give her my best wishes the next time you see her. I'm sure she'll make a wonderful mother."

"It's a pity her own mother won't be here to witness the happy occasion. But that's life – it deals us some terrible blows, but gives us moments of great joy in return. Now, Miss Bessie Hardwicke, I seem to be wasting your precious time. What can I do for you?"

"It's just Mrs Grist's tonic. She's run out of it and her nerves are especially bad today."

"Ah, the famous tonic!"

"I don't know what you put in it, but it certainly seems to do her good."

"Well, that's the thing. She thinks it does her good and that's the pick-me-up she needs. There's nothing medicinal or addictive in what I prepare, but she believes it's a cure for all her ills. Don't tell her I said that though. It's our little secret."

"No, of course not. I'm just glad it has a positive effect on her mood. I benefit from that as well."

"Bessie, my dear, I know Fanny Grist can be difficult

at times. But don't judge her too harshly. She's had a difficult life. Her husband was… well, not easy to live with, and her youngest son continues to trouble her. Do you know if she still relies on liquor to help her sleep?"

"I don't know if it's every night, but I've seen her add a drop of brandy to a cup of Horlicks before going to bed. And occasionally she'll have a glass of gin with lime cordial in the evening. Oh and just the other day she sent me to the house of a man called Hornby to buy a bottle of sherry. She wanted it mixed with egg yolk for her sore throat. I have to admit that going there wasn't an errand I particularly enjoyed."

"She shouldn't have sent you there. He's not a respectable man and you were risking your good name by calling at his house. Don't go there again, Bessie. Make any excuse. Fanny will understand. And she shouldn't be buying spirits from him, though I suppose he… Never mind. I've heard that some of the liquor he sells is adulterated and that could be bad for her health. I'll try to have a word with her when I get a chance."

"Oh, please don't let her know I told you! She hates anybody knowing about her personal business."

"I wouldn't dream of it, Bessie. I'm grateful to you for mentioning it though. She'll listen to me, even though she always says I don't know what I'm talking about. Here's the tonic. Our secret, remember?"

Goodness me, Mr Fielding and I now have a secret! But I feel a bit troubled. Despite the fact that he insists that Mrs Grist's bark is worse than her bite, I'm sure she'll dismiss me if she finds out that I've been talking to him about her drinking habits. I'm equally sure he won't let me down, but she's bound to become suspicious if he brings up the subject. She keeps telling me not to spend time chatting with him – it's as if she knows he's going to ask me questions about her. And what am I to make of the advice he gave me about not going to Mr Hornby's house if I value my good name? Could he be running a brothel? It wouldn't surprise me after what I witnessed there. Now what is the connection between an educated, respectable lady and a common man who sells adulterated liquor and appears to be running a brothel? And what on earth am I going to say if Mrs Grist asks me to go there again? Make any excuse, Mr Fielding said. That's easier said than done!

But awkward moments aside, I have to admit that I look forward to my visits to the pharmacy. The kind and confiding way in which Mr Fielding speaks to me gives me a warm feeling inside. I've not felt this way in the presence of a man since Arthur. Dear me, what on earth am I saying? I cannot believe I'm comparing Mr Fielding – whom I barely know – to Arthur, who was not only a childhood friend but also, from the age of sixteen, my one and only sweetheart. I think my imagination must be running away with me. I'm sure Mr Fielding – being such a good and caring man – treats everyone in the same way, or at least those he feels need a bit of kindness in their lives. The important thing is not to react in a way that's likely to reveal my feelings, like blushing when he pays me a compliment, for instance. I don't want to come across as a foolish woman desperate for friendship. It's probably too late though – I think he already suspects my loneliness and the fact that I'm in dire need of a kind word or two.

Robert has written to me, as promised. He says he's sent a letter to the Mother Superior at the Sisters of Gethsemane Convent that runs the orphanage in Hammersmith, but has not yet received a reply. Since it's almost the end of the week, he suggests that we again meet in the park on Sunday for Michael's second reading lesson. If he's received a response by then, he'll pass me a note to let me know, but tells me not to say anything to Michael at this point. We need first to be sure that we can meet with Harriet and find out whether she's willing and able to correspond with her brother.

I feel a bit disappointed. I wanted to give Michael a bit of good news, but Robert is right – we cannot raise his hopes until we have some positive information to impart.

In church on Sunday morning, I pray for Michael and his sister. It's a strange coincidence that the sermon is about so-called untimely death. The Reverend Thomas Wilson tells us that no death is untimely when ordained by God, who always knows how much suffering we can bear. I feel somewhat guilty for having always dwelt so much on my own bereavements – my parents, Ethel, Arthur – rather than thinking about those who've endured greater losses. Michael and his sister are still so young and yet they've witnessed the death of both their parents in tragic circumstances. I cannot dispute the fact that God knows best, but it's hard to understand why children have to suffer in this way.

After a quick lunch in the kitchen – my private domain on a Sunday – I set out to meet Robert and Michael. The weather is cooler than of late and a bit cloudy, but I think we can still have our lesson in the park. It hasn't rained for the last few days, so the grass won't be too damp. By the time I arrive in Clapham, the sun is peeking through the clouds and it feels a couple of degrees warmer, though that might be because I've been walking so briskly.

Robert and Michael are already in the park, busily engaged in collecting conkers. There is a mass of them strewn on the grass beneath the horse chestnut tree. Michael's pockets are already full of the glossy brown treasures and he seems reluctant to accept the additional ones Robert insists on giving him. It looks to me as if Robert is enjoying the activity much more than Michael is.

"Hello Bessie," Robert says. "We're collecting conkers, as you can see. Michael tells me he knows how to play the game of conkers and all he needs is some string. As it happens, I always carry a length of string in my pocket, so he's all set to have a game with his classmates later on today."

Michael looks doubtful as to whether such a game will be possible, but I decide to support Robert's optimistic approach.

"That game is so much fun," I say. "We used to play it as children, but for some reason the boys always won. I think it was because they always managed to nab the biggest and hardest conkers. Or perhaps it was because they cheated."

Michael gives me a forced smile as he rubs a shiny conker between his palms. I look at Robert, wondering if he has a note to give me. But he shakes his head before bidding us goodbye.

"How are you today, Michael?" I ask as we settle down in the same spot as before. "Were your lessons any easier this week?"

"No, not really," he says. "I couldn't concentrate. I kept thinking about Harriet. Do you know where she is yet?"

"No, not yet. It's probably going to take another couple of weeks. But I've made a start and am hopeful that I'll find her. Don't worry. You don't know your Aunt Bessie. Once I make up my mind to do something, I don't rest until I've accomplished it."

Perhaps I shouldn't sound so confident, especially since I'm far from sure that Harriet is still at the orphanage. And Robert told me not to raise Michael's hopes, yet that's just what I've done. But Michael's little face looks so pale and anxious that I can't bear disappointing him. I decide to change the subject quickly."

"Oh, before I forget," I say. "Here are some sweets for you to take back to school to share with your classmates." I dig deep in my bag and produce a bag of toffees.

"Thank you, Miss, I mean Aunt Bessie," Michael says. "Can I have one now, please?"

"Yes, of course, but you won't be able to read while chewing a toffee. I'll start first. Now, let's see what young David Copperfield has been up to since we last met."

I decide to skip a couple of chapters. I'm not sure that Michael needs to hear about how badly David is treated by his mother's new husband, Mr Murdstone. I begin with the chapter about his trip to Yarmouth with his nurse Peggotty, an episode that's sure to bring a smile to the boy's face. I was right; he is fascinated by the notion that Peggotty's family live in an upside-down boat and says that would be his dream home.

"Have you ever been to the seaside?" I ask him.

"Yes, we went to Southend-on-Sea on holiday when I was eight," he says. "The doctor said Mother needed some sea air for her health, so we spent almost a week there. Every day I went down to the beach with Harriet and we played in the sand. It was too cold to go in the sea, but we loved watching the fishermen in their boats. They were friendly too and gave us cockles and whelks - at least that's what Harriet said they were called. But I didn't see anyone living in an upturned boat!"

"You're lucky to have such a special memory, Michael. I've never seen the sea. I used to live in the countryside, which was lovely but it wasn't close to the coast. There was a river nearby though and we sometimes swam in it. I liked the idea that the river would eventually flow into the sea."

Michael looks at me in astonishment. I think he finds it hard to believe that a person as old as I am has never seen the sea. I move on to the chapter where David is sent away to school and suggest that Michael reads. I want him to appreciate just how difficult David finds it to adjust to life at Salem School, and to understand that his own suffering as a victim of bullying is not uncommon.

He looks incredulous when he hears that David is forced to wear a placard on his back stating, 'Take care of him, he bites'. "At least that didn't happen to me," he says, pausing to look at me with wide eyes.

"But it seems to me," he continues thoughtfully, "that David is bullied by the masters, not the other boys. It wasn't his classmates who made him wear the placard, it was the masters. It's different at my school. It's the boys who bully me."

"You're right," I say. "The masters at David's school are so harsh that the boys are less cruel to each other. But wait, let's read on a bit. I think you'll find that there *is* a bully at the school, though in this case David isn't the one who gets picked on."

"You see," I say once we've read about how one of David's classmates, Traddles, is bullied by the popular James Steerforth, "Traddles is a kind-hearted fellow and is appalled by Steerforth's treatment of the homely master, Mr Mell. Steerforth taunts him with the name of 'Miss Traddles', calling him a girl, after the poor boy has already been caned for being discovered in tears. I don't want to give anything away, but later on we discover that Traddles is a real friend to David, while Steerforth is anything but."

Michael nods and says, hesitantly, "In my first week at this school, one of the bigger boys said I was weak like a girl. The other boys laughed."

"I'm sorry to hear that, Michael. How is it now with the other boys? Did you take my advice and try to ignore their teasing?"

'Yes, but some of the bigger boys still do it. One of my classmates stole my essay and spilt ink all over it. So I had to write it again. But I think a boy called Thomson might become my friend. He asked me to show him my penknife – it's the one Harriet gave me for my last birthday. She saved some money from running errands for our neighbours and bought the one I'd been wanting for ages. Thomson said I was lucky to have such a good penknife."

"I'm glad to hear that, Michael. Try to get to know him better and you'll probably find you both have a lot in common. But do keep your penknife in a safe place. You don't want to lose it, do you?"

"No, never! I always keep it close to me. At the moment I'm hiding it under my mattress. But please don't tell Mr Cartwright. We're not allowed to keep penknives in the dormitory."

"Of course I won't. But do you trust Thomson not to tell anyone?"

"Yes, because he has a penknife too. But not such a good one as mine. He told me that last term one of older boys tried to stab a classmate with his penknife. Since then it's become a rule that all knives should be given to Brother Francis for safekeeping. But I don't trust him with mine."

"Why don't you trust him?"

"He has his favourites and I'm not one of them. I'm afraid he'll give my penknife away to one of the boys he likes more."

"I'm sure he wouldn't do that, Michael. You should always trust people until you know for sure that they're *not* to be trusted."

"Well, Thomson said he took his marbles away from him for no reason at all. Other boys were playing with their marbles too, but he didn't take theirs."

"Oh dear. Well, just make sure you don't get on the wrong side of him. Always be polite and don't answer back."

"He's hasn't yet said one word to me, nor I to him."

I don't think it's wise to pursue this topic of conversation any further. I wonder whether I should have a word with Robert about Brother Francis, but it's not my place to interfere and I wouldn't want him to know that Michael's been telling me such tales. After all, it's supposed to be a reading lesson, not an opportunity for him to complain about school life. And schoolboys are not exactly reliable witnesses. I should just stick to the task at hand, however tempting it is to find out more about the interactions between the boys and their masters.

Our hour together is almost up, so I put away my book.

"Shall we look for a few more conkers?" I suggest.

"Yes, all right," Michael says, but he doesn't sound too enthusiastic. He's already collected more than his pockets can hold.

"Might you be able to have a game of conkers with Thomson when you get back?"

"Thomson goes home at weekends, but perhaps during break tomorrow. Unless Brother Francis confiscates my conkers before then."

"I'm sure he won't do that. Come along, Michael. Let's see who can find the biggest one."

When Robert reappears a few minutes later, he tells me that Patty is waiting for me and will accept no excuses this time. We walk Michael back to school together.

The school and its dormitories are housed in a large red brick building that looks much less daunting than I had imagined. Robert says it's quiet at weekends as the majority of boys go home to their families. Clearly, Michael is expected to stay at school until the Christmas break. I ask him if his uncle ever visits on the weekend, but he shakes his head and says he's glad he doesn't come to see him. His woeful response makes me even more determined to reunite him with his sister, who must surely miss him as much as he misses her.

Patty welcomes me into her parlour and chides me for not having come sooner. Celia is again sitting in her chair by the window and says she's suffering from asthma, an affliction that seems to have worsened since her move to London.

"The pharmacist gave me a nasal spray," she says. "It's made my breathing much easier. I don't think our village pharmacy would have had such a thing in stock."

"You're probably right," I say. "The pharmacies back home are so old-fashioned compared to the ones here. There's one I go to near Mrs Grist's house – the pharmacist's name is Mr Fielding. Mrs Grist has a number of different ailments – none of them really serious – but he always knows exactly what to prescribe. There's never a need to call the doctor."

I find myself blushing when I say Mr Fielding's name. I'm sure Patty notices, but she says nothing. I'd like to tell her about my fondness for this gentleman – we've shared secrets since early childhood – but certainly not within earshot of her mother and husband.

"And how is your young pupil, Bessie?" she asks me as she pours the tea. "I might have guessed you'd be reading *David Copperfield*. I remember it was a favourite of yours when you used to read with Walter on Sunday afternoons."

"Yes, it's still a favourite," I say. "I'll never tire of reading that book. Walter loved it too. Michael actually reads quite well. I think he must be nervous in class, poor lad. He's very shy and unsure of himself, but he's a sweet boy. I do hope we can reunite him with his sister – I think that not knowing her whereabouts is affecting both his friendships with the other boys and his ability to do well in his lessons."

"Well, let's hope Robert hears from the Sisters of Gethsemane this week. It's sad that the children were separated like that so soon after losing their parents. What on earth was the uncle thinking, taking just the boy and not the girl?"

"It does seem cruel, but apparently, he felt he'd be unable to cope with a girl of Harriet's age. He could at least have given it a try. Still, he is paying for Michael's education, so that's something, I suppose – though it's too early to tell whether the child will benefit from it. He's desperately unhappy at the moment."

I spend a pleasant hour taking tea with my closest friends, who always manage to cheer me up. But as I walk home, my mind is again preoccupied by the fate of Michael and Harriet. I begin to have doubts about how we can help Harriet, even if we do succeed in making contact with her. I know Robert's goal is simply to put her in touch with her brother, but do we then just abandon her? What damage will an institution like the orphanage do to such a strong-willed girl? Sadly, none of us is in a position to help her. Mrs Radford might have been willing to take her, were she in a better financial position and not afraid of her husband's reaction upon his return. As for me, as usual I can do nothing, and I know Patty and Robert's circumstances are constrained. Despite their happy home, it's my belief that the three of them are only just about managing to get by on Robert's meagre wages and the few sewing jobs that Patty and Celia are able to do for their neighbours.

Life is so unfair, I think, not for the first time. But then I spot a group of dirty, bare-foot, ragged children looking in the dustbins for their next meal and sheltering who-knows-where at night to escape being rounded up and taken to the workhouse. It's a stark reminder that I should be counting my blessings. At least I'm not so unfortunate as not to know where my next meal is coming from and, for all my troubles, I've never lacked a warm and comfortable bed in which to rest my weary body at the end of a working day.

7

Despite having taken two full teaspoonfuls of her restorative tonic, Mrs Grist is again suffering from her nerves. She's snapping at everyone, me included. Not only that, but this morning, much to my horror, she asks me – or rather tells me – to go to Mr Hornby to buy a bottle of brandy.

"I don't know how the one in the pantry can be empty already," she says. "You've seen how much I take with my Horlicks. It's barely a thimbleful."

"I don't know either," I say. "Perhaps Mrs Hopper uses it in some of her recipes."

"Recipes! She has none. Her meals couldn't be simpler if she tried. Not that I mind. It's the rich food that my sister-in-law's French cook serves that disagrees with me. Don't ask me why Doris doesn't have an English cook – that's something I'll never understand. I don't think I've once come away from her house without indigestion. Now, Elizabeth, will you kindly pop over to Mr Hornby's and buy a bottle of brandy. I don't want to be without it tonight. I didn't sleep a wink last night."

"Mrs Grist, I promise I'll do anything else, but please don't make me go to Mr Hornby's again. I can't help feeling he runs a house of ill repute. A partially dressed young woman was clearly visible the last time I went there. She made no attempt to cover herself even when she saw me standing on the doorstep. I don't want people in the neighbourhood seeing me knocking on his door. You know how they gossip – you've said so yourself. Perhaps the boy you hired for clearing the garden could go there for you."

She looks at me in surprise, frowns deeply, and is silent for a moment.

"You talk like a young girl who's afraid of losing her honour," she says finally. "I would not have thought, at your mature age, you'd be so sensitive. I'm certainly not going to trust that ignorant boy with a task that involves carrying money. That would be the last I'd see of him. But never mind, I'll ask Mrs Hopper to go. She's a married woman and is not afraid of wagging tongues."

"Thank you, Mrs Grist," I say, feeling relief. It wasn't tactful of her to make reference to my mature age, but I can hardly point that out. I'm just thankful I don't have to go to that horrible man's house, even though I expect I'll suffer more abuse when Mrs Hopper finds out she's being sent on an errand that I've refused.

Later on my employer tries to justify the fact that she buys liquor from Mr Hornby, which makes me think that she values my opinion, however slightly.

"Just so you know, Elizabeth," she says haughtily, "I've been told to go to Mr Hornby if I'm in need of brandy or any other spirits for medicinal purposes. As you can imagine, it's difficult for a woman to buy such goods in places that are typically the domain of men. And I've been led to believe Hornby sells his bottles at a good price, certainly for less than that charged by the city's wine merchants."

"But, Mrs Grist," I say, "are you sure they're recognised brands? There wasn't a label on the bottle of sherry he sold you last time, which made me think that perhaps the spirits he sells are adulterated. But I'm sure someone would have already tipped you off if that were the case."

"Are you implying, Elizabeth, that I'd do business with a man who sells contaminated alcohol?"

"No, of course not. I just thought it odd that the bottle didn't have a label on it. And, in the case of brandy, how would you know the good stuff from the bad if you only add it to your Horlicks? I certainly wouldn't be able to tell the difference."

"I'm not a connoisseur, it's true, but I believe my late husband had business dealings with the Hornby family. That's how I came to be aware that Basil Hornby is a supplier of spirits."

"I just think you can never be too careful as far as alcohol is concerned. Do you remember, at the turn of the century, there were a large number of deaths due to arsenic poisoning? Apparently, arsenic had been used in the brewing of beer. My brother Edward stopped drinking it as a result."

"I have never touched beer, and I never will. As for the brandy, I'll ask Mrs Hopper to taste it when she returns. She's sure to know whether it's of good quality or not. Now, can we please return to *Jane Eyre*?"

Mrs Grist informs me the next day that Mrs Hopper believes the brandy to be pure. I am not surprised. Even if she is able to differentiate between 'good' and 'bad' brandy, she's hardly likely to tell her employer that Mr Hornby has been duping her, especially if she's well acquainted with the man. She's been working for Mrs Grist for some years now and he lives so close by that he's unlikely to be a stranger to her. And since she's clearly helping herself to spirits stored in the pantry – if the empty bottles are anything to go by – she won't want to admit to herself that she's been fooled. I can do no more. The next time I see Mr Fielding, I'll tell him that I've spoken to Mrs Grist about the matter. If he mentions it himself, she's bound to think that we've been talking about her drinking habits and I'll risk losing my job.

I've been feeling a bit down in the dumps for the past couple of days, but a letter from Robert cheers me up. He's had a reply from the convent. Sister Martha, one of the resident sisters, has written to say that Harriet is indeed staying with them and that he's welcome to visit on Sunday afternoon. This is exactly what we'd hoped for. I won't think further ahead than Sunday; our meeting with the sisters and with Harriet will determine our next move, if any.

In the meantime, I have to get through another three days with Mrs Grist and Mrs Hopper who, as I predicted, is angry with me for not going to buy the brandy. Despite the fact that I've told myself time and time again not to become upset by the unkind behaviour of the two servants, I just can't help comparing them to the mild-tempered women I knew at Farringdale House; even those of a higher rank were kind and friendly towards me. I'd been warned that city people, especially Londoners, were difficult to get to know – but was told that once you did get to know them, they'd be your friends for life. Sadly, I'm not on friendly terms with anyone yet, unless I count Mr Fielding who, if I'm honest, I hardly know at all. Robert, of course, is a Londoner, though you'd never guess it. He quickly picked up our village ways through his association with Patty and Celia, but I think it's fair to say that he was cast in a different mould to begin with.

I decide to take a walk to Wandsworth Park to clear my head of the negative thoughts that keep recurring despite my attempts to think positively. It's late afternoon and should be light for at least another couple of hours. Mrs Grist went to her sister-in-law's for high tea and won't be back until much later, probably complaining of indigestion and asking for her tonic.

Taking a stroll out-of-doors may lift my mood, but breathing in the Wandsworth air isn't exactly a healthy exercise. The neighbourhood, with its iron mill and brewery, is dirty and polluted, and even though the park and the common are welcome spaces where one can breathe a little more easily, it's impossible for me not to pine for the green paradise that was my home for almost forty years. But since there's little I can do to relieve that particular ache in my heart, the less I dwell on it the better.

The park is just under a mile's walk from Mrs Grist's house and is situated on the south bank of the River Thames. I've been there a couple of times before, usually when I yearn to see more than a spattering of the colour green. A riverside path borders the park and makes for a pleasant stroll. Of course, the Thames is not a river I'd ever want to bathe in, even in the warmest of weather. I'm told that even though there's less sewage flowing into it now than in the last century – thanks to underground sewage pipes – it's still full of industrial waste that would probably poison any unsuspecting swimmers. Different indeed from the clear water of the river that runs through my village and is popular with bathers on hot summer days.

Today is cooler than of late and overcast, but I hope to avoid the rain, which I believe may be coming our way this evening or even earlier. I'm walking at a fairly brisk pace – as I usually do when I'm alone – but I hear someone coming up behind me, appearing to be walking even faster.

"Is that Miss Bessie Hardwicke?" says a familiar voice. I turn around in surprise. It's Mr Fielding, the very person I was thinking about just minutes before.

"Oh, hello, Mr Fielding," I say, feeling a little awkward at meeting him outside his place of work. I'm used to seeing him in his white pharmacist's coat and he looks so different in his three-piece suit and bowler hat, quite the city gentleman in fact. He carries a black umbrella and has a raincoat over one arm.

"What are you doing on this… this not so fine day?"

he asks me.

"I just needed to get out the house for a little while. So I thought I'd walk to the park, even though I'll probably get caught in the rain. I keep thinking about how much I used to enjoy strolling along the country roads and across the fields back home in the West Country. I know it's a poor comparison, but today I'm going to have to make do with Wandsworth Park."

"Ah, London has its own splendours, but I agree, it's no substitute for the countryside. May I walk with you a little way? I'm going to Mathilda's. I closed the shop early to make sure I'd be there in time for tea."

"Yes, of course. How is Mathilda?"

"She's much better, thank you. No more morning sickness, I'm pleased to say. How is our friend Mrs Fanny Grist?"

"Well, her nerves are still bad, but she's gone to her sister-in-law's for tea. Yesterday she asked me to go to Mr Hornby's for another bottle of brandy, but I took your advice and refused. She was upset with me at first and made an unkind remark, but didn't insist. She asked the cook to go instead. Later, I think she realised she'd spoken in haste and explained that it was easier for her, as a woman, to buy liquor from Mr Hornby than to visit a wine merchant, and that her late husband used to do business with him. I said I suspected that the spirits he sells are adulterated, as they didn't carry a label. She wasn't happy at my implication that she may be buying tainted liquor, but said she'd ask the cook to taste the brandy for her. Of course, Mrs Hopper said it tasted fine.

"Mr Fielding, I know you said you'd speak to Mrs Grist yourself, but I really can't have her suspecting that I've spoken to you about the matter. She wouldn't forgive me and I'm sure I'd lose my position."

"Bessie, my dear, I would never say anything that

would result in such an outcome. We certainly can't have that happening. But you can trust me. I've known Fanny Grist for many years and she knows I'm well aware that she takes the occasional drop of brandy as a nightcap. She regards it as medicinal. And I also know that her son Phillip sometimes drinks too much when things aren't going well for him. I'll raise the subject of their liquor source when I have an opportunity to talk to Fanny about her health and Phillip's in general. But don't worry. I won't compromise you in any way. Please believe me when I say that."

He is such a kind man and I feel so miserable generally that I can feel the familiar onset of tears. I mustn't let him see or he may well suspect that his friendship is more important to me than it should be.

"Thank you, Mr Fielding," I say in as steady a voice as I can manage. "I do trust you. It's just that it's… it's so testing at times. I know Mrs Grist is not a bad person, and now that you've told me about her difficult life and her son's problems, I can understand why she's often short-tempered. But she's just so unpredictable and I find her moods hard to fathom. And the cook and the housekeeper – they're not friendly at all. Perhaps it's my fault, but I can't seem to do anything right."

"Listen to me, Bessie. One thing I'm certain of – it's not your fault. I'm acquainted with Mrs Hopper and I think I'm right in saying that she's related to Basil Hornby. She also has a husband who's a lazy, good-for-nothing fellow, so I suspect that she's an unhappy woman. Some people who aren't happy themselves don't like to see others who are content or doing well in life. It's human nature I'm afraid."

"Well, I'm sure I don't look particularly content. Far from it, in fact. Those women know nothing of my life and yet they still judge me. It's so unfair."

"I know nothing of your life either, Bessie, but I'm judging you as a good, honest young woman. Your position at Mrs Grist's is of a more prestigious nature than that of cook or housekeeper, so it's obvious to me that they're jealous of you. And you're younger and far more presentable than Mrs Hopper – and probably the housekeeper too – so that's another reason for their envy."

"Oh, Mr Fielding, I'm not so young, as you well know, and as for being more presentable... well, I'm sure both those women were better looking than me in their youth. But thank you for your kind words. As for my life, there's not much to know. I grew up in a village in the countryside – my father was a wheelwright. I have two brothers still living and one sister who died young. My father passed away when I was fourteen – he'd never enjoyed good health since fighting in the Crimean War – so in order to help my mother, I left school and went to work as a servant at Farringdale House – it was known in the village as the 'big house' and was the ancestral home of Lord and Lady Radcliffe. I was employed there for twenty-five years – a lifetime it seems. Earlier this year, the Radcliffes were beginning to talk about having to cut down on servants because of financial difficulties – and because the children were growing up and leaving home – so when my good friend Patty, who lives in Clapham with her husband Robert, told me about the job at Mrs Grist's, I applied for it. I never thought I'd get it, but to my astonishment I did. And here I am. That's my life in a nutshell. Quite ordinary really."

"It doesn't sound ordinary to me, Bessie. No one's life is ever ordinary, despite what they themselves may think to the contrary. May I ask you, if it's not too personal a question, why did you never marry? Or perhaps you're a widow?"

"No, I never married. I was engaged to a young man I grew up with, but he passed away before we tied the knot. After that, I didn't have much interest in courting anyone else, despite my mother's despair over my remaining unmarried. I spent many years grieving for Arthur and then my dear sister Ethel, and finally came to the conclusion that it was my fate to live a single life."

"And your mother – is she still alive?"

"No, sadly she died less than a year after Ethel. Like me, she was devastated by her death and her health suffered as a result. Ethel left a son, Walter, who was only five when his mother died in childbirth. My brother Edward took him in when his father Frederick left the village to search for work in the north of England. Frederick claimed he'd return for Walter, but he never did. Edward and his wife Mabel did their best, but I felt that Walter, who was a sensitive boy, needed more love and attention than they were prepared to give him. So I spent as much time as possible with my little nephew. He's nineteen now and we're still very close. In fact, he's like a son to me."

"Well, that just goes to show that you're not ordinary at all. Thank you for telling me your personal history, Bessie. Now I feel I know you a bit better. We'll talk more another time. I'm afraid I have to leave you here. Mathilda's home is on the other side of the river. I'll see you again soon no doubt?"

"If Mrs Grist's nerves don't get any better, you'll probably see me sooner than you'd like. Thank you for walking with me and for your kind words."

"It was my pleasure, Bessie. And I would like to see you sooner rather than later. Look after yourself, my dear."

Mr Fielding takes my gloved hand and gives it a light squeeze. I am almost overcome with emotion, but I manage to smile and say goodbye. He walks away, but turns his head after a few steps and raises his hand in a gesture of farewell. My thoughts are racing. Is it acceptable for a man to pay such compliments to a woman he barely knows? Is this commonplace among Londoners? I have so little experience in these matters that I really can't say. The only man who ever paid me such attention was my beloved Arthur. Later, there were a couple of widowers in the village who were said to be considering me as a possible wife, but they showed me no fondness whatsoever and I could never have subjected myself to a life with either one of them. In any case, Mr Fielding is of a different class completely. I can't think about it anymore, or I'll start imagining a future that could never come to pass. I'm already getting ahead of myself, believing that his kind words mean much more than they actually do.

For my own emotional sanity, I cannot afford to let this unexpected and rather thrilling encounter go to my head. But he took my hand! And looked into my eyes in such a sincere way, as if he really cared for me. I know it's ridiculous, but I already find myself thinking about him when I lie in my bed at night. I relish these thoughts and am powerless to stop them, even though I feel that they border on the sinful and am plagued with guilt at the idea that anyone could ever take the place of Arthur in my affections.

I continue my walk and soon reach the park. Once again, it surprises me that the soothing gifts of nature can exist side by side with the busy and filthy London streets. The assortment of trees in the park astounds me – I cannot name them all but I recognise the common ones like oak, poplar, plane and ash. On the other side of the wide river is a striking silhouette of trees that haven't yet lost their leaves, and I spot many birds and wildfowl, including some I've never seen before. Of course, glimpses of nature in the city cannot be compared to the wonder of the countryside by any stretch of the imagination, but there's a certain grandeur here that's missing in the quiet copses, gentle streams and peaceful meadows that I used to take for granted. Back in the village, I had all the time in the world to enjoy Mother Nature, but that's not the case here. So I must never allow myself to be unmoved when I chance upon her splendours, especially in a place that is far from her natural habitat.

There are benches facing the river so I sit for a few minutes to catch my breath and to enjoy my surroundings, rather than let the conversation with Mr Fielding eclipse all other thoughts. This is my tonic; I don't need it bottled like Mrs Grist does. I'd like to suggest that she try a walk in the park as a possible remedy for her nerves, but I know full well that she'll dismiss the idea as mere foolishness.

I resolve to write to Walter as soon as I get back to the house and tell him about Wandsworth Park and its proximity to the River Thames. Writing to my dear nephew will take my mind off Mr Fielding and bring me back to the reality of my own social class. It still irks me that Mrs Grist looks down on Walter's occupation. But I suppose her remarks mirror my own view that he could be something more than a stonemason. Not that I don't respect the skills that are required for such a trade – I know how hard Walter has worked, and he learnt the craft in record time. He's never sought a higher profession and is proud of what he does. But he was always such a clever boy and, as I've said before, deserved to learn more than what the village school had to offer.

My brother Edward, who never cared much for

education himself – although he had more years of learning than the rest of us – insisted that Walter learn a trade from an early age. He had Walter's best interests at heart and met no objections. I, of course, had no say in the matter. What could I have said? I wasn't able to offer any alternative. Besides, Walter has done remarkably well; he's now working independently and he loves his work. But I'm sure that, given the opportunity, he could have successfully pursued one of the respected professions, like medicine – if that were his calling – or perhaps the bar. Walter has always possessed a strong sense of justice and would have made a worthy solicitor.

Dear me, if Mother were to know my thoughts now, how she would scoff! She always said I was Miss High and Mighty and needed to learn to accept my humble status in life. I suppose she was right – at least insofar as my own ambitions were concerned – but when it comes to Walter, it's a different matter. My aspirations for his success know no bounds.

8

I'm to meet Robert at the Wandle Bridge at three o'clock. The weather is not so pleasant today – in fact, it begins to drizzle soon after I leave the house. Fortunately, I have my umbrella with me, which protects my blue woollen cloak – a gift from Lady Sophia Radcliffe before she left for Italy – but the hem of my dress and my well-worn boots become splattered with mud in no time at all. Even though I arrive a few minutes early, Robert is already there, leaning over the railings, watching a flock of mallards float under the bridge.

"I suggest we tell the sisters that we'd like to take Harriet to see her brother next Sunday," he says, once we're in the shelter of a Hansom cab. "What do you think, Bessie?"

"Yes, I think that's a good idea," I say. "I can't see why the sisters would object. It's not a prison, is it?"

"I would certainly hope not. I'm sure they want the children to be happy. Sister Martha sounded very reasonable in her letter. She said they encourage visits from relatives or friends."

"Was she going to let Harriet know that we're coming, and that we have news of her brother?"

"She didn't say. I hope so. We don't want to startle the girl. She's had enough shocks in the last few weeks to last her a lifetime."

I feel a bit apprehensive when we are dropped off next to a high fortress-like wall, behind which is the tall Gothic building of the orphanage. I'm keen for our meeting with Harriet to yield a positive result, yet the austere surroundings fill me with dread. Robert, however, observes with approval the Benedictine convent on the other side of the road, which he believes enforces the notion of the children's home as a sanctuary. But for me, there's an unnerving stillness surrounding both buildings, giving me the disturbing sense that they deter visitors from entering their interiors rather than welcome them.

As we approach the heavy wooden door that looks as if its sole purpose is to shut out the world and all its prying eyes, Robert tells me that, as well as running an orphanage, the sisters also provide a home for the old and infirm. He says he's made a few local enquiries and discovered that the sisters make it their lives' work to look after the needy, both young and old, and that there are presently about 250 children being cared for, as well as more than 200 elderly residents. It is not for me to judge, and it's not in my nature to be so cynical, but instinct tells me that the care they provide may be spread a little too thinly, if Robert's numbers are correct.

The cast iron doorknocker looks almost too heavy to lift, but Robert succeeds in raising it just enough for a couple of knocks and we wait patiently for someone to arrive. Finally, we hear shuffling steps from within and an elderly sister with wire-rimmed spectacles opens the door a few inches and peers through the gap.

"Who are you and what is your business here?" she asks in a voice that sounds accusatory. But Robert is unfazed and quickly states our purpose, saying that Sister Martha has told us we're allowed to visit. When he shows her the letter, she opens the gate a few more inches.

"But it's Sunday," she says. "This is our day of prayer and visitors are not usually permitted. Sister Martha should not have told you to come on a Sunday. She doesn't yet know the rules – she's new to the sisterhood."

"I'm sorry," Robert says. "But we're here now and we've travelled some distance. If it's not too much trouble, could we please meet with Miss Turnbull? I promise we won't keep her long."

"It really is most irregular, but since you're here you might as well come in. Let me first introduce myself. I'm Sister Agatha and I attend mainly to the older residents. Please wait in the entrance hall and I'll have one of the other sisters find the child you've come to see. You say her name is Turnbull, correct? What is her age?"

"Yes, Miss Harriet Turnbull," Robert confirms. "She's thirteen or thereabouts."

Sister Agatha nods and we follow her inside the orphanage. She points to two hardback chairs placed against the wall underneath a heavy wooden cross, and instructs us to sit and wait. I have a feeling it may be some time before Harriet is found. It's cold in the hall and I'm glad I'm wearing my warm cloak. Robert, bless him, sees me rubbing my hands together and makes a joke about the need for Roman Catholics to suffer before they're welcomed into the heavenly afterlife. "Suffering improves our souls," he says, "and makes us worthy of God's acceptance. So the longer we sit here in the cold, the better it is for us in the long run."

Just as I'm about to give up on our ever meeting Harriet, a young sister appears, followed by a slim, dark-haired girl in a grey tunic.

"Good afternoon," the sister says shyly in a slight foreign accent. "I am Sister Marie-Thérèse. This is Miss Harriet Turnbull. I understand you wish to speak with her."

"Yes, thank you, Sister," Robert says, standing up. "My name is Robert Cartwright, and this is my relative, Miss Hardwicke. Might we talk to Miss Turnbull in private? We have news of her brother."

"Of course. I will wait in the next room. But please don't be too long. We have prayers that begin at four o'clock sharp."

I'm flattered that Robert refers to me as his relative.

As I've said before, I do regard him as a brother, so it's good to know that the familial feeling is mutual.

Sister Marie-Thérèse gives Harriet's hand a squeeze before leaving the entrance hall. She looks young, not much older than Harriet herself, and her habit accentuates her pretty, delicate features.

Robert invites Harriet to sit in the chair he's vacated.

"Miss Turnbull," he says, "may I call you Harriet? You must be wondering who we are. I work at the school in Clapham where your brother Michael is a boarding pupil. Miss Hardwicke here is giving him private lessons in reading. He's been in state of anguish since the two of you were separated following your parents' tragic deaths, so we promised him that we would try to find you. He misses you terribly. Your former neighbour, Mrs Radford, told us you were here. Tell me, Harriet, how are you settling in?"

Harriet has so far said nothing. She looks pale and drawn, poorly even, yet at the same time determined and resolute.

"I'm not settling in because I'm not going to stay here," she says fervently, pushing a greasy strand of hair back from her face. "But I'm glad Michael is at boarding school and not with Uncle Gordon. I hate that man. I wrote to my brother at his address, but I suppose he didn't bother to forward my letter to the school."

"Michael says he hasn't heard from you. He has no idea you're here. But Harriet, what do you mean when you say you're not going to stay here? What plans do you have? Do you have somewhere else to go?"

"Not yet, but I'll find somewhere. I can't stay here. They want to train me to be a sister!" She gives a wry laugh. "They did the same with Marie-Thérèse. She's sixteen and is an orphan too. When her aunt died, she had no other relatives she could live with. She didn't want to become a sister but had no choice. But they're not going to do the same with me! I would rather die!"

"Harriet my dear, I think you're exaggerating. I'm sure the sisters mean well. And I strongly advise you not to leave unless you know where you're going. At least here you have shelter and regular meals. London is a frightening city and you can't live on the streets."

"I'm not frightened of London. I've lived here all my life. But I am scared of staying in this place. You've no idea what it's like. The sisters think they're helping us just by giving us somewhere to live, but most of them are cruel and are always looking for ways to hurt the younger children. I've seen them slap a baby just for crying in the night. And we're always being punished in class. Look at this mark on my arm."

Harriet pulls up her sleeve and the sight of a painful-looking red mark just above her elbow makes me gasp.

"That's from a ruler," she continues, "and it's the least of the injuries I've received in the short time I've been here. I was punished for answering back when all I did was question the spelling of a word Sister Beatrice had written on the blackboard. It was obvious even to me that she'd spelt it wrongly."

"I'm sorry you're finding life here so difficult, Harriet. But trust me, it's better than being on the streets where you risk being seriously harmed or taken to the workhouse. If you can just stick it out for a little while longer, perhaps you'll be able to find work once you turn fourteen. We may be able to help you with that."

"In the meantime," I say, "we can arrange regular meetings between you and your brother. Perhaps next week we could take you to see him? Would you be willing to come with us to Clapham next Sunday?"

"I'd like to, of course I would. I miss Michael just as much as he misses me. But the sisters will insist that a chaperone comes with me. Despite what they say, they don't encourage the orphans to leave the grounds. They're afraid that once we're outside we won't return. The younger children obviously have no choice but to stay, but the older ones often do escape."

"Perhaps Sister Marie-Thérèse could accompany you? Should we ask permission from one of the senior sisters?"

"I don't think they trust her. They know we talk together and I've noticed Sister Beatrice – she's the worst of them all – giving us disapproving looks. One of the older nuns would be asked to accompany me, or rather keep an eye on me. And it would need to be a Saturday, not a Sunday. They're very strict about prayers on Sundays."

"Then perhaps we could bring Michael to see you here," Robert says. "We'd come earlier so as not to interrupt your prayers. How does that sound?"

"It's going to upset him to see me here. I know how sensitive he is. It's better for him to think I'm in a place where I'm happy. If he comes here, he won't believe I'm in a good situation. He'd only have to look at my face to see how miserable I am. Listen, I'll write him a letter now and you can give it to him. But don't let him write to me – I don't think the sisters will give me his letters. Believe me, they're like spies. If you give me his address at the school, I'll try to write to him regularly, though I'll have to ask Marie-Thérèse for envelopes and stamps. She'll need to post the letters for me as well. The sisters don't like us writing to anyone."

"All right, Harriet, though I don't see why they would object to an exchange of letters. I can give you a few coins for stamps. If you write him a note now, I'll tell him that you'll send him a longer letter in a few days. I'll give you his address. Bessie, do you have a pencil and paper in your bag by any chance?"

I delve into my handbag and produce a notebook and a pencil. "Here Harriet," I say. "Tear out the page once you've written your message."

Harriet looks at the blank page for a few moments and then begins to write furiously. She fills one side, turns the page over and writes on the back. At the bottom she does a quick sketch. Then she tears out the sheet, folds it carefully and hands it to Robert. He writes down Michael's address and both of our names on another sheet and gives that to Harriet.

"I did a drawing of our kitten, Romeo," Harriet says. "Michael doesn't know that I managed to find him and that Rosamund Radford has promised to look after him. He'll be pleased to know he's safe."

"Can we visit you again, Harriet?" Robert asks.

"I don't think it's a good idea. The sisters hate it when we receive visitors, especially on a Sunday. It might get me into even more trouble if they think I've asked you to come."

"All right. But we'll keep in touch through Michael. Let him know if you need any help from us. You have our names – Mr Robert Cartwright and Miss Bessie Hardwicke. I can see Sister Marie-Thérèse hovering in the doorway so it's clearly time for us to leave. Remember what I said, Harriet. Just be patient – don't do anything rash. However much you hate it here, there are worse situations you could find yourself in, believe me."

Harriet bids us a quick farewell before turning and hurrying off with the young sister. In spite of the note she's scribbled to Michael and her promise to stay in touch with him, I feel that our visit has been nothing more than a fool's errand. We've not been able to help her in any significant way and the more she suffers punishment at the hands of the sisters, the more she's going to want to escape their tyranny. As if to deter us from ever visiting again, a piercing scream is heard as we descend the front steps, making me shudder.

"What on earth was that?" I exclaim. Even Robert, who's so far been trying to condone the sisters' draconian behaviour, looks shocked.

"Not exactly a sound that gives us confidence in the love and care the children are receiving," he says. "But I think it came from the building next door where the elderly – poor souls – are housed. Don't look so disheartened, Bessie. For the moment, Harriet has no choice but to stay here. At least we've found her and she says she'll write to Michael. You didn't promise the boy anything more than that, did you?"

"No, not really. But I'm worried about the girl, Robert. The fact that she told us not to bring Michael to see her, or take her to see him, and not to let him write, suggests that she doesn't intend to be here much longer."

"Let's not give credence to her talk of running away. She's young and is prone to imagining all sorts of things. I know when I was about her age and was hospitalised for a week, I was constantly thinking of possible ways to escape and return home. In reality, Harriet won't be given the opportunity to leave. You've seen how secure the building is."

Robert's words don't exactly make me feel any better, but I can see his point. The building is a prison – both young and old are incarcerated; they can't possibly get out. I begin to think that Harriet's only hope is for Robert and myself to free her. But I need to be patient. Robert doesn't see the urgency as much as I do, and I can't possibly help her on my own. I'll talk to Patty and see if she can persuade him to start looking for a position for the girl – as a live-in servant perhaps – and thereby release her from the clutches of the Sisters of Gethsemane.

I pass a sleepless night worrying about Harriet, but force myself to rise early on Monday morning to write another letter to Walter. I want to tell him about the Turnbull children and my desire to help them. He's the only person, apart from Patty, to whom I can open my heart. But I don't want him to worry on my behalf, so I won't relate the more sorrowful details, like Michael's tears or Harriet's injuries. Still, knowing Walter, he'll probably be able to read between the lines.

But it's much harder to write about the siblings than I had imagined, and I need to have breakfast before Mrs Hopper arrives. So I fold my unfinished letter in half and place it between the pages of *David Copperfield* before going downstairs. By coincidence, there's a postcard addressed to me on the doormat, and it's from Walter, of course. He doesn't just send me cards – he writes letters as well – but he knows that I love picture postcards and have collected at least a hundred over the years. I couldn't be persuaded to part with any of them when I left the village, even though they took up no small amount of precious space in my carpetbag.

A photograph of Walter's territorial unit at camp in Swanage last August is printed on the front of the card. The whole unit is on its knees in prayer. The photo, which gives me goose pimples the instant I look at it, is captioned 'At Divine Service'. Walter's message is a short one. He writes:

'Dear Aunt, I hope this will find you well as it leaves me. This is a photo of our company at camp last summer. I meant to send it to you before, but better late than never. I hope Aunt Patty and Mr Cartwright are well and that you are able to visit them regularly.

Edie wishes to be remembered to you. Best love, Walter'

The postcard and its message mean so much to me. While the photograph alone is enough to make my day, Walter's closing words, 'Best love', give me added pleasure. He is, without doubt, my best love. I just hope he hasn't sent me the only picture he has of his unit in Swanage. It's such a unique memento, one that he can look back on with pride in later years. Of course, it's impossible to pick out my nephew from the hundreds of men in the photograph, all kneeling on the grass in their smart uniforms, but just to know that he's there is enough.

It was considerate of Walter to ask after Patty and Robert. He knows how much Patty means to me and that she doesn't always enjoy the best of health. Oftentimes I used to take him to visit Patty and her parents at their cottage in the village and he was always well behaved, even when he was a small boy. He would sit quietly sipping his lemonade while we drank our tea, and would politely refuse a second piece of cake, probably knowing full well that Patty or Celia would cut him a slice anyway.

How I wish I could hold him in my arms – all six foot of him – right at this moment. I miss him so much and would give anything to talk to him in person just for a few minutes. Edie Bancroft is surely the luckiest girl in the world! It would delight any girl in the village to step out with Walter – he could have his pick – yet he has chosen Edie as his sweetheart. Of course, the feeling is mutual, but I hope she never forgets how fortunate she is to have captured my dear nephew's heart.

The yearning I feel when I think about Walter – which is most of the time – reminds me of just how much Michael must be missing Harriet. At least I can take comfort in the knowledge that Walter keeps in touch with me regularly and is in good health and spirits, but poor Michael is completely in the dark about Harriet's wellbeing, and doesn't know if he'll ever see her again. I cannot let the boy continue to suffer. However much Robert might caution me about raising his hopes, I will not let him down. I will pursue with determination the goal of reuniting the siblings, however many hurdles are thrown in my path.

9

Mrs Grist says she's in the mood for poetry and asks me to fetch a volume by Alfred Lord Tennyson from the bookcase. She picks an epic poem and says we will recite three verses each. I'm a bit nervous. If I stumble over the words, it will spoil the rhythm and my employer will become annoyed. Before we begin, she asks me if I've heard of the famous quotation: 'Tis better to have loved and lost than never to have loved at all'. I tell her I *have* heard of it and that it's one of my favourite quotes.

"Well, did you know" she says, "that it was penned by Tennyson and is embedded in the last stanza of the poem we're about to recite?"

"No," I say, "I didn't know that. I had no idea of its origin. I'm learning something new every day!"

She goes on to tell me the poem is called *In Memoriam,* that it was written over a period of seventeen years, and is an elegy to the memory of Tennyson's close friend, Arthur Henry Hallam, who died suddenly at the age of twenty-two.

Am I in the mood for such a sad poem? Probably not, but I have no choice. It's Mrs Grist's mood that's important, not mine. She begins to read and the sadness and beauty of the words captivate me. To my great embarrassment, my eyes fill with tears when I hear the words:

> 'So find I every pleasant spot
> In which we two were wont to meet,
> The field, the chamber, and the street,
> For all is dark where thou art not.'

Mrs Grist hands me the volume and I manage to

compose myself enough to read aloud. But my dry eyes are short-lived. Three verses later, Tennyson mentions 'my lost Arthur's loved remains' and my tears well up again. Mrs Grist reads the final verse of that canto:

> 'My Arthur, whom I shall not see
> Till all my widow'd race be run;
> Dear as the mother to the son,
> More than my brothers are to me.'

At this point I can no longer control myself and have to pull a handkerchief from my sleeve to wipe my overflowing eyes.

"What on earth is the matter with you, Elizabeth?" Mrs Grist asks.

"I'm so sorry, Mrs Grist," I blurt out. "It's just that the words are so moving. It's such a sad poem."

"A lot of poems are sad – that's their particular charm – but rarely to the extent that one is reduced to tears. There must be something else. What is it?"

"You'll think I'm silly if I tell you."

"That's for me to decide."

"Well, when I was a young woman, twenty years old, I had a sweetheart whose name was Arthur. We were engaged to be married. But he had a terrible accident and died. He was a thatcher and he fell off a roof during a sudden storm. His foot slipped and he couldn't right himself. He met his death instantly. He was twenty-two, the same age as Tennyson's friend."

"And you are still grieving for this man, all these years later?"

"Yes, I can't help it. He was the love of my life and is the reason why I never married. He was in his prime, strong and healthy, and then suddenly there he was, lying lifeless on the ground. Arthur was an only child and his mother didn't get over the shock – she died the following year. She was the age that I am now."

"It's a sad story, no doubt about it, but you must remember what I quoted to you, the words that Tennyson himself wrote: 'Tis better to have loved and lost than never to have loved at all'. You knew the love of your Arthur and you have precious memories of him as a healthy young man, full of life. You must be thankful for that, Elizabeth."

"Yes, you're right, Mrs Grist. Believe me, I am thankful. At least I've known true love. I feel better now. Shall we continue?"

"I think that's enough for today. Why don't you take the volume and read the poem in the quiet of your room. Then you can cry to your heart's content. It might do you good. Sometimes it helps to know that others have endured grief similar to your own."

"Thank you, I'll do that. And sorry for breaking down like that in the middle of the poem."

"You don't need to apologise. We all have our crosses to bear. Life is not, nor ever has been, a bed of roses."

I pick up the book and leave the room, telling Mrs Grist to call me if she needs anything. She's being unusually kind. Perhaps Mr Fielding is right – her bark *is* worse than her bite. I feel so embarrassed that I was unable to control my emotions, but the fact that the poem concerned a young man called Arthur, who died at twenty-two, was too much of a coincidence and came as such a painful reminder of my own loss. And of course I've been thinking a lot about Arthur lately. Whenever I'm feeling under the weather or have a problem that's niggling me, I begin to feel sorry for myself, and question why he was taken from me. That's selfish of me, I know. *He* was the one who lost his life, not me, and his mother's suffering took *her* to an early grave. But sometimes, to my shame, I forget the sanctity of life and wish that my own had ended with Arthur's.

I sit by the window in my room, solemnly looking out at the garden. I won't read any more of Tennyson today. I need to be in a better frame of mind to be able to appreciate the beauty of his words without taking them too personally. It's a breezy day and gusts of wind are blowing leaves all over the garden. The lawn is a carpet of browns, oranges and yellows. I'm reminded of my childhood when Ethel and I used to jump up and down on the crunchy piles of leaves, having such fun. We'd each hold one of Patty's arms so she could enjoy it too. Whatever blows the last two decades have dealt me, I can at least say with all honesty that I had a happy childhood.

My thoughts inevitably turn to Michael whose childhood has not been so blessed. At least I was already grown up when tragedy struck twice within a few short years and I lost my beloved fiancé Arthur and my cherished sister Ethel. Poor Michael lost both his parents and his home at the tender age of eleven. When I think about his terrible losses, my heart aches for him.

I'm about to resume my letter to Walter when Mrs Grist's bell rings. I pass Mrs Evans on the stairs and I greet her cordially, but she ignores me. The downward turn of her mouth makes me think that she's been scolded for something, and the fact that I've now been called for has probably angered her.

"Elizabeth," Mrs Grist says, "I'd like you to go to the pharmacy right away. Mrs Evans has brought me the wrong type of soap. She should know by now that I only use Pears, yet she's gone and purchased Lifebuoy. She insists Pears wasn't available, but I know Mr Fielding has it in stock. I can't take my bath until I have my favourite soap. It does wonders for my skin."

She fumbles in her purse and hands me some coins.

"Don't waste time chatting," she says. "I want to take my bath the minute you get back."

Why does she think I spend so much time chatting to Mr Fielding? This is not the first time she's warned me against it. I'm disturbed by such a thought. Where is the sympathetic Mrs Grist of earlier today? How quickly her mood changes! I don't really want to go to the pharmacy. I shall feel too embarrassed after the way Mr Fielding took my hand at the end of our walk together the other afternoon. He may think I'm finding excuses to go to his shop. But hopefully he'll understand that the purchase is for Mrs Grist and that I have to do as she instructs. I don't even have a chance to look in the mirror before I leave the house. My eyes must still be puffy from my earlier tears and this wind is so strong that I have to pull my hat down over my ears to stop it from blowing off. I hate having to face Mr Fielding looking such a sight, but perhaps it's just as well. It might deter him from paying me more compliments.

"Good afternoon, Bessie," he says as I walk through the door. "To what do I owe this pleasure?"

"I'm on another errand for Mrs Grist," I say matter-of-factly. "She needs a bar of Pears soap. She says you have a stock of them."

Mr Fielding laughs. "What makes her think that? I think I have just two bars left. But you shall take both of them. Two for the price of one. How does that sound?"

"I think Mrs Grist may be annoyed if I accept your kind offer. She has a suspicious nature and will think she's being tricked in some way. I think it's best that I just take the one bar."

"Then you shall have the second one for yourself, Bessie. No, don't look like that. I insist on it. I'll order some more tomorrow in case Fanny runs out again. We can't have her using Lifebuoy, now, can we?"

"It's very kind of you, Mr Fielding, but I really must refuse. Let me just buy the one bar for Mrs Grist."

"Bessie, I won't take no for an answer. You *will* accept my offer. And not only will you take this bar of soap for yourself, but you'll also take this bag of pear drops to go with your Pears soap."

Mr Fielding produces a bag of pear drops from one of his many drawers. He comes out from behind the counter and thrusts the soap and the sweets into my hands. Despite myself, I have to laugh at his antics. And since I don't want to appear ungrateful or impolite, I have no choice but to accept the gifts.

"And now, Miss Bessie Hardwicke," he says. "You will follow the example of Mrs Lillie Langtry and state to all the world that you 'prefer Pears' soap to any other'. You are certainly no less beautiful than that popular actress."

"Please, Mr Fielding, you're making me blush. Thank you ever so much for the soap and the pear drops. But I beg you, let this be the last kindness I receive from you, or I shall be hesitant to come here in the future."

"Oh, Bessie, don't say that. I do so look forward to your visits. But, if you insist, I will think twice before offering you any small item as a token of our friendship."

Before he can say anything else to make me redden even more, I give him the money for Mrs Grist's one bar of soap and make a quick exit. As I've said before, I'm so inexperienced in accepting compliments that I become flustered every time he expresses words of a personal nature. And yet I like him enormously. I just feel unequal to him on so many levels – class, status, knowledge, wealth – you name it. The fact that he continues to flirt with me – though I hardly know if you can call it that – makes me wonder if he's making fun of me. But I'm sure he's too honourable a man to play such a game on a poor single woman like myself. With Mrs Grist, it would be different – she always gives as good as she gets – but I cannot utter a single sentence without getting tongue-tied. Ah, Mr Fielding, you're giving me pleasure and disquiet in equal measure!

Robert has written suggesting that we meet at the school gates on Sunday and that my session with Michael take place in the library, as it's now too cool to sit outside for long. It surprises me that we're allowed to use the library over the weekend – after all, Robert is not one of the masters – but he tells me that Brother Luke is his good friend and is happy to give us access.

The school is called a college, which sounds very grand and adds to my unease at setting foot inside an educational establishment – other than the village school – for the first time in my life. But the main building looks so much more welcoming that the Hammersmith orphanage, and the grounds are a pleasant mixture of shrubs, late-blooming flowers and newly mown lawns – thanks to Robert's hard work, of course.

Robert and Michael are waiting for me when I arrive, breathless from hurrying. I'm curious to know Michael's reaction to Harriet's letter, but will wait for Robert to leave before I talk to him about it. We enter a long hallway where one of the walls is completely bare except for a large, framed reproduction of 'The Last Supper'. Trophies and plaques recognising student achievements are displayed on mounted shelves on the opposite wall. At the far end of the hallway is the library – a spacious room with bookshelves that reach right up to the ceiling. The top shelves are lined with thick tomes that look as if they haven't been touched for decades. I feel privileged to enter such a place of learning, and I breathe in the room's musty aroma with appreciation. I love being in the presence of dusty, ancient books that transport me to another age without my even having to open their covers.

"It's so quiet," I whisper to Robert as Michael chooses where he wants to sit. "Where are all the other boarders?"

"There are only a few," Robert tells me. "And today they've been taken to a mass at Westminster Cathedral. It's All Saints' Day on Tuesday and the school thought it would be an appropriate outing for the boys. Brother Luke said Michael could be excused unless he particularly wanted to go. When I asked him, he said he'd rather stay here and meet with you."

"Oh, I hope he wasn't just being polite."

"No, I don't think so. Most boys of his age prefer to avoid mass if they can, and even the grandeur of Westminster Cathedral is unlikely to tempt them."

"Well, I'd better make the session interesting for him since he's declined the school excursion."

"I'm sure all your sessions are interesting, Bessie. I'll leave you now and come back in an hour. You'll take tea with us, won't you? You know how much Patty looks forward to it."

"Thank you, Robert. You're both very kind."

Robert leaves, closing the door behind him, and I sit down next to Michael at the reading table nearest the window. There's still enough natural light for us to read by.

"Harriet wrote to me," Michael says as I retrieve *David Copperfield* from my bag. "She told me she's in an orphanage – a Catholic one – but won't be there for much longer. She's planning to run away and will then come and find me. Until that happens, she promises to keep writing to me."

I'm not sure how to respond. I find it disturbing that Harriet has admitted to Michael that she intends to leave the orphanage, even though I suspected as much. I wonder if Robert read the note she wrote to her brother. Of course, it wouldn't have been the proper thing to do, but I would have found it hard to resist, given that she'd been unable to enclose it in a sealed envelope.

"You'll let Mr Cartwright know if she contacts you again, won't you Michael?" I say finally. "If she does intend to leave the orphanage, we want to make sure she's in a safe place and is being looked after."

"Oh, Harriet can look after herself," Michael says confidently. "I told you, she looked after all of us. We knew Mother was dying, but she kept her alive even though the doctor only gave her a week to live. In fact, she lived for another three months before…"

"It's all right, Michael," I say quickly. "I know that Harriet is remarkable in many ways. But London is a big city and danger is lurking at every corner. We don't want to interfere with her plans, but she should know she's able to come to us for help if she needs it. Even someone as capable as Harriet has to have friends she can turn to."

"All right. But I'm sure Harriet will know what she's doing. She'll plan everything carefully. You don't know her like I do."

I think it best to leave it at that. I don't want him to feel as anxious as I do about Harriet's determination not to stay in the orphanage. I place Mr Fielding's bag of pear drops on the table.

"Do you like pear drops, Michael? I say. "Help yourself. If there are any left when we finish, you can take them with you. Now, let's do some reading. Where shall we begin today?"

I decide to skip the chapter concerning David's departure from Salem House School due to his mother's death. It's sure to remind Michael of the terrible loss of his own mother, which also resulted in a change of school. And I certainly intend to omit the chapter about

David's cruel stepfather who sends him to work in London, the same dangerous city in which Harriet might well find herself as destitute as poor David. Instead, I move on to the more cheerful episode of his reunion with his aunt, Betsey Trotwood, in Dover. Michael is incredulous at the idea that David has run away from the London wine-bottling factory and walked over seventy miles to Dover.

"How old was he at that time?" Michael asks.

"I'm not entirely sure," I say. "But I believe he was only ten when Mr Murdstone sent him to London, so probably not more than eleven."

"That's my age." Michael stares at me in wonderment and I begin to suspect that he may be entertaining the thought of running away from school, buoyed on by Harriet plan to 'escape' from the orphanage. I quickly tell him that David's situation was desperate; he had no friends once the kindhearted Mr Micawber was imprisoned, and no one cared whether he lived or died.

"So you see, Michael," I say. "David wants to find the only living relative he's aware of – his aunt, Betsey Trotwood – even though she walked out of his life at the time of his birth because he was a boy and not a girl. But I think you'll find that we can forgive her for that. Let's find out how David gets on once he reaches Dover."

Michael is amused by Aunt Betsey's eccentric ways and those of her lodger, Mr Dick. It's good to see the boy chuckling. He's definitely becoming more at ease with me, which is exactly what I'd hoped for. His reading skills are good; there's hardly a word he's unable to pronounce and he can understand the story without difficulty, despite all the bits I've left out. I'm certain that he doesn't really need a tutor at all – definitely not in reading – just someone with whom he can unburden himself of his troubles. But if those concerned want to call me a tutor, then who am I to object? This hour or so every other Sunday gives the boy some relief from the constraints of school life and, at the same time, gives me a chance to forget *my* worries. Killing two birds with one stone, as Father used to say.

The hour passes quickly and neither of us hears Robert entering the room. We are both laughing about Aunt Betsey's decision to rename David, 'Trotwood Copperfield'.

"She can't do that," Michael exclaims. "Trotwood isn't his Christian name!"

"I think you'll find Aunt Betsey can do any number of things that others would find peculiar," I say, closing the book.

"It's good to hear laughter," Robert says. "You seem to be enjoying David Copperfield's escapades, Turnbull. And are those pear drops I see? Miss Hardwicke seems to have forgotten to offer me one."

"Help yourself," I say. "Michael will take the rest with him. But remember, Michael – no eating sweets after cleaning your teeth, which I hope you do every evening. Now that's an order!"

Michael gives me a shy smile and offers the bag of sweets to Robert before depositing it safely in his trouser pocket.

"You know your way back to the common room, Turnbull," Robert says as we leave the library. "Miss Hardwicke will be back to continue David's story next Sunday week."

I follow Robert into the hallway. Michael begins to climb the stairs at a very slow pace, as if delaying his return to the common room for as long as possible. My heart goes out to the boy. I feel that in locating Harriet, we've given him a measure of hope, but have nothing more to offer him. Who knows when he'll hear from her again? If only we could have arranged for him to visit her at the orphanage, or for her to come to the school to see him. But Harriet was adamant that neither approach would work. Is it because she's already hatched a plan for fleeing the orphanage and intends to set out on her own through the streets of London, in much the same way as our fictional hero, David Copperfield?

10

I never did finish my letter to Walter, and now it won't be necessary. To my great surprise and joy, he's written to tell me that he'll be coming to the big city this Sunday. He's cycled all the way to Maidenhead, his place of work for the next fortnight, and says he plans to catch the train to London on Sunday morning, arriving at twelve o'clock. I cannot wait to see him!

Mrs Grist is wondering why I'm grinning like a Cheshire cat this morning, so I show her the postcard of Cliveden House, near Maidenhead, that Walter enclosed with his letter. She tells me that our late queen was a frequent visitor at the country house, but that it's now the home of the Astor family who, she says, love to entertain the rich and famous. Well, Walter certainly won't be receiving a welcome there, but he'll receive a most heartfelt one from me when he steps off the train at Paddington station.

I tell her how thrilled I am that he's finally coming to London and ask where she thinks I should take him for tea.

"The obvious choice," she says, "is a Lyons tea room. There's one in Piccadilly – in fact, it's the first one Mr Joe Lyons opened. If your nephew hasn't visited London before, he'll be impressed by the liveliness of Piccadilly Circus and its surrounding streets. And if it's a nice day, you can show him some of London's famous sights on foot from there. I know how much you dislike public transport."

"Thank you, Mrs Grist," I say. "Yes, this will be his first time in the city. He travels a lot for his work, as I've told you, but not usually to large cities. He's a country boy at heart and prefers to work in rural settings if he has a choice."

"Where does he stay when he has to work far from home?"

"Oh, he usually finds lodgings upon arrival. Mostly it's just for a few nights, though this time he says he'll be in Maidenhead for two or more weeks."

I don't tell her that Walter often spends the night in the open air when he arrives at a destination late in the evening. On more than one occasion he's found shelter under a hedgerow or in a farmer's hayloft during the summer months, though obviously he tries to avoid having to resort to such measures in the winter.

I excuse myself from church on Sunday morning, as I'm too excited about Walter's visit to be able to concentrate on the Reverend Thomas Wilson's sermon, which is seldom a short one. And since his train arrives at midday, I must give myself enough time to get to the station. Fortunately, the weather gods are on my side and it's a clear, crisp autumn morning. I set off in good time, wearing my blue woollen cloak and my best leather gloves, and manage to board the motorbus, thanks to Mrs Grist's instructions. She's right about my loathing of public transport; travelling alone still makes me anxious, even after several months in the city. She's given me a map of London, as well as a pocket underground map, although the thought of being transported through a tunnel beneath the city streets still terrifies me. But after careful study of the city map, I've decided that we can easily walk from Paddington to Piccadilly by way of Hyde Park and St James's Park. For me, and probably Walter too, that'll be much more pleasant than risking an attack of claustrophobia on the underground railway.

I remember arriving at Paddington station on my first day in London. I'd come up from the West Country and was a bundle of nerves. Patty and Robert wanted to meet me, but then I received a letter from Mrs Grist stating that she'd be waiting for me at the station, so I had to refuse my friends' kind offer. Even though I'd never met Mrs Grist before, she seemed to know who I was and approached me directly. I suppose there were not many unaccompanied women alighting from the train and I was conspicuously carrying all my worldly goods in a cardboard suitcase and an old carpetbag. We took a motor cab to Wandsworth and I should have treasured the experience, but was too anxious in the presence of my formidable employer to enjoy the ride. It must have cost her a lot of money and I hoped I thanked her sufficiently, though I can't remember whether I did or not. Come to think of it, she was kind to me those first few days, and I wish I'd been more appreciative at the time. But I was still getting used to her changeable moods and, for several days, I was a nervous wreck as I tried to understand and perform properly my duties as her companion.

Still, for all my timidity and anxiety, I've had more new experiences in the last few months than in all of the many years I worked at Farringdale House. So I don't know why I keep wishing I was back there, but I do. Perhaps if I'd had this opportunity earlier in my life, I'd have been able to tackle it with more self-confidence and courage. As it is, I wake up every morning filled with dread as to what the day will bring, and constantly question whether I'm fit for new challenges.

Enough of my pondering, here is my stop and everyone seems to be getting off the bus. The street upon which I'm deposited is so crowded and unfamiliar that it takes me a few moments to find my bearings. But I see now that Paddington station is almost directly opposite the bus stop, so it's impossible for me to get lost. Everyone around me is moving so quickly that I too feel the need to hurry towards the station concourse. A large three-faced clock on platform one tells me the time and I'm alarmed to discover that I'm five minutes late. Walter's train must already have arrived. But fortunately, before I can start panicking, I spot my dear nephew striding towards me.

"Walter!" I cry. "I'm sorry I'm late. Oh, it's wonderful to see you!"

"Dear Aunt Bessie," Walter says, giving me a hug. "You're not late at all. I've only just got off the train. How are you, Aunt?"

"I'm so much better for seeing you, Walter. You're looking extremely well. Can it be that you've grown even taller?"

Walter laughs. He's used to relatives commenting on how tall he is. The only other male member of the family who comes close to his height is his cousin Joseph, who's five foot ten. Walter reached six foot when he was just sixteen. I look at him with pride, as though he were my own son. His dark wavy hair is combed back and his blue eyes sparkle. He's wearing a double-breasted grey suit and a navy tie, so different form his usual work clothes. How handsome he is!

"*And* you're looking exceptionally smart today, Walter," I say, linking my arm in his. "I'm proud to be your companion. Since the weather's fine, I thought we might walk to Piccadilly. I have a map in my bag and have worked out the route. When we reach Piccadilly, Mrs Grist suggests that we take tea in a Lyons tea room. How does that sound to you?"

"It sounds perfect, Aunt. My train back to Maidenhead doesn't leave until six o'clock this evening, so we have plenty of time. But first let me enjoy the splendour of Paddington railway station. Just look at that glazed roof and those magnificent arches! Brunel was truly a visionary, don't you think? And believe it or not, only this morning I was lucky enough to see another of his astonishing achievements. He built the Sounding Arch railway bridge across the Thames in Maidenhead, the widest arched bridge ever constructed. Just listen to me! I haven't been in London for five minutes, yet I'm already talking about architecture."

"That's all right, Walter. I love hearing you speak about things you're passionate about."

"Well, just let me know if I start to bore you. I'm told I can go on a bit."

"You never bore me, my dear. But tell me, are you hungry? Would you like to have a bite to eat before we leave Paddington?"

"No thank you, Aunt. I had a cooked breakfast and, just as I was leaving, my landlady gave me a couple of sausage rolls, which I ate on the train. So I can easily wait until teatime. What about you? Have you eaten something?"

"Oh yes. I didn't go to church so I had breakfast late. I'm not hungry either. Let's get away from these crowds before we lose each other."

A few minutes later we're sauntering through Hyde Park under cloudless skies. We stop to watch the children playing with their boats on the Serpentine. It moves me when Walter says he's reminded of the afternoons we used to spend on the riverbank. He goes on to say that he and Edie often walk there on a summer evening and my name is always mentioned. I take the opportunity to ask him how his courtship is progressing.

"Hmm, Edie," he says pensively. "She has a mind of her own, Aunt. Not that I'm against that, but sometimes I wonder where it's going to lead her… and us. I can't think about marriage just yet. She's not ready for it, and neither am I."

"Well, you're only nineteen, Walter," I say. "You shouldn't need to think about settling down for a while. But what do you mean exactly when you say Edie has a mind of her own?"

"Well, to begin with, she wants to have a career. And, as you know, nurses must give up their jobs once they marry. This rule infuriates Edie, and rightly so. She says, if that's the case, then she won't marry at all. I think perhaps she'll change her mind about that, but then again, she may not. And not only that... You'll have heard about the Suffragettes, Aunt – the followers of Mrs Emmeline Pankhurst, who are campaigning for women's rights and are prepared to take all kinds of drastic measures to further their cause. Well, Edie is a keen supporter of that movement and I'm not sure she knows what she's getting herself into."

"Just a minute, Walter. I've heard folk talk about the Suffragettes here in London, but never in the village. You're saying Edie supports these women and their marches?"

"Yes, that's exactly what I'm saying. In fact, walking through this very park reminded me of something she said when I told her I'd be spending a day in London. She suggested that I visit Hyde Park, not because of its beauty but because there was a rally here last July in support of the Conciliation Bill. This bill, if passed in Parliament, will give some women – mostly wealthy property owners – the right to vote. Edie is adamant that women should have the same rights as men and, although I can understand the reasons behind the campaign, I worry about where it's all going to end, for Edie at least. If she had half a chance, she'd be here in London working with the WSPU – that's the Women's Social and Political Union – which is the organisation founded by Mrs Pankhurst."

"Goodness me, Walter. Here I am, a woman myself, living in the very city where all this is happening, and yet I know almost nothing about it. I really should follow the news more regularly. But I don't think you should worry too much. Edie is young, like you, and passionate about just causes. If you're convinced she's the right one for you, then give her time. Despite what she says about preferring a career over marriage, she won't want to give up the chance of having a family of her own, will she?"

"I don't know, Aunt. Even before she became fascinated by the Suffragette movement, she was the most headstrong lass I've ever met. It's what attracted me to her in the first place. Now, after hearing about Mrs Pankhurst and her campaigns, she's more determined than ever to pursue her own goals. For now, I'm ready to wait to see what happens. As I said, I'm in no rush to marry, but I can't wait forever."

"I'm sure she'll change, given time. Her interest in the movement will probably start to wane once she realises that there are other more important things she needs to pay attention to – like a future life with you."

Walter just nods. I can see that he's worried about Edie, and I have to admit that I'm also disturbed by what he's told me. I had no idea she had such modern ideas. I'm not saying I disagree with them, but I just haven't thought that much about whether or not women should be given the right to vote. I suppose I'm just stuck in the last century where politics was always the terrain of men and any reform had to receive their sanction first. It does seem likely that women will have to put up a fight if they want things to change. Men will never accept giving women a voice unless they feel they have no choice but to do so. I feel ashamed for my lack of knowledge, but living all my life in a village, where tradition and respect for the old ways are more important than so-called 'newfangled' ideas, hasn't exactly helped me to keep up with the times. Well, Edie's a village girl too, but she's much younger and is now mixing with more worldly young women, who no doubt encourage her to think for herself. I just hope and pray this new passion doesn't crush the love she must surely feel for Walter.

With the help of Mrs Grist's map, we manage to locate Buckingham Palace, which I've seen once before but only from the top deck of a motorbus. Looking at the royal family's residence for the first time reminds Walter of the late King Edward VII, who took his last breath there just seven months ago at the age of sixty-eight.

"It's a shame," Walter says, "that he reigned only for ten years. He spent most of his life waiting for the throne, so it's no wonder he gained a reputation for being a playboy. But, despite that, he was a popular monarch."

"Hmm," I say, "I'm not sure that his long tenure as Prince of Wales is a valid excuse for his philandering. But you're right – he was already past his prime when he was crowned king. At least his son George has more of a chance to reign for a longer period. I think he's only in his mid-forties."

"Yes, that's true. He never expected to be king, did he? His older brother Albert was the heir apparent, but died young. But perhaps that was for the best given the number of scandals that surrounded *him*. I think George V promises to be a more respected monarch than Albert would ever have been."

"Let's hope so. Did I tell you that Patty and Robert have invited me to watch the coronation procession with them when it takes place next year? I'm already looking forward to it."

"Oh, that's wonderful, Aunt! Lucky you! It's sure to be such a memorable experience. I'll expect you to write to tell me all about it. And please send me any newspaper articles you're able to lay your hands on. Unless you want to keep them yourself, of course."

We spend a few minutes admiring the statue of Eros in Piccadilly Circus, a rather controversial monument honouring the 7th Earl of Shaftesbury, who campaigned to replace child labour with school attendance. Walter, clever boy that he is, knows all about the history of this and many other monuments in London, and puts me to shame for not having sufficiently educated myself before coming to live in the city. Some people, Walter tells me, find Eros too sensual a figure for such a memorial, but he believes that the winged Eros – Greek god of love and romance – is a fine depiction since it was love of humankind that inspired Shaftesbury's good works. I find that hard to dispute.

Our walk has given us an appetite and the tea room is hard to miss. The sign of J. Lyons & Co Ltd is displayed in large lettering above its entrance. It's crowded inside, but Walter attracts the eye of a pretty young waitress and we're given a table right away. Sitting with Walter in an elegant London tearoom is an extravagance I could never have imagined would be mine to enjoy. I feel a little bit like a fish out of water, but I decide to ignore the thought and behave as though this is an everyday occurrence. Walter certainly doesn't look out of place; both his attire and his manners are perfectly attuned to London life. Although still young, he's travelled far more than I have, and has no doubt eaten many meals in taverns or public dining rooms. In contrast, I have never before taken a meal outside my own abode or that of my friends. I intend to savour every moment of this indulgence! I do, however, experience a pang of remorse that it is not Walter's dear mother enjoying his company instead of me. How proud Ethel would be to see him now!

Once our tea is poured and we are enjoying a

mountain of tiny sandwiches and cakes, I start to tell Walter about Michael and the misfortunes he's had to endure.

"I'm reading *David Copperfield* with him," I say, smiling. "How many times did we read it? At least three or four, I think. My – or rather your – ancient copy is practically falling apart."

"You're making me envious, Aunt," Walter says. "I wish I was Michael's age again and reading about David's adventures with you. From what you're telling me, there seem to be some similarities between Michael and myself. He's lost his parents and is living with an uncle who doesn't particularly care for him. And now he's found an aunt – a substitute one I admit – who's taking an interest in him."

"Yes, that thought crossed my mind too. But Walter, Edward does care for you, even though he might not always show it."

"I know. I shouldn't have said that. But you were the only one who showed me any real affection. You were like a mother to me."

"It's kind of you to say so. I just wish I could have spent more time with you. It was difficult since I lived and worked at Farringdale House, as you know, and was only allowed one day off a week."

"Well, I used to look forward to that one day for most of my childhood."

"I'm gratified to hear that, Walter. The other thing I wanted to tell you concerns Michael's sister, Harriet."

I pause while the pretty waitress refills our teacups. She wears a spotless white apron with a heart-shaped bodice. For some minutes she's been looking at Walter, waiting for a chance to come over to our table. But Walter barely notices her and just says, "Thank you kindly," without even looking at her. Poor girl! I want to tell him to make her day by saying something complimentary, but he's too much in love with Edie to notice any other young ladies.

"Michael's uncle wouldn't take Harriet who, at thirteen, is a little bit older," I continue. "He's a bachelor and said he wouldn't be able to cope with a girl of her age. He did what he could for Michael by sending him to a good boarding school, but has no interest whatsoever in his niece. She's been sent to an orphanage run by a Roman Catholic convent. Robert and I visited her there and she's terribly unhappy. She says the sisters in charge are strict and often punish the children for no reason. She showed us a painful-looking mark on her arm where she'd been hit with a ruler just for questioning the spelling of a word. I wish we could do something for her, but I think Robert is reluctant to get involved, though he did say that perhaps we could help her find work when she's a bit older."

"I'm sorry to hear that, Aunt," Walter says. "It doesn't sound as if she has much of a future ahead of her. Poor girl. She must still be grieving for her parents."

"Yes, for her mother at least. According to Michael, Harriet did everything at home. Their mother was an invalid and their father was intoxicated more often than not. So she had to leave school to care for her sick mother and her brother. She's a plucky girl and deserves better. I'm concerned because she seems intent on running away from the orphanage – though where she plans to go is unclear. Robert told her that if she does run away, she risks being caught and taken to a workhouse – or she could find herself in an even worse situation – but I don't think that'll deter her. She says she feels imprisoned and is determined to find a way to escape. Robert doesn't think she's serious and says I shouldn't worry about it, but Michael insists that his sister won't stay in an orphanage a minute longer than she has to."

"I can understand why you want to help the girl, Aunt Bessie. But perhaps Mr Cartwright is right – you shouldn't worry too much about her. It would be wrong to mistake London for our village where folk take care of each other. Here, it's everyone for himself. Harriet may be only thirteen, but if she's always lived in the city and taken on the responsibilities you say she has, she's probably quite capable of looking after herself. You're helping her younger brother and I think that's more than enough."

"I suppose you're right. I just feel so sorry for her, trapped as she is in that orphanage. Anyway, despite what she says, I think it'll be difficult for her to leave. Robert says there's no way she can get out – they keep all the doors locked and the gates bolted. But she's made a friend of one of the young sisters, a French lass called Sister Marie-Thérèse, who's just as unhappy as she is. I suspect she may enlist her help if she does decide to run away."

"Well, let's hope she knows what she's doing and has somewhere to go if she does find a way to leave. But promise me you won't worry about her, Aunt. If she has a good head on her shoulders, she'll be all right, I'm sure."

I nod my head and smile. It seems that our roles are reversed. Walter is now the one reassuring me, not the other way round. I'm enormously proud of him, but at the same time I feel a bit sad that he's no longer the little boy who never wanted to let go of my hand.

"Today has been a real treat," he says, looking at his pocket watch. "This Lyons tea room is such a popular place – people are queuing up for a table. Perhaps we should vacate ours now if you're ready to leave. I don't want to miss my train from Paddington."

He puts his hand into his trouser pocket and draws out

some coins. I place my hand over his.

"Walter, no," I say resolutely. "This is my treat. You've already had to pay for your train fare. Put your money away, please."

"Are you sure, Aunt?"

"Yes, quite sure. If I can't treat my favourite nephew to a high tea, then I must be in a sorry state indeed."

"All right, if you insist. Thank you. Let's try to find a motorbus to take us back to Paddington station – unless you want to go straight back to Wandsworth from here."

"Oh no. I want to see you off at the station. I thought you might want to go on the underground railway. I've not been on it myself but if you want to give it a try, then I'm willing to accompany you. I'm told it's very fast."

"Let's do that the next time I visit. It's such lovely weather today that I think I prefer to stay above ground."

"Good, that's my preference too." I hand Walter a florin. "Here, you pay the waitress. She's been looking at you for the last hour, so the least you can do is smile at her. And give her a ha'penny tip too, since she's been so attentive."

Walter looks at me with a shocked expression. Then he laughs and says, "Good gracious me, Aunt! What will Edie say when I tell her you've been matchmaking!"

11

Walter's visit has cheered me up no end. He says he'll try to come again if he's working reasonably close to London. Knowing that I might see him from time to time gives me the strength to carry on in my less than perfect present situation.

He asked me what my plans were for Christmas. I have not even thought about Christmas yet and can't believe it's drawing close. I told him that I would probably spend the day with Patty and Robert – assuming of course that Mrs Grist gives me the time off work. When I asked him what *his* plans were, he said he didn't have any. That made me feel sad and guilty. Since Mother died, I've always gone to Edward's on Christmas Day, laden with baked goods from Farringdale House's kitchen. Edward is not the most sociable of men – he is a silent person, preferring his own company to that of others – but Walter and I would try to make it a festive occasion, though Edward could never hide the fact that he was itching to return to his workshop.

I think Walter was hoping I'd say that I planned to come home – to the village, that is. But I would need a minimum of three days for such a visit, and I don't feel I've been working for Mrs Grist long enough to be allowed such a release from my duties. And besides, I can ill afford the train fare and the gifts of food and drink that I'd feel obliged to bring with me. I suggested that Walter might like to spend the day with brother Harold and his family, but he said he couldn't leave Edward alone – though I'm sure Edward wouldn't mind in the slightest. After all, it's not as if my eldest brother has nowhere else to go; his son Victor invites him every year, but he never accepts the invitation. Walter then hinted that he might go to Edie's in the afternoon, if Edward doesn't mind, which made me feel a bit better. But talking about Christmas made me realise how difficult it is to be far from family at such times and, of course, for the hundredth time, I questioned my decision to move to the city.

The first thing Mrs Grist says to me the next morning is, "How was your day with Wilfred, Elizabeth?"

"His name is Walter, Mrs Grist," I say. "Walter, like Sir Walter Scott, whom you admire so much. The day was a success, thank you. The weather was good and we walked a lot. We had tea at the Lyons tea room in Piccadilly, as you recommended. It was a lovely treat for both of us. How was your day? Did you spend it with your son?"

"I have three sons, Elizabeth," she says. "And, to be honest, I don't always want to see them. Phillip, yes, but the other two not so much. Their wives can be irritating, though the children are always a delight. But to answer your question, no I did not. I stayed home and it was just as well. I had a visitor and for some reason he seemed to expect you to be here. In fact, I would go so far as to say that you were missed."

"Who on earth was that?" I ask, astonished that anyone in London should be acquainted with me, let alone miss me.

"It was Lionel Fielding. He came to bring me a new tonic and he asked where you were. I told him your nephew was in town and that you were entertaining him. He said he was pleased to hear it, though I fail to see why your comings and goings should be of any concern to him."

"Oh, Mr Fielding is such a gentleman," I say, blushing. "I daresay it's normal for him to ask after everyone, regardless of how well he knows them."

"Well, he seems to know you *very* well, Elizabeth."

"Only from going to the pharmacy so often for you, Mrs Grist. I've noticed that he makes everyone feel like his most valued customer. He doesn't distinguish between the young and the old, or the rich and the poor. And he's very kind. He often doesn't charge those who can't afford to pay."

"I'm sure you intend such a remark to be a compliment, but I think he would do better to respect his customers' social statuses, especially in his role of shopkeeper. But I know only too well how he is. He's egalitarian to the core and doesn't care if that offends people. His daughter is the same. His late wife was different. She was a quiet, mouse-like creature, but she understood the rules of social class and treated people accordingly."

I say no more. Mrs Grist makes 'shopkeeper' sound like a dirty word. And Mr Fielding is not just a shopkeeper – he's a registered pharmacist, a profession that surely requires the passing of exams and a lot of training. As for her remarks about his late wife, well, I'll think about those later.

"Anyway, Elizabeth," she says after a short while, "I want you to return this tonic. It didn't do me any good at all and made me feel sick. Tell Mr Fielding that I thank him for the thought, but that I'd like my usual concoction. He wouldn't let me pay for this one – not that *I* can't afford it – so it's not an exchange. Here's the money for my regular tonic and ask him for some cod liver oil as well. My sister-in-law tells me it's good for rheumatism."

I pocket the money and the bottle of tonic that Mrs Grist wants me to return. It's a pity that Mr Fielding's good deeds are so unappreciated. Still, I doubt that he'll be surprised. As he said himself, he's known my employer for many years and has become accustomed to her fussiness and biting remarks.

There is one customer ahead of me in the pharmacy, so I wait patiently. A middle-aged, well-dressed lady is asking for an ointment for her skin complaint. She has a blistery rash on her face and hands, probably made worse by constant scratching. Mr Fielding tries to insist that she see a doctor, as he is unable to diagnose the cause of her rash.

"It could be one of a number of things," he says. "If you're feeling unwell generally, it might be shingles. Or it could be impetigo or a bad case of eczema. Or an allergy to something you've eaten or touched. I don't want to make it worse by giving you the wrong medication. Once you've seen a doctor, I'll be happy to provide you with whatever he prescribes."

The woman is not at all pleased with Mr Fielding's advice and expresses her dissatisfaction in no uncertain terms. As a consolation, he hands her a small pot of skin cream and says it may relieve the itching until she's able to see a physician. But he insists that it's not a cure. He tells her it's complimentary and wishes her well. She leaves with barely a thank you. Sometimes I wonder how he makes any profit at all; he's always giving things away for free.

"Another unhappy customer," he sighs as the woman leaves the shop. "It's not easy being a pharmacist these days, Bessie. Those who are too embarrassed to go to the doctor, or can't afford the fees, come to me. And then they're disappointed and sometimes angry that I can't do more to help them. But you, Miss Bessie Hardwicke, are the exact opposite. I know you will never ask me for something I'm unable to provide."

"If I come here only for myself," I say, trying not to blush, "then you're right. I won't ask you to cure my illnesses, though I should add that I'm hardly ever sick.

But I come for Mrs Grist, as you know. And I'm afraid you might consider *her* an unhappy customer. She's returning this tonic, which you kindly gave her yesterday. She says it made her feel worse and has sent me to buy a bottle of her regular one, as well as some cod liver oil for her rheumatism."

"Ah well, I'm not surprised," he says with a laugh. "Mrs Grist doesn't like anyone to suggest that she change her habits or routines. Why don't you take the tonic, Bessie? You say you're in good health and you certainly look extraordinarily well, but I'm sure there are days when you feel a bit under the weather. It might help lift your spirits, as there are some magic ingredients in it. But I promise you it contains nothing harmful."

"Thank you, Mr Fielding. That's very kind of you. I may be tempting fate by saying I'm rarely sick. Perhaps a winter in London will prove me wrong."

"I hope not. But it's good to have something to take just in case. Now tell me, Bessie, where were you yesterday? I was hoping to see your friendly face when I called on Mrs Grist."

"Yes, I'm sorry I missed you. I was with my nephew, who's presently working in Maidenhead. I met him off the train at Paddington and we spent a very pleasant afternoon together. I miss him so much – as I've told you, he's like a son to me. We write to each other all the time, but it's not the same as talking face-to-face."

"Indeed it isn't. What is he doing in Maidenhead, if I may be so bold as to ask?"

"Walter works as a stonemason and is assisting in the restoration of an old building – a chapel, I think he said. He served a parish apprenticeship from an early age – he was just a child really – but now he's working on his own. He hasn't had any problem finding work so far, though sometimes he has to travel a long way from home, as on this occasion."

"That's a worthy profession and he must be a strong and fit young man. The next time he comes to London, I'd like to meet him."

"That's kind of you to say, Mr Fielding. But I don't know when that will be. I suspect it won't be for some time."

"I'm sure he'll be back to see you before too long. I'm glad you enjoyed your time together. Now, I want to tell you about my visit to Mrs Grist. Would you mind if I close the shop and invite you for a cup of tea in my back parlour?"

I am so shocked at this last remark that I don't know what to say. Mr Fielding, a London pharmacist, well respected within the community, wants to invite *me* into his parlour for a cup of tea! Finally, I find my voice.

"Oh, Mr Fielding," I say, trying not to become too flustered. "I do appreciate your invitation. But I really must get back to Mrs Grist, otherwise she'll want to know what took me so long."

"Just tell her there was a queue or that a difficult customer was ahead of you. That's the truth, after all."

I can tell he won't take no for an answer, so I reluctantly – or willingly, I really don't know which – wait while he locks the door. I follow him into the back of the shop. It's a small room with two chairs, a table, and boxes piled high against one wall – pharmaceutical supplies no doubt. A fire is already lit and a copper kettle is suspended above the hearth. Mr Fielding opens the window and retrieves a bottle of milk from the windowsill, then busies himself with making the tea. He says the water is already boiling. I offer to do the honours, but he refuses.

"No, Bessie, you sit there and be waited on. I'm sure it doesn't happen very often, does it? And it gives me great pleasure, believe me. Now, do you take milk and sugar with your tea?"

"Yes, please," I say. "Just one sugar. You really are too kind, Mr Fielding."

"I think we need to get one thing straight. If I'm to call you Bessie, which I already do without properly asking your permission, then you must call me Lionel. It's a bit of a mouthful, I know, but it *is* my Christian name and I'd like you to use it."

"Oh no, Mr Fielding. I couldn't possibly. Whatever would Mrs Grist say?"

"What does it matter what Fanny Grist would say? If there are others around, you may be more formal if you wish, but when there are just the two of us, I insist that you address me as Lionel."

I feel more embarrassed than ever. How can I possibly call him Lionel? I suppose I'll end up not calling him anything at all. But he's sure to notice and chide me for it.

"The tea is ready," he says, "but we'll let it steep for a minute or two. Oh, I almost forgot. Garibaldi biscuits." He opens a cupboard and takes out a tin. "Mathilda brought me these yesterday. She continues to spoil me, while I should be the one spoiling her."

"You'll soon have a grandchild to spoil," I say. "Is she hoping for a boy or a girl?"

"Oh, I don't think she minds. Boys are usually the preference for a first child, but Mathilda scoffs at such a notion. She's all for gender equality. If she wasn't with child, I think she would be joining Mrs Pankhurst and her crew on their marches, married woman though she is."

"Really? I have to admit, I don't know much about the Suffragettes, but Walter told me yesterday that his sweetheart, Edie, supports their goals. He seems rather worried about it and is not sure where it all might lead, at least as far as Edie is concerned."

"Well, we'll just have to wait and see. Certainly, the movement is not going to go away and at some point, Parliament will have to sit up and listen. It's not such a bad thing that younger women are giving their support to the cause, so I wouldn't worry too much. At least Walter's girl is not living in London and actually participating in the demonstrations, is she? I don't think she'll come to any harm."

He pours me a cup of tea, adds a spoonful of sugar and a splash of milk, and passes me the tin of biscuits.

"Now," he says. "Suffragette marches aside, I want to talk to you about Mrs Grist. She was rather put out at my arriving uninvited, but I thought I'd take a chance since I was going in that direction. And, to be honest, I thought I might find you alone in the house and then we could have taken a walk in the park. But, as it turned out, she was home and you were out. I was a little bit disappointed, but never mind.

"I used the excuse of the tonic to invite myself into her drawing room. She said I should excuse the fact that she couldn't offer me tea since there was no one around to make it, but asked if I'd like a glass of sherry. I accepted. The offer of a drink gave me the perfect opportunity to raise the subject of where she obtains her spirits. She told me that Phillip usually supplies her with sherry – it was a good bottle of Pedro Ximénez, though a little too sweet for my liking. I complimented her on Phillip's taste, which pleased her. I pointed out that one can never be too careful when buying alcohol, especially since I'd heard that her close neighbour, Mr Basil Hornby, is selling cheap liquor, and what he fills his bottles with is anyone's guess. She looked a bit alarmed, but said coolly that Phillip always obtains his spirits from one of the best wine merchants in the city.

"My hope is that she'll now think twice before buying bottles of brandy or sherry from Hornby. She's always been concerned about her health – you'll have noticed she's a bit of a hypochondriac – and while she may enjoy the odd drink or two, she's unlikely to overdo it. It's Phillip I'm more worried about. When he's feeling low, I think he's prone to drowning his sorrows, as they say, and I believe he's also one of Hornby's customers, despite what Fanny says. The man sells spirits for a fraction of the price you'd pay elsewhere.

"I have to tell you something about Phillip, Bessie. He was a childhood friend of my Mathilda and they were sweethearts for over a year. It broke his heart when she left him for Ronald and I think it broke his mother's too, as she was also fond of Mathilda, though she'd never admit it now. It hadn't been long since Frank Grist died of a heart attack, so their grief was two-fold. And seeing me always reminds Fanny of the pain she and Phillip suffered at that time, so she's not always welcoming when I call on her. I understand that. But I'd like to do something to help Phillip – to stop him from becoming melancholic, which causes him to drink too much – but unfortunately, he's become a stranger to me. I hope his mother will warn him about Hornby to deter him from imbibing that particular poison, but all alcohol in excess is a form of poison, don't you agree?"

"Yes, I've seen what it can do to the best of men. Walter's father, Frederick, took to the bottle after my sister Ethel died. It was very hard for Walter, who was only five years old at the time. Frederick then left the village and returned to his hometown in Lancashire, leaving Walter behind. I think I've already told you this story, so forgive me for repeating myself. But I'm glad my brother Edward and his wife Mabel gave him a home, as I was in no position to do so. I don't know how things would have turned out had Frederick stayed. I think eventually he stopped drinking and remarried, though he's never made contact with Walter."

"That's very sad, Bessie. Is Walter still living with your brother?"

"Yes. Each go about their own business and some days they hardly see each other. I hate to say it, but Mabel – may God rest her soul – wasn't a proper mother to Walter, even though she watched him grow up. She wasn't keen on taking in Edward's young nephew and felt he'd been forced on her. That's partly why I became so attached to Walter – I tried to be a substitute for Ethel in his affections. I certainly didn't have to compete with Mabel for that. She didn't really show Walter much fondness, but I suppose she compensated in other ways. He grew up to be a fine young man, and it's not all thanks to me.

"Mr Fielding – oh sorry, it's going to take a while for me to stop calling you that – I'm grateful to you for telling me about Mrs Grist and Phillip. Now I understand why she's sometimes down in the dumps. She obviously knows that Phillip has personal problems and is at a loss to see how she can help him. It's no secret that he's her favourite son – I don't even know the names of the other two – and it must be painful for her to see him making wrong decisions. If only you could help him in some way!"

"I haven't given up, Bessie. I'll try to find a way to make contact with him. Sometimes I think what he needs is a good talking to! His mother has always been too soft with him. But I'll need to tread carefully so as not to make matters worse."

"I truly hope he'll listen to you. Now I really must be getting along. I know Mrs Grist will be wondering where I am. Thank you for the tea – it was so considerate of you to wait on me in this way. You're right, it doesn't happen very often."

"Then we must repeat it. If you'd like to, that is. I'll let you go now, Bessie, though you know you're welcome to stay longer. Still, I suppose my customers will be wondering why my shop is closed at such an odd hour."

As I walk back to the house, I ask myself why Mr Fielding confides in me and treats me so affectionately. He's not an unattractive man, though he must be on the wrong side of fifty. His hair and his whiskers are a rich auburn – like Mrs Grist, he doesn't appear to have a single grey hair – and his brown eyes are warm and honest looking. He wouldn't have any difficulty in finding another wife – a widow of his own age and class perhaps, or even a much younger lady looking for stability in life. I cannot bring myself to entertain the thought that he might be interested – in a romantic sense – in me. I know I'm putting myself down – an all-too-common fault of mine – but it would take too great a leap of faith for me to believe that I mean more to him than any other customer with a friendly face and a sympathetic ear.

12

I'm on my way to Clapham for another session with Michael. Menacing rainclouds loom overhead and a gusty wind slows my pace. But I feel cheerful enough. At church this morning, the Reverend Thomas Wilson said much to improve my mood – he referenced the Gospel of Matthew and read from the Sermon on the Mount, which is one of my favourite passages from the Bible. Jesus' words 'Blessed are they that mourn, for they shall be comforted' was a great consolation to me following the deaths of Arthur and Ethel, and even now it helps me to know that I'm not alone in my sorrow.

Michael and I are to meet in the library again. When we are alone, I ask him if he's heard anything more from Harriet.

"No, nothing," Michael says, looking at me glumly. "Aunt Bessie, do you think you could go and see her again? I want to know if she's still at that orphanage."

"Oh, Michael," I say, "I'm sure she is. It's probably difficult for her to send a letter if she hasn't access to writing materials, or money for a stamp." I don't reveal that Robert gave her a few pennies for postage. "Also, she'd have to ask someone to post the letter for her, and it would need to be someone she could trust."

"Harriet is not going to stay in a place that forbids her even to go out and post a letter. She's not used to that. Before the… the fire, she used to go everywhere on her own or with her friends – to the corner shop to buy food for us, to neighbours' houses, to the park. Once she even went to a fairground at Hampstead Heath where she rode a carousel and saw a moving picture. She's never going to stay locked up in that orphanage!"

It grieves me to hear the pain in his voice. He knows

his sister better than anyone and if he doesn't think she'll stay with the Sisters of Gethsemane, then I think it's fair to say she won't. He seems to have already concluded that the orphanage is a secure building, that there are locks and bolts which prevent the inmates from leaving. Inmates! What am I saying? I mean residents. Even if I'm beginning to view the place as a prison, I don't want Michael to think of it like that. I must try to put his mind at ease, even if it means telling him a white lie or two.

"Michael," I say, laying my hand on his. "I'll try to find out whether she's still at the orphanage if that will stop you from worrying. But believe me, she's safe there. She's receiving three square meals a day, she has regular lessons in the schoolroom, and she's in good health. By now I'm sure she's made some friends, so may not be in such a hurry to leave. Once she turns fourteen, then perhaps it'll be time for Mr Cartwright and myself to talk to the sisters about her future. For the moment though, I think we have to be patient."

"She won't be fourteen until March. I don't think she'll wait that long."

"March is only four months away. That's not long at all. But like I said, I'll make some enquiries so as to put your mind at rest. But I'm certain Harriet is settled now and not thinking any more about escaping. Now, let's see what new adventures await young David Copperfield. He's presently living with the kind Mr Wickfield and his daughter Agnes, and is about to start his new school, Doctor Strong's Establishment for Boys. Perhaps we should call him Trotwood, as that's the funny name his aunt has given him and that's how he'll be addressed at his new school."

Michael is struggling to hold back his tears, but manages a slight smile for my sake. As we take it in turns to read, I suspect that he's beginning to feel a kinship with David, especially when we learn that he was 'so unused to the sports and games of boys' and that he felt 'awkward and inexperienced in the commonest things belonging to them'. Not to mention the fact that he 'was put into the lowest form of the school' and was troubled by his 'want of boyish skill, and of book-learning too'.

In fact, David's first day at the school was not unlike Michael's own experience. He tells us: '… I felt distrustful of my slightest look and gesture; shrunk within myself whensoever I was approached by one of my new schoolfellows; and hurried off the minute school was over, afraid of committing myself in my response to any friendly notice or advance'.

But although Michael is trying his best to enjoy *David Copperfield*, and the comparisons are helpful, I can see that his heart isn't in it today. I feel I'm not being fair to him. All that I'm able to offer him is an hour of reading and a friendly chat, but the only thing that's on his mind is my foolish promise of reuniting him with Harriet. I've made a blunder and I don't know how to make it right. But did I say I'd *reunite* him with his sister? I think I only said I'd *find* her, and Robert and I have found her. But what's the point of finding her if they can't be reunited? It's just making the poor boy become even more fretful, especially since he insists that she's going to escape the orphanage at the first opportunity.

Our hour is up before we've even read a full chapter. I put away my book and hand Michael a bag of liquorice allsorts.

"Put them away before Mr Cartwright returns," I say, "or he's going to want to steal them from you. You know what a sweet tooth he has."

Michael mutters his thanks and stuffs the sweets in his trouser pocket. A minute later Robert enters the room, and I bid the boy a fond farewell. He leaves us no less dolefully than when he arrived. My cheerful mood of this morning has all but disappeared.

Robert and I walk towards the school gates. It's already started raining so we share my umbrella, although it doesn't provide much protection as the wind keeps blowing it inside out.

"I couldn't say anything before, Bessie," Robert says, "but there's been a development with Harriet."

"What's happened?" I ask in some alarm.

"Well, she did what she said she was going to do. She's left the orphanage."

"Oh no! I knew she would. How did you find this out?"

"Well, it seems she went back to her old house and hid in a broken-down shed in the rear garden for two days. Somehow, she made contact with Mrs Radford's daughter, who took her food and blankets. When Mrs Radford found out – she was wondering why her provisions kept disappearing – she wrote to me immediately. She's taken Harriet into her home again, but says it can only be a temporary arrangement. She asked me for advice on what she should do.

"I spoke with Patty and she insists that Harriet should come to live with us, at least until she's able to find a job. She's still young, but looks older and is mature for her age, so I think she stands a good chance of securing a position, perhaps with a family that has young children."

"Oh, Robert!" I exclaim. "That's so kind of you and Patty. And while she's with you, she'll be able to see Michael at the weekends. He'll be so thrilled when he finds out."

"Yes, I'll tell him when everything is settled. She first needs to agree to the arrangement. It won't be an ideal situation, as the house is small and she'll have to share a bedroom with Celia. But my dear mother-in-law says she doesn't mind – she claims she'll be glad of the company, bless her. The girl will be able to lend a hand with the housework and the cooking, which will help Patty a lot. But she'll need to start looking for paid employment as soon as possible. Our means are already quite stretched."

"I understand. I wish I could help in some way. When do you plan to talk to her? Have you already replied to Mrs Radford? And what about the Sisters of Gethsemane? Will they go looking for her? Sorry, Robert – I'm bombarding you with questions."

"I don't really know what the sisters do when a child runs away from the orphanage. But, once I've talked to Harriet, I plan to let them know that she's safe and has a new home. Mrs Radford should receive my letter tomorrow. I'll go over there one evening this week and ask Harriet if she's willing to come and live with us."

"I'm sure she'll agree. What other option does she have? This has taken such a weight off my mind, Robert, you've no idea – though I'm sure it's put an additional weight on yours. But thank you so much for all you've done. I feel responsible somehow. I just couldn't bear to see Michael so unhappy."

"You and Patty are much more soft-hearted than us Londoners, Bessie. I fear for you sometimes. Well, not for Patty as I can protect her, but for you, my dear. You can't become personally involved with every injustice or tragedy you witness. London is a breeding ground for crime and misfortune. You need to become a lot tougher if you're going to survive in the city."

"I know, Robert. My nephew Walter was telling me the same thing. I'm trying, believe me. I think I'm beginning to get used to Mrs Grist's ways and not become so upset every time she complains or says a sharp word. There's hope for me yet."

"That's good to know, Bessie. Now, since it's

beginning to get dark and you've declined our invitation to tea, I'll say goodbye and let you be on your way. I'll write to you this week to tell you how things stand with Harriet. Hopefully, the next time you're in Clapham, she'll be here too."

This is such good news and I'm so grateful to Patty and Robert, especially Patty, who successfully persuaded Robert to overlook his misgivings. I can't see any reason why Harriet should object – she'll be in such good hands and close to her brother's school. The responsibility of looking after her mother and brother, while her father became intoxicated at the local pub, took away her childhood from an early age. And the loss and devastation she's since experienced, not to mention the horrors of orphanage, could easily have scarred her for life. But her darkest days are surely over. I'm confident that the Cartwrights will not only reunite her with Michael at the earliest opportunity, but will also make her feel she's amongst friends and, most important of all, give her hope for the future.

When I arrive back at Mrs Grist's – I still hesitate to call it home, though it's the only one I have – I hear voices in the drawing room. There's a male voice, but it's not Mr Fielding's, I'm certain of that. I'm about to go straight to my room, but Mrs Grist has heard me come in and calls out to me.

"Elizabeth! Come here a moment, please. There's someone I'd like you to meet."

I quickly glance in the hall mirror. I look a fright. My hair is an untidy mop and the cold wind has made my eyes water. I run my fingers through my hair and wipe my eyes before entering the drawing room. A young man is sitting on the settee, drinking tea.

"This is my son, Phillip, Elizabeth," Mrs Grist says.

"You've heard me speak of him. Phillip, this is my companion, Miss Elizabeth Hardwicke."

Phillip stands up to greet me. He's a fine-looking young man in his early twenties, but his grey eyes are bloodshot and his face is pale and drawn. I get the impression that he hasn't slept for several nights.

"Phillip is feeling a bit under the weather and is going to be moving back home for a short while," Mrs Grist continues. "He'll be in his old room, which is the one opposite mine."

I hardly know what to say. I have no idea whether his return home is a move that he welcomes or is because his mother wants to keep an eye on him. Somehow, I manage to string together a few words about how I hope he'll soon be feeling better and how pleasant it will be for Mrs Grist to have his company. I'm sure I sound quite unintelligible, but Phillip thanks me politely. When I turn to leave the room. Mrs Grist stops me in my tracks.

"Elizabeth, I know it's not your job, but would you mind lighting a fire in Phillip's room? Mrs Evans is not here, as you know, and the room is chilly. The bed's already made but perhaps you could fill a hot water bottle and place it under the covers. I'd be much obliged to you."

"I can take care of the fire, Mama," Phillip says, "and I won't need a hot water bottle. There's no need to disturb Miss Hardwicke on her day off."

"No, please, it's no trouble at all," I say. "I'll be happy to take care of warming up the room and the bed. Is there anything else either of you need? Would you like me to prepare something for your supper?"

"No, that will be all, thank you, Elizabeth," Mrs Grist says. "We've both had a substantial lunch and can help ourselves to bread and cheese or cold meats later on, if we feel like it."

"Very well. Just ring the bell if you do need anything. Have a pleasant evening."

I don't mind doing these types of household tasks. In fact, I rather wish I had Mrs Evans' job instead of my own. It's not a big house – at least not compared to Farringdale House – and I would make light work of keeping it clean and tidy. In fact, I'd be much more thorough than Mrs Evans. She tends to cut corners, though I don't think Mrs Grist realises it, or perhaps she does but says nothing. But I'm sure Mrs Evans knows that *I've* spotted her shoddy work, which probably accounts for her worsening attitude towards me.

I find a spare hot water bottle in one of the kitchen cupboards and heat some water in the kettle on the range. In Phillip's room, there's already a half-full coalscuttle and some kindling in the grate, so it takes no time at all to get a fire started. The coals should still be burning when he retires for the night, and the room will be warm and cosy.

Once back in my own room, it occurs to me that Phillip Grist's presence in the house might have an impact on my position. If Mrs Grist has the company of her son – even if he's at work most days – will she continue to need the presence of a person such as myself? I'm supposed to be her companion, but since my competence in this role is surely questionable owing to my very evident lack of conversational skills, it would not come as a surprise if she tells me she doesn't need me anymore. What would I do in that case?

I think I would have to throw myself at the mercy of my brother Edward. I could offer to keep house for him and Walter, while taking in sewing and laundry to supplement the household income by a few pence a week. It would even be a relief from the uncertainties I'm experiencing on a daily basis living here in London, which are only eased by the time I spend with Patty and Robert, and with Michael. And I'd be able to spend more time with my dear Walter, at least until he's ready to embark on a future with Edie. But to go back to the village would mean admitting failure – people would say that I tried to rise above my station and fell flat on my face. Could I face such ignominy? Well, I may have no choice if Mrs Grist decides to give me notice to leave.

But I mustn't pre-empt her next move. Phillip may only stay for a short while, and she may have no intention of getting rid of me. I hope she tells me more tomorrow, so that I may either rest easy or make plans for my uncertain future. My immediate concern is how to handle the presence of a man in the house, when up until now it's been all womenfolk. Mrs Grist has her own water closet and bathroom, equipped with a clawfoot bathtub, in which she performs her daily ablutions. As for myself, I wash every morning at the washstand in my room, making sure that I always have a full pitcher of water handy. I use the outhouse to empty my chamber pot first thing in the mornings and to relieve myself during the day. Before bed each Saturday evening, I fill a tub in the kitchen with hot water and scrub my whole body so as to be scrupulously clean for church on Sunday morning. Mrs Evans and Mrs Hopper both leave early on a Saturday and Mrs Grist rarely enters the kitchen, so I have no fear of being intruded upon. But with a man in the house I'll have to take some precautions. Phillip may feel like a bite to eat and enter the kitchen while I'm in my altogether! I don't know who would have the greater shock – him or me!

Well, I took my bath yesterday, so no need to worry about that for another week. Let me not spoil the day by worrying about how I'm going to adapt to Mr Phillip Grist living in the house, or whether Mrs Grist will decide to dismiss me. I have my letters to write – to Walter and Edward, and to Lady Sophia Radcliffe, now Contessa Sophia Boncompagni – and I want to enjoy the thought that Harriet will soon be living with Patty and Robert, within easy reach of Michael. It occurs to me that Celia could perhaps teach Harriet the basics of dressmaking. She had to stop using her old Singer sewing machine because of her arthritic hands and failing eyesight. Patty has never been able to master the machine – and neither have I for that matter – but I'm sure Harriet would take to it like a duck to water. But, as usual, I'm getting a bit ahead of myself. I need to wait until Harriet is actually living with the Cartwrights before I start imagining her as a skilled seamstress, following in the footsteps of the talented Mrs Celia Harris.

13

After an early breakfast, I return to my room to finish writing to Walter. Since he'll be back in the village this week, I want my letter to be waiting for him. I've finished my letter to Edward, which is long overdue – not that he will have noticed. Still, I do try to keep up a correspondence with him; he *is* my brother and I may well need his help in the future. He never replies to my letters. If there's something important he wants me to know – like a birth or a death – he'll ask Walter to convey the news. It doesn't bother me too much – I know he's not a letter writer. Nothing really interests him besides his woodworking and he's becoming more and more of a recluse, despite Walter's presence in the house and a weekly visit from his eldest son Victor. Victor works as a cobbler and is married with two young children. He's a bit like his father – wedded to his work – but fortunately his wife Marian is a lively character and won't allow him to spend more than eight hours a day in his workshop.

I told Edward that, sadly, I won't be seeing him this Christmas and suggested he and Walter spend the twenty-fifth with Victor and his wife, or with brother Harold. I know he won't go to either of them – Walter has already told me as much – but it doesn't hurt to point out that he does have a family who would be pleased to see him, however much of a curmudgeon he's determined to become.

Thinking about Christmas reminds me that I need to start making or buying presents. I have only a small amount of money saved, so most will have to be made by hand. I want to make Patty a lavender handkerchief case. I've seen Mrs Grist with one that has a sprig of lavender embroidered on the front and is edged with lace. It looks so pretty and easy to make. I can enclose a small bag of dried lavender inside, which will give it a pleasant fragrance. I intend to knit Robert a pair of socks – not very original, I know, but always well received. Every time I visit the Cartwrights, I see a basket of socks that need darning next to Celia's window seat. I'll knit her a pair of mittens that she can wear while watching the world go by in the draughtiest corner of the room. Admittedly, despite her arthritis, her hands are not often idle, but she does complain of icy fingers when she's not sewing – unsurprising really, since she insists on sitting so far from the fireplace.

I shall have to give Mrs Grist something, but what? I have no idea what will please her. She seems to have everything she needs. And what should I give Michael? A book would probably be the most welcome gift; perhaps an adventure story that will transport him to another world and help him forget about his troubles. I regularly pass a second-hand bookshop on my walks in the neighbourhood, so I can easily pop in to see if there are any children's books for sale. If I could find a copy of *Treasure Island*, I think that would be perfect. I've heard that Robert Louis Stevenson's tale of pirates and buried treasure is enormously popular among boys his age. And while I'm in there, I can look for a novel for Harriet too. I still need to think about what to send Walter and Edward – men are always the most difficult – but that's a long enough list to be getting on with.

I stay in my room until Mrs Grist rings her bell. In the drawing room, everything is as normal. My employer is sitting in her easy chair with her copy of *Jane Eyre*, which we have not yet finished, on her lap.

"I thought we'd read a bit more this morning," she says. "I like Jane's character very much indeed. She's extremely modest, but at the same time is remarkably self-assured. An admirable combination, don't you think?"

"Most definitely," I say, wondering if my employer is indirectly criticising my own lack of self-assurance.

"But before we begin, Elizabeth, could you please go and ask Mrs Hopper to bring me a cup of Camp coffee? I didn't sleep well again and need something to help me stay awake."

"Yes, of course, Mrs Grist."

I've heard it said that Camp coffee is mostly chicory essence and contains no caffeine, but if Mrs Grist thinks it will help her stay awake, then who am I to argue? As Mr Fielding says, it's often just the idea that something is good for you, or is going to give relief, that produces the required effect.

As I approach the kitchen, I hear my adversaries chatting. I'm reluctant to enter without knocking, but to knock would imply that I have no right to use the kitchen. Still, I hate it when they stop talking in my presence and give me the evil eye. I wait for a moment to pluck up some much-needed courage and cannot help overhearing part of their conversation.

"She's brought him back here so she can keep an eye on him," Mrs Hopper says in a disapproving tone. "He's taken after his father – thinks he's a class above the rest of us. But I blame her – she always spoilt him to death."

"But how did she know he was going *there*?" Mrs Evans asks.

"It was that pharmacist – what's his name? Yes, Fielding – Lionel Fielding. He told her he'd seen the boy leaving Basil's house in a bit of a hurry. If you ask me, it wasn't booze he was after, but the *other* thing. Now, I'm not saying I approve of such goings-on, but Basil has to make a living like the rest of us. And you can call me what you like, but I'm no prude and no hypocrite neither."

"How do you know all this, Enid?"

"Ah, I just keep my ears and eyes open. I had to come back here yesterday afternoon, as I needed a handful of the good tea she buys from Lyons. She has plenty of it, so I just helped myself. I had our Louisa's future mother-in-law coming to tea and wanted to make a good impression. Anyhow, I could hear them – her ladyship and her darling son – talking in the drawing room. For once she was really having a go at him. So I listened outside the door. Miss Hoity-Toity was out, thank goodness – I wouldn't have wanted to bump into *her*. He's weak, that Phillip. I thought he'd tell her to mind her own business – after all, he's a grown man now – but he said nothing. He's old enough to stand up for himself, but he's still clinging to her apron strings – not that she'd ever wear one! – and is terrified of answering her back."

Miss Hoity-Toity! That's me! I want to listen to more of this conversation, but I daren't. Mrs Grist is waiting for me and for her beverage. I cough loudly and enter the kitchen. Of course they stop their conversation immediately. I convey the message and leave promptly.

The two women are terrible gossips but I can't disbelieve what I've just heard. Mr Fielding told me he's concerned about Phillip's health and the fact that he might be drinking too much. He didn't mention that he'd actually seen him leaving Mr Hornby's residence – a brothel, no less – but probably didn't want to embarrass me, gentleman that he is. The fact that Mrs Grist appears to be turning a blind eye to the goings-on at Hornby's house confounds me. I wonder why she continues to do business with him. While she might withhold criticism of his illegal sales of alcohol, I would have thought she'd be deeply disapproving of that other, more shameful wrongdoing.

All this listening behind doors! I suppose I'm as bad as Mrs Hopper, but I didn't *deliberately* listen to their conversation. I only paused because I was afraid to enter and face their silence and scowls. I wish I wasn't such a coward!

Back in the drawing room, Mrs Grist obviously feels she owes me some explanation as to why Phillip has returned home.

"It's only temporary," she says. "He's been living in lodgings near his office for the past six months, but I'm worried about his health. He's never been as strong as his brothers and I don't think he's eating properly. He's lost weight and looks pale and sickly – to me at least – and his mood is... well, let's just say he's not the lively young man he used to be. He's so sensitive and suffered enormously when his father died. And, as if that wasn't bad enough, he had his heart broken shortly afterwards. I don't think he's over either sorrow, though it's been two years now.

"He hasn't given up his lodgings so will be going back there eventually, but I managed to persuade him to stay here, at least for a couple of weeks. I said it was because *I'd* been unwell and needed looking after, or he would never have agreed to come. But at least he'll get some breakfast and a proper meal in the evenings. And I'll have Mrs Hopper make him beef and mustard sandwiches – his favourite – for his lunch at the office. Ah, Elizabeth, you have no children of your own so you don't know the worries that torment a mother."

I don't really need reminding that I have no children, but I make sympathetic noises. I suppose what she's omitted to tell me is that she intends to prevent him from drinking too much, if indeed that *has* become a cause for concern.

"I tried to persuade him to take a few days off work," she continues. "Like me, he doesn't sleep well and some rest would do him good. But he refuses to stay home. He knows you're here and that I'm not alone.

"Oh, I almost forgot – before we begin again with *Jane Eyre*, I'd like you to go to the pharmacy and ask Mr Fielding if he has any tonic or tablets that Phillip can take for his... his melancholia. He told me he's worried about him, but didn't give me any advice as to treatment. Here's a shilling – buy whatever he recommends."

In spite of my musings, I sincerely hope Mr Fielding doesn't invite me into his back parlour a second time. I don't feel confident enough to face another personal conversation with him just yet. I suppose I should look to Jane Eyre for guidance on self-confidence! I have no idea how to behave when he pays me compliments; like I've said, I have received so few in the last twenty years. I want to dismiss them, but I know it's not gracious to do so. Whatever I might conjure up in the darkness of my room at night, in the here and now I just want him to treat me as he would any other customer who visits the pharmacy on behalf of an employer.

He's alone in the shop and greets me with a smile as usual. I don't prolong the pleasantries; I get straight to the point.

"Phillip is staying at the house for a while," I say. "Mrs Grist wants to keep an eye on him. She says he's suffering from melancholia – I think you know that already – and she's sent me to buy some tonic or tablets for him, whatever you recommend."

"Ah, Bessie," he says, "I'm glad she's looking after him. I did mention to her that I suspected that he was keeping questionable company and may be drinking too much. I don't think he's severely melancholic, but it's not good for him to be alone. He's not a bad boy – not at all –

but he doesn't have a strong enough character to resist harmful influences. There's really nothing I can recommend, but I know Fanny is not going to accept your returning empty-handed. Just give her this tonic – it's the same one I gave you, the one she returned. If she's able to persuade him to take it, it might lift his mood even though it contains nothing to warrant such an effect."

"You don't think he should see a doctor?"

"No, Bessie, I do not. We don't want to give a doctor the chance to diagnose mental illness. That might involve him being admitted to an asylum, which would be the worst possible outcome. No, what he really needs is to meet another young lady and to forget all about Mathilda. I think it was the news that she was with child that caused this latest crisis. He was doing well until that information reached him. When I last spoke to Fanny, I suggested that she arrange some informal gatherings where he can socialise with those of a similar age and background. I actually meant young women, but I didn't specify that. I'm sure her sister-in-law Doris would be willing to help her – she loves to entertain despite her physical limitations. Fanny used to be famous for *her* dinner parties, but she's not held any, as far as I'm aware, since Frank died. I know she's taken a dislike to me because of Mathilda and is reluctant to follow my advice, but at the same time she's well aware that I'll do anything I can to help her son, as I feel partly responsible for his misfortune."

"You shouldn't feel responsible. There was nothing you could have done. Phillip isn't the first young man to be thwarted in love. I'll take the tonic and tell Mrs Grist you think it might help lift his spirits. I hope she doesn't recognise it as the one you wanted *her* to take."

"No, she won't. They're all brown tonics, and most of them taste the same. The lemon verbena that I use in the mix gives all my concoctions a similar flavour."

"That's good to know. Thank you, Mr Fielding."

"Mr Fielding? Didn't I ask you to call me Lionel, Bessie?"

"Yes, you did. I'm sorry."

I pay for the tonic and leave the pharmacy. He doesn't try to engage me in further conversation. Now I feel disappointed, even though I entered the shop hoping that he wouldn't subject me to any special treatment. Never mind. It's probably for the best. I'll never be more, in his eyes, than the middle-aged companion of his friend, Mrs Fanny Grist.

I didn't see Phillip at all yesterday, but I know he came in from work at about six o'clock and sat down to dinner with his mother at seven. Mrs Hopper stayed late to serve each course separately, which meant that I ate my supper much later than I usually do. There was a pile of washing up left in the sink, but I've learnt my lesson not to touch it.

This morning I hear Mrs Grist and Phillip talking in the drawing room. He appears not to have gone to work. Mrs Grist hasn't rung the bell, but I decide to knock and ask her if she needs me. If not, then I'll go for a walk and post my letters to Walter and Edward.

"Good morning," I say upon entering the room. "Is there anything you'd like me to do this morning, Mrs Grist?"

"Good morning, Elizabeth," Mrs Grist says. "Yes, I'd be grateful if you could you deliver this invitation to Mr Fielding. I'm inviting him to have dinner with Phillip and myself tomorrow evening."

"Yes, of course. I'll take it right away."

I don't want to go back to the pharmacy, but I have no choice. Mr Fielding is going to get sick of the sight of me at this rate, and my role of messenger is hardly an enviable one. It occurs to me that if he accepts the invitation, Mrs Hopper will have to stay even later to serve them dinner and I'll be stuck in my room until goodness knows what time, waiting for her to leave so that I can have a bite to eat. Well, that's certainly better than being invited to join them. I'd be a nervous wreck, unable to say anything intelligible, and Mr Fielding would see me for what I really am – a woman from the village who's not fit for the position she occupies.

He's serving a customer when I walk into the shop. He looks surprised when he sees me again so soon after my last visit, and probably thinks I'm returning the tonic. The elderly woman he's attending to seems difficult to please; she keeps questioning his advice and won't take the tablets he recommends. But he responds patiently, not showing any sign of irritation. I wonder if I should just pass him the invitation and make a quick exit. No, that would be rude and, besides, Mrs Grist probably wants me to return with his response.

Finally, the customer leaves – without buying anything at all – and as soon as the door is closed, Mr Fielding breathes a sigh of relief.

"Sorry, Bessie," he says. "This has been a trying morning. I don't know why these people come to me if they're not prepared to accept my advice. Mark my words, she'll be back tomorrow, asking for the tablets I wanted her to take."

"I don't know how you can be so patient," I say. "She was quite impolite, wasn't she?"

"Yes, she was. Not all my customers are as easy to please as you, dear Bessie. Now what can I do for you today?"

Dear Bessie! Ah, now that's what I like to hear, even if it means nothing.

"I'm just a messenger today, delivering a note from Mrs Grist," I say. "She told me she's inviting you to dinner at the house tomorrow evening. She probably wants me to return with your response."

"Tomorrow evening?" he says, opening the envelope. "Yes, I'd be delighted. I've been hoping that Fanny will begin to entertain again, but never expected an invitation myself. Do you know who the other guests will be? You'll be present, won't you Bessie?"

"No, of course I won't. It'll just be you, Mrs Grist and Phillip. I don't think she's inviting anyone else."

"Just a cosy dinner then. I'd look forward to it much more if I thought you'd be joining us, Bessie."

"I would never expect to be asked to join you. In any case, I take my meals in the kitchen, not the dining room. In that respect, I'm not treated differently to the other servants, and I don't expect to be."

"Bessie, dear Bessie. You do enjoy belittling yourself, but you really shouldn't. Believe me, compared to many of the folk I meet on a daily basis, who put on airs for no reason at all, I find your modesty extremely appealing. So you see, however much you put yourself down, it's not going to change my respect for you or diminish our burgeoning friendship. I'll be sorry not to see you tomorrow evening, but I suspect you wouldn't enjoy the evening so I'll say no more. Though I hope there'll be other occasions when I might be afforded the pleasure of your company."

"Thank you, I hope so too," I say, reddening at his last remark. "So should I tell Mrs Grist that you'll come at seven o'clock?"

"Yes, certainly. I'll be there, right on the hour."

"Very well, I'll let her know," I say brusquely, just as another customer enters the pharmacy. I turn to leave a little too quickly.

Oh, I hope he doesn't think I was rude, but I can't risk revealing my fondness for him, though he's probably already aware of it. Our burgeoning friendship! What does he mean by that? Is he hinting at the beginning of a closer acquaintance? Ah, Mr Fielding, if you knew how seriously I take your casual remarks and how thoroughly I pick them apart for hidden meanings, I'm sure you'd refrain from talking to me in such an informal way. I must never let it be known just how much even the most commonplace conversation with you means to me!

Mrs Hopper is none too pleased that she has to prepare dinner for three persons. She's become too accustomed to cooking solely for Mrs Grist and gets into a panic when there's extra work to do. But she's been with the Grist family for more than five years, having been hired when Mr Frank Grist was still alive and when Phillip and perhaps the two other boys were living at home. So, in my opinion, dinner for three should not be a cause for alarm. Needless to say, I'm staying well out of her way – I don't want to catch the sharp edge of her tongue, which is particularly cutting towards me even when she's not in a bad mood.

Mrs Evans has also been asked to stay for the duration of the meal. She's to receive Mr Fielding, show him into the drawing room and, much to her disdain, wait on the three of them in the dining room. While normally I'd be happy to take on any of Mrs Evans' tasks, I'm glad Mrs Grist didn't ask me to serve the meal. It would make me so nervous that I'd be all fingers and thumbs and would likely drop a dish or spill wine on the tablecloth. Not that I haven't served many, many meals at Farringdale House, sometimes for twenty or more guests, and I've never once had such an accident. But here it would be different – all eyes would be on me, especially Mr Fielding's, and since

Mrs Grist makes me anxious at the best of times, I would be sure to upset the apple cart in one way or another before the end of the evening.

Mrs Hopper's been on her feet all day long; when I pass through the kitchen to go to the outhouse, she's red in the face and muttering to herself. So as not to get in her way, I decide to skip lunch, though I know that by late evening I'll be starving. The menu for this evening consists of mushroom soup, followed by baked salmon, chicken vol-au-vents, venison with green beans and mashed potatoes, a strawberry trifle, and cheese and biscuits. Sherry is to be served with the first course, followed by a bottle of hock, then a claret to accompany the venison. Port will be served after the coffee. I know all this, not because I've been told, but because Mrs Grist gave Mrs Hopper handwritten notes, specifying the menu and detailing the recipes for each course, and I surreptitiously glanced at these when I had my breakfast this morning. I actually felt a bit sorry for Mrs Hopper when I later overheard her asking Mrs Evans to read aloud Mrs Grist's notes. I don't think she's able to read herself, though she's obviously kept that fact well hidden from her employer.

Mrs Grist told me that were there any leftovers – she was sure there would be – I was to help myself to whatever took my fancy. But I daresay Mrs Hopper and Mrs Evans are looking forward to taking home as much as they can carry, so I'll be left with just bread and cheese, or bread and dripping at the end of the day. It's quite funny really that such a lot of fuss is being made over a dinner for just three people, especially given the fact that the one and only guest is a family friend. Dinner parties were a regular occurrence at Farringdale House; there were many more courses and everything was handled smoothly and without complaint. At the end of the evening, the servants would assemble and have a nightcap together. I especially enjoyed the air of camaraderie as we discussed whether or not the evening had been a success, and gossiped about the appearances and manners of the guests.

It's close to eleven o'clock at night when I finally go down to the kitchen for a bite to eat. I feel weak from not having eaten since breakfast. Not one bit of washing up has been done and it pains me not to be able to make a start on it. I'm too tired to put together a meal from leftovers – not that there is much to choose from – and besides, it's not pleasant to remain in the kitchen surrounded by dirty crockery and glassware, and greasy pots and pans. I quickly cut a thick slice of bread, spread it generously with butter, take a chunk of cheese from the selection in the pantry, pour myself a glass of milk, and return to my room.

14

There was a bit of a row this morning about the state of the kitchen. Phillip rose early with the intention of making himself a cup of coffee and some buttered toast before leaving for work, but because of the mess left by Mrs Hopper, he decided not to bother. He is in the hallway putting on his coat when she arrives, and he tells her in no uncertain terms that she should have done the washing up before going home. The dirty dishes and leftover food, he says, are an invitation to rats and other vermin, and he will henceforth refuse to eat anything she's prepared unless he's convinced that minimum standards of hygiene are being observed in the kitchen.

Mrs Hopper does not take kindly to Phillip's admonishment. She's already disgruntled about having had to work so hard and stay late yesterday and is now about ready to explode. As soon as Mrs Evans arrives, she proceeds to tell her all about Phillip's reproach and is so upset that she doesn't even notice my presence in the kitchen. If she hadn't been so nasty the one time I did the washing up, she'd have arrived this morning to find everything spick and span and would thus have avoided the confrontation. I can't help feeling a bit self-righteous, especially since I was as disgusted as Phillip at the disarray I witnessed last night.

Mrs Grist is oblivious to the row. She breakfasts late and it's mid-morning by the time she rings her bell.

"Elizabeth," she says. "Mr Fielding left his monocle here last night. He must be missing it by now. Could you return it to him, please?"

"Yes, of course, Mrs Grist," I say. "Is there anything you'd like me to buy while I'm at the pharmacy?"

"No, nothing. Thank you."

Another visit to the pharmacy! I carefully wrap the monocle in my clean handkerchief and place it in my coat pocket. It's a cold, blustery morning so I wrap a thick woollen scarf around my neck and put on an old pair of mittens. My grey everyday coat is warm but shapeless; it has weathered many cold winters and will probably survive a good few more. I know I don't look the slightest bit stylish, but Mr Fielding is used to seeing me this way and since it doesn't seem to bother him, I won't let it trouble me either.

I haven't walked more than a hundred yards when the man himself comes striding towards me.

"Bessie!" he exclaims. "What a surprise. I was just about to call on Mrs Grist as I forgot my…"

"Your monocle," I interrupt. 'I have it here. I was on my way to return it to you. Mrs Grist guessed you'd have missed it by now."

I hand him the monocle, wrapped in my handkerchief. He slips both items into his pocket.

"Yes, indeed. Thank you, Bessie. Do you have time to walk with me for a short distance? I've closed the shop early, as Mathilda's invited me for lunch. I'm being spoilt with all these invitations! If you could accompany me as far as the park, I'd like that very much."

"I don't have much time, but perhaps for five minutes. Mrs Grist knows how long it takes for me to walk to the pharmacy and back, and she'll be watching the clock."

"She seemed in good spirits yesterday evening, but was probably making an effort. On the other hand, Phillip was rather quiet. I think he was embarrassed that his mother had invited me. I still remind him of his ill-fated love affair with Mathilda."

"Perhaps it would have been better if she'd invited a few other guests. Though I don't know how the cook would have handled that. She could barely cope as it was."

"Yes, you're right. A few more guests would have made it easier for everyone. Apart from the cook that is! But I think Fanny has lost touch with many of her former friends and acquaintances. As I mentioned before, after Frank died, she began to decline invitations and rarely left the house. She stayed in touch with me because, well, she needed me. So I think I'm the only person she felt she could invite – someone who knew Phillip and would be able to converse with him easily."

"Perhaps now, for Phillip's sake, she'll start to socialise more. On Sundays she sometimes goes to her sister-in-law's home and often stays overnight. But I've never seen this lady at the house since I've been living there."

"I'm well acquainted with Doris. She's an invalid, but she has a loving family – a husband, a son and two daughters – who care for her, and she and Fanny have always been close. I'm glad she still accepts her invitations.

"Anyway, that's enough about the Grists. How are you, Bessie? And how are your friends, the ones who live in Clapham?"

"They're well, thank you. I see them every other Sunday when I go to read with a student at the Roman Catholic school where Robert works as a groundsman. The boy is a boarder there and is having difficulty settling in. His parents died in a fire – it was the most tragic of accidents – and his sister was put into an orphanage. Michael was taken in by an uncle, who pays for his education, but unfortunately that gentleman did nothing to help the girl."

"That sounds like a sad story, Bessie. How old is this boy?"

"He's eleven and his sister is thirteen."

"It's good of you to spend time with him. Is his reading improving?"

"His reading was already good. But he was so distressed when he started at the school that the teachers thought he was behind the other boys in most subjects. Still, he's a clever lad and I'm sure he'll catch up quickly. He was terribly worried about his sister Harriet – he had no idea where she was – but Robert and I managed to locate her and put them in touch with one another."

"It seems unfair that the girl had to go to an orphanage. It's a pity the uncle couldn't have done something for her as well."

"As it happens, she's no longer at the orphanage She was so unhappy there that she ran away, back to her old house, even though it was badly damaged by the fire. When the neighbour found her sleeping in the garden shed, she wrote to Robert for advice on what to do. In the end, Robert and Patty decided they would let Harriet live with them until she can find some type of work. She might be able to get a job in service, though I'm sure she aspires to something better than that."

"That's very kind of your friends. Tell me, is Harriet an educated girl?"

"Yes, I think so. She left school at eleven, but Michael speaks highly of her abilities. Their mother was bedridden and their father wasn't able to cope – he began drinking too much and was often rough with the children – so Harriet had to do everything at home. Now, thank goodness, she has the chance of a normal life. I'm hoping that Patty's mother, Celia – who lives with them – can teach her dressmaking. That might help her avoid having to go into service, which she'll probably hate."

"Poor girl. But I'm glad your friends are helping her for now. How is she settling in?"

"I don't know. I haven't yet heard from Robert to say

he's picked her up from the neighbour's house. He said he'd write to me as soon as she was with them. I do hope everything's all right. She's a strong-willed girl and may have other plans."

"I'm sure she'll accept the offer of a roof over her head. It's certainly better than having to return to the orphanage, or even worse, ending up in the workhouse."

"Yes, that's what Robert says. I'm sorry Mr Fielding – I mean… Lionel – but I really must go now. Mrs Grist will be wondering where I am."

"All right, Bessie. Thank you for returning my monocle. And please relay my thanks to Fanny for finding it and also for the splendid dinner last night. I'll be sending her a thank you note as soon as I return from Mathilda's. Goodbye, my dear."

Whatever induced me to call him Lionel! What will he think? I know he's told me more than once to address him by his Christian name, but surely that puts our friendship on a different level. I shouldn't have allowed myself to be so familiar. Now I won't be able to call him Mr Fielding ever again, and I always think of him as Mr Fielding, never as Lionel. How could I have been so foolish?

Well, one thing I've just realised is that he's now in possession of my lace handkerchief with my initials, E H, embroidered in the corner. I shan't ask for it back – let me see if he attempts to return it. It's my favourite hankie, but I don't want it back. It pleases me to think of him treasuring it as a keepsake, though such a notion is surely just a figment of my wild imagination.

Phillip looks tired and upset when he returns from work. I overhear him telling his mother that Basil Hornby cornered him on the street and asked him when his mother was going to buy another two bottles of brandy.

The last time he went there, he said, he came away without buying the spirits because the man kept insisting that he take advantage of the 'other services' that were on offer. He didn't even set foot over the threshold, but that was the time, apparently, when Lionel Fielding saw him making a quick retreat and jumped to the wrong conclusion.

"What am I supposed to do, Mama?" he asks. "Hornby knows my movements. I try to avoid him, but he always tracks me down. He never goes after Godfrey or Jack – it's always me."

"It's because you're the youngest," Mrs Grist says. "He thinks you're more easily influenced. But don't worry, darling. Lionel Fielding has promised to help us put a stop to this blackmail. I know, it's a harsh word, but that's what it is. Look at this note Hornby sent me today. He says he can't wait much longer for the money I owe him. As if I haven't paid his extortionate interest a hundred times over!"

"Oh no! What are you going to do?"

"I'll send Mrs Hopper with the money in an envelope and tell her it's for brandy – the two bottles he told you about. But this is the last time. It has to stop. Hornby thinks he can continue to intimidate us because of the feud between your father and his, but that's in the past. I'll no longer be held hostage by the likes of that family. Let him threaten us. What have we got to lose?"

"Do you have to send the cook? Surely you know how close they are. I don't think it helps. I had words with her this morning because she left the kitchen in such a mess overnight. I'm not in her good books, never have been in fact. Can't you ask Miss Hardwicke to go?"

"No, Phillip. Miss Hardwicke is a single woman and, although not young, she shouldn't be seen going to such a place. Don't worry about Mrs Hopper. She'll do whatever

I tell her to do."

Mrs Grist and Phillip are talking in the hallway while I'm in the drawing room packing up my sewing for the day. The door is ajar so I cannot avoid overhearing every word of their conversation. I don't want them to know that they've been listened to, so I pass through the dining room and then down the stairs into the kitchen. I linger there for a few minutes to make sure that the coast is clear before retreating to my room. As I climb the stairs, I see Mrs Hopper putting on her hat and coat, about to run that unfortunate errand for Mrs Grist. Clearly still in a foul mood, she slams the front door on her way out.

One of the first things I do in the mornings is to check if there's any post. Today, however, Phillip has beaten me to it. He hands me a letter and a postcard.

"For you, Miss Hardwicke," he says with a smile. "No post for anyone else today."

"Oh, thank you, Mr Grist," I say. "I've been waiting for this letter, and the postcard will be from my nephew. He's my most regular correspondent."

"Please call me Phillip. Mr Grist is much too formal for me. You must find it rather dull here after working at a country house. My mother told me you used to work for nobility."

"Yes, I did, but my role wasn't an enviable one, though I was treated well. I was in service for many years. I can't deny that it's different here, but certainly not dull. I'm grateful to your mother for giving me employment. I've been extremely fortunate. I don't get as tired as I used to at Farringdale House where some of the tasks were physically taxing."

"But I think you still feel like an outsider, am I right? Try to feel more at home, Miss Hardwicke. I know my mother isn't the easiest person to get along with, but she needs your company. The two servants are not loyal to her – she's aware of it but refuses to take any action against them. If it weren't for you, she'd be very lonely indeed."

"Oh, thank you for your kind words. It's true that it's taking me a while to adjust to living here, but it's not because of your mother. She's been kind to me. It's just that I've always lived in the countryside, and London's such a big city – so different to what I've been used to."

"Well, I'm sure you'll soon learn to love it. I've never lived in the countryside so I can't make a comparison, but I believe the city has much more to offer in terms of opportunities. And we have history on our doorstep, as you'll begin to discover."

"Yes, you're right, of course. I *am* beginning to appreciate the advantages of living in the city, even though I might appear to be making slow progress."

"I'm glad to hear it. You'll have to excuse me now – I must be off. I promised to arrive at work on time today. Good day to you, Miss Hardwicke."

With that, Phillip picks up his briefcase and leaves the house. I'm flattered that he took the time to talk to me so kindly. He seems to be a decent young man and is clearly as concerned about his mother as she is about him.

Back in my room, I slit open the envelope. I know from the handwriting that it's a letter from Robert, and I pray that it brings good tidings. I retrieve a single sheet of paper, covered in Robert's inky scrawl. The letter reads:

'Dearest Bessie,
I'm delighted to tell you that Harriet is now with Patty, Celia and myself. It wasn't easy getting her to agree to come home with me, but I was able to persuade her when I promised that she'd see her brother every weekend. I also told her that she should look upon her

stay as temporary. Once she decides on a sensible course of action – and we will help and advise her on that – then she'll be free to leave.

She came to us only yesterday, but has already made a great friend of Celia. Today the ancient sewing machine saw the light of day and Celia is teaching her to make alterations to some of Patty's old dresses and skirts. As you will have guessed, her own clothes were destroyed in the fire and she arrived at the orphanage in the dress she was wearing that fateful day, which was then confiscated. When she ran away, she still wore the uniform the sisters gave her. I will return it to them, washed and pressed. Mrs Radford gave her a dress and a coat, which she insists she keeps, but the girl is in dire need of warm clothing. If you can spare anything at all, Bessie, it will help us enormously.

I will invite Michael to the house for tea on Sunday to reunite him with his sister. If you would like to join us at the usual time, you will be more than welcome.

Affectionately yours,
Robert'

Just the news I was praying for! I'm so relieved that Harriet is now with Robert, Patty and Celia, safely ensconced in the bosom of that small family. Not only that, but Celia is teaching her dressmaking, just as I'd hoped! I've spent the last few nights worrying in case she refused to return with Robert, intent on some alternative plan, which might put her at risk. Thank goodness Robert succeeded in his mission!

Now, as soon as I have time, I need to see what I can spare from my – admittedly small – wardrobe of clothes. I gave away several old dresses before coming to London – they would have been too shabby anyway – so I don't have much to offer and am doubtful if any of my old-fashioned clothes will appeal to a girl of thirteen. Still, at least we're about the same size, give or take an inch or so – so anything that I am able to part with will most likely fit her without much alteration.

I suppose my reading with Michael will be coming to an end. The siblings will have so much to talk about that reading will be the last thing on the boy's mind. Never mind. I'm just glad he's to be reunited with his sister and that the sweet smile he occasionally graces me with will at last be a genuine one.

Now that my mind is at rest concerning Harriet, I can indulge in the pleasure of reading Walter's postcard. As I've already mentioned, he usually sends me a postcard from any new place he visits for work, and this time I see that it really is close to home. The picture on the front of the card is of the village of Woodchester, seen from a distance within the wider Cotswold landscape. Walter writes:

'Dear Aunt, I hope this will find you in the best of health as it leaves us all at present. I think you will like this card, though it might make you homesick. But I'm sure you will not miss the damp weather we are now experiencing. It's most unpleasant just now and has not stopped raining for almost a week. Yesterday I visited Uncle Harold and Aunt Dorothy and they send their love, as do Edward and Edie. Your affectionate nephew, Walter'

Walter's postcards usually precede a letter so I can probably expect more news by the end of next week. But whether I receive a card or a letter, hearing from him always makes my day. And he's right, the picture does make me homesick, but I mustn't dwell on it. I need to remember my conversation with Phillip and hope that, in due course, I will learn to love London and all it has to offer.

15

Phillip brings us some disturbing news this evening. Apparently, there has been a protest at Westminster by the women of the Suffragette movement, some of whom tried to break into the House of Commons. The women were met with violence from the police and many of them were injured, several seriously. Phillip says the clash erupted because Prime Minister Asquith has delayed passing the Bill of Conciliation, which would give some women the right to vote. The reason for the delay, he says, is the decision to call for another election in order to pass through Parliament the so-called 'People's Budget'. I should add that all this would have been meaningless to me had Walter not alerted me to the activities of the Suffragettes and Edie's support for the movement. Now that I know the news will affect the young couple that occupies such a special place in my heart, I'm keen to take an interest.

Mrs Grist is not at all supportive of the women's protest, and says they deserved the treatment they received at the hands of the police, who were only trying to maintain law and order. Phillip, on the other hand, is sympathetic towards the Suffragettes. He tells his mother that times are changing and women should no longer be denied their rights; they should be allowed the same education, career choices and suffrage as men. Mrs Grist is shocked by his views and tells him to keep them to himself.

"What do you think, Miss Hardwicke?" Phillip asks me, to my embarrassment.

"Well, I can't really give an opinion," I say cautiously, not wanting to disagree with him but not wanting to offend Mrs Grist either. "I think if I knew more about it, I might sympathise with some of the women's demands, but I can't support the protests if they lead to violence. Is there not a more peaceful path they could follow?"

"I think you'll find they've tried to make their voices heard through peaceful means, but have failed. Postponing the discussion of the Conciliation Bill at the point when it was about to be passed into law was the tipping point for Mrs Pankhurst and her followers. How much longer are these women supposed to wait before they're taken seriously?"

"Women should be satisfied with their lot," Mrs Grist says. "Putting ideas of suffrage and equal rights into their heads will only lead to more grief, mark my words. Do you think a man who already treats his wife badly is going to listen to her when she claims to be equal to him? He's going to make her suffer even more."

"Oh, Mama," Phillip sighs. "No woman should be subjected to ill treatment at the hands of any man, especially not her husband. If equal rights were passed into law and women were given the chance to earn a decent living of their own, then there would be no need for them to marry such appalling men in the first place. Change will not come about without a fight, but in the long run it surely has to be worth it."

My goodness, Phillip's views are very modern, but the more I hear him speak his mind, the more I respect him. I remember Mr Fielding telling me that his daughter Mathilda supports the women's suffrage movement too, and I wonder if she and Phillip discussed such issues when they were sweethearts. What a pity they parted company. I think they would have made a perfect couple.

Saturday's newspapers are full of reports about the women's protests. The 18th of November has come to be known as 'Black Friday'. The *Daily Mirror's* headline reads, 'Violent scenes at Westminster, where many

Suffragettes were arrested while trying to force their way into the House of Commons', and underneath is a photograph of a woman, named as Ada Wright, who was knocked to the ground by a policeman. Phillip claims that the Home Secretary, Mr Winston Churchill, had himself sanctioned the police brutality, but subsequently decided not to prosecute any of the women who were arrested so as to prevent an inquiry into police actions.

I think I need to write another letter to Walter to tell him all about yesterday's news in case he hasn't had time to read a newspaper or speak with Edie. Unlike many in the village, he does try his best to keep up with current affairs, and this is definitely something that will interest him. There's little doubt that Edie will already have heard about the protest and its aftermath; in fact, she's probably much more informed than I am regarding Friday's unsettling events.

I tell Mrs Grist that my friends have taken in a girl whose parents died in a fire, and they've asked me if I could bequeath any clothes that I no longer wear. So as not to disappoint them, I've spent the last hour going through my things to see if there's anything I'm able to part with.

"But you have so little, Elizabeth," she says. "You arrived here with such a small amount of luggage. You keep your things – I have a chest full of clothes I no longer wear. You can take whatever you think will be useful. None of the items fits me anymore. If they're too big for the girl now, she may grow into them, or you or your friend might care to try them on. Let's go upstairs now and you can decide what to take."

I certainly didn't expect Mrs Grist to be so generous. I only mentioned Harriet because she accused me of being distracted and asked me what was on my mind. I was in fact wondering whether I should give Harriet one of the two good dresses Lady Sophia Radcliffe presented me with back in the spring before she left on a trip to the continent. Neither one fits me well as I am less well endowed than she is, and I suspect they will be a loose fit on Harriet too.

The only time I've entered Mrs Grist's bedroom was on the one occasion she was sick, so I've not really had a chance until now to observe the décor. The four-poster bed is striking; its floral drapes are pulled back to reveal a rose pink candlewick bedspread. A beautiful dressing table with three adjustable mirrors is lined with bottles of scent, jars of face cream, and a silver-backed hairbrush and comb. And a heavy mahogany chest of drawers and matching two-door wardrobe, both with cabriole legs, give evidence to the fact that Mrs Grist is not short of a dress or two.

"Are you sure you can spare this, Mrs Grist?" I say, holding up a lilac silk blouse with billowing sleeves and ruffles down the front. "Some of these things are so elegant and look as though they've hardly been worn."

"Yes, I'll glad to be rid of them. I was going to give them to Mrs Hopper or Mrs Evans, who between them have five daughters – but I'd rather they go where they're needed and appreciated. I've given so many things to those two over the years and I never receive a word of thanks."

"Well, *I* can't thank you enough, and I'm sure young Harriet will be just as appreciative. My friend's mother is a seamstress so she'll know what alterations are needed, if any. Harriet is not yet fourteen but is tall for her age, so I think most of these clothes will fit her."

"I'm glad to hear it. Why don't you put all the clothes in this old carpetbag that I no longer use. I don't want it back – my travelling days are over – so the girl can keep it. And here is a handbag that's still in good condition.

Oh, and what about boots? I don't suppose you know her size, but if these are a size too big, she can still wear them with a pair of thick woollen stockings. And she's going to need a hat and some gloves, isn't she? Here, take these. I've barely worn them."

Mrs Grist is being so kind that I feel guilty for always thinking the worst about her. It just goes to show that you can't judge a book by its cover, as Father used to say. Even though Mr Fielding insists that she isn't a bad person, I've stubbornly persisted in my ill feelings towards her. I'm not saying she doesn't still address me with a sharp word or two from time to time, but I can see now that she's a caring person at heart and bears no hostility towards me. That knowledge makes me a lot happier.

Despite my own dearth of clothing, I feel I should make some contribution towards Harriet's new wardrobe. Lady Sophia's dresses are no longer necessary since Mrs Grist has provided some equally fine ones, as well as several blouses and skirts, but no one has mentioned undergarments. I have a spare front-fastening corset and chemise, a petticoat that's seen its better days but is still serviceable, and a pair of drawers that I bought a month ago and still haven't worn. I also have a pair of black woollen stockings that are almost new, so I'll include those too in case they're needed to make the boots fit. I think that should be enough. Without doubt, Miss Harriet Turnbull is going to be the best-dressed young lady in Clapham!

I can't wait to see Harriet's face when I present her with such an abundance of clothes and accessories. Of course, an even greater joy will be to witness the long-awaited reunion between brother and sister. I'm too excited to attend church on Sunday morning and instead spend an hour or more arranging and rearranging the contents of the carpetbag, which is only just big enough for all Mrs Grist's discarded finery.

As the bag is so heavy, I catch a motorbus from the Wandsworth stop, but it doesn't take me all the way and the last half mile I have to walk. Would that I had a male friend to carry the bag for me! No sooner has this thought flashed through my mind than a young man dressed in his Sunday best asks if he can help me with my load. At first, I refuse, not wanting to trouble him, but he ignores my protests and takes the bag from me. He insists that he knows the street where I'm headed, and says he's going that way himself. I'm so grateful to be relieved of my load that I make no further objection.

The young man deposits the bag right on Patty's doorstep. I thank him profusely and even offer him a coin, but he refuses to take it. He's gone before I can insist, but not before I glance at his face and notice that his eyes are a striking shade of green, framed by long dark lashes. Such a handsome boy and so kind too!

I knock on the door and Patty opens it instantly, welcoming me in.

"What on earth do you have there, Bessie?" she asks, eyeing the bulging bag.

"Clothes for Harriet!" I exclaim. "Mrs Grist has been extremely generous. She's given me so many items of clothing she claims she no longer needs. And a hat, gloves, a pair of boots, a handbag and this carpetbag!"

"Good gracious. I thought your Mrs Grist was a bad-tempered character. When did she change into a fairy godmother?"

"To be honest, I think I've probably painted a false picture of her. I realise that now. But it's true, she does seem to have changed, especially since her son Phillip came to stay at the house. She's certainly been a lot nicer to me recently."

"Well, Bessie, please convey our sincere thanks. Harriet is desperate for a change of clothes."

"Where is she, Patty? And where is Michael? Is he here yet?"

"Yes. They're both out in the garden. There's little space in here for privacy so I suggested they go outside to talk. They're so excited to see one another that I don't think they'll feel the cold."

"How is it going? Is Harriet beginning to feel at home? Robert said in his letter that your mother was teaching her how to use the old sewing machine. It'll be wonderful if she can become skilled in dressmaking. Where is Aunt Celia, by the way?"

"She's just gone upstairs to have a lie-down. All the excitement is a bit much for her. Yes, I'm sure Harriet will succeed in anything she turns her mind to. She's a clever girl and quick to learn. And she has a willing pair of hands, always ready to help me with the housework and in the kitchen. She certainly doesn't need anyone to teach her domestic chores. But she's still a bit reserved – guarded I would say – and doesn't talk much unless she's spoken to. Still, it's early days yet."

"Is Robert now resigned to her living with you? I know he was undecided at first and you needed to persuade him that it was the right thing to do."

"Yes, but he was only hesitant because he didn't want any conflict with the sisters at the orphanage. Don't forget, he's a Roman Catholic, brought up to respect others of that faith – especially those dedicated to a life of worship – so he'd hate to offend them. Anyway, he wrote to them, explaining the situation and returning Harriet's uniform, but has received no response. He takes that as a good sign and is now satisfied that we've done the right thing. As for there being one more person living here, that doesn't bother him in the least. He was raised in a large family that had just two rooms between them, so for him, this house is a mansion."

I follow Patty into the kitchen where she's getting the tea ready. She says Robert will be in shortly; he's helping a neighbour – whose eyesight is failing him – write a letter to his landlord. According to Patty, he's always doing little favours for the neighbours and is popular with the older folk, most of whom are less literate than he is. Through the kitchen window I can see Michael and Harriet deep in conversation. Michael is clearly amused by something Harriet says, so much so that he bursts out laughing. What a joyful sight! It takes him a minute or more to control his giggles.

"It's good to see them together," I say. "Their closeness reminds me of Ethel and myself. Do you remember the fun we used to have growing up? Ethel could always make us laugh, even when we were feeling miserable."

"Yes, I shall never forget those days. We had a happy childhood, I think. Of course, our parents struggled and there were many shortages, but compared to the way children live here in the city, I think we were lucky to grow up in the countryside. Don't you agree?"

"Indeed I do. Am I right in thinking that you miss the West Country as much as I do, Patty?"

"Oh yes, I miss it every single day. But I wouldn't give up my life here with Robert to return there. I've been very fortunate. What about you, Bessie dear? You don't regret coming to London, do you?"

"If you'd asked me that a couple of months ago, I might have said yes. But no, not so much now. I think my life is more interesting here – each day gives me some new experience – and I'm slowly beginning to overcome my fear of everything I'm not used to. I was even brave enough to catch the motorbus by myself today, though I had to walk part of the way. Mind you, my feelings about living in the city do tend to change fairly frequently, depending on my mood. Earlier this week I was ready to pack my bags and throw myself at the mercy of Edward. I thought Mrs Grist might not need me any more since her son Phillip is now back home. But she assures me it's only temporary. And *he* actually told me that she needs me much more than she lets on."

"Oh, I'm so glad. What's her son like?"

"Well, he's a lot nicer than I'd imagined, though a bit unstable at times. I think he has a nervous disposition. That's why Mrs Grist persuaded him to come back home for a short while. Mr Fielding, the pharmacist, thinks he suffers from melancholia and is concerned for him. He's been thwarted in love and hasn't yet fully recovered from his heartbreak. I do feel sorry for him. But he goes to work most days and clearly doesn't want to be fussed over. The rumour is that Mrs Grist spoiled him since he's the youngest of her three boys and that his sensitivity is her fault, but I don't think that's necessarily true."

"You've always been a good judge of character, Bessie. I'm glad you get along well with him. Now, tea is almost ready. I think we'd better call the children inside."

Michael enters the kitchen, followed by Harriet. His face is flushed, and he looks at me shyly.

"Harriet is here, Aunt Bessie," he says.

"I know, Michael," I say. "Isn't it wonderful? I'm so pleased that she's now living with Mr and Mrs Cartwright, especially since your school is close by."

"I wish I could live here too and not have to go to school."

"Come now, Michael, school isn't so bad. And Harriet wants you to do well, don't you, Harriet?"

"Yes, of course," Harriet says. "Michael has to study hard and become top of his class. Then, when he leaves school and is earning a lot of money, we can both live together."

"That sounds like a good plan. You look well, Harriet, and a lot happier than when I last met you."

"Yes, I'm much happier. I hated it in the orphanage. Thank you for helping my brother, Miss…"

"Call me Aunt Bessie, Harriet. It was my pleasure. Besides, Michael didn't really need my help, and I'm sure I enjoyed our meetings much more than he did."

"Harriet," Patty says, "Aunt Bessie has kindly brought you a bag full of clothes. Once Michael goes back to school, you and Aunt Celia can go through them and see what fits and what doesn't. Now that you're learning dressmaking, you can help with any alterations that are needed."

"Oh, thank you so much, Aunt Bessie," Harriet says, her eyes widening when she sees the bulky carpetbag. "Clothes are what I need more than anything else."

"Well, they're mostly from my employer," I say. "I'll thank her on your behalf. I'm not a follower of fashion – far from it – but some of the garments appear very stylish. I'm sure they'll suit you beautifully."

"Tea is nearly ready," Patty says. "Wash your hands at the kitchen sink, Michael, and you too, Harriet. Uncle Robert won't let you sit down at the table with hands like that. Here he is, back just in time."

"Hello, Bessie," Robert says, taking off his boots at the door. "Our household has grown since you were last here. We even have Romeo to add to our number, though he refuses to be stroked by anyone except Harriet."

"Oh, is the kitten here too?" I ask, looking around the room.

"Yes. He refused to be left behind. Here he is now, following Harriet as usual."

Harriet bends down and picks up a sleek black cat

with golden eyes. Michael strokes the glossy fur on the cat's neck and he immediately starts purring.

"He lets me stroke him," Michael says.

"Of course he does," I say. "He hasn't forgotten you, Michael. Now, Harriet, you'd better put Romeo down before Aunt Patty comes in with the tea, or she'll make you wash your hands a second time."

It's such a pleasure to see Michael and Harriet – and Romeo! – so happily reunited. The siblings' troubles are far from over, but they can forget them for one afternoon at least. Celia comes down from upstairs and I can that a bond has already been established between the old lady and the young girl. Celia is a great one for jokes and she makes the children laugh with her teasing and old-fashioned ways. After tea, Michael looks sad when Robert tells him he must take him back to school, but cheers up at the promise that he'll see his sister every Sunday and perhaps mid-week too, if the brothers will allow it.

"Remember our friend David," I say, as he reluctantly puts on his jacket. "He has to go away to school too, but he knows that his Aunt Betsey still cares for him. He's confident that he can turn to her if ever he finds himself in trouble. And you should know that you're able to turn to any one of us if you're worried about something or have a problem – however small – that's keeping you from falling asleep at night. Now, run along my dear, and make sure you do well in your lessons so that your big sister can be proud of you."

16

Free of the heavy carpetbag, I walk back home. I still can't get used to calling Mrs Grist's house 'home', but I have no other. I manage to reach Rosehill Road just before a heavy fog engulfs Wandsworth and its neighbouring parishes. I'm glad I left Patty and Robert's when I did, because for the last half mile it's been difficult to distinguish one house from another. The fog that regularly descends upon the metropolis is another thing I haven't yet become accustomed to. Mr Fielding says it's smoke pollution – smog – rather than the type of valley fog we often experience back home, and that's why many people in the city suffer from respiratory illnesses. He says that as long as London's factories continue to burn coal and emit harmful chemicals into the atmosphere, and as long as Londoners use coal to heat their homes, then the so-called 'pea-souper' fogs will continue to plague the city.

I feel my way along the railings, moving slowly and counting each house until I reach Mrs Grist's. I unlock the front door with a sigh of relief. Now that I'm safely inside, it does actually feel like home. Unexpectedly, there are voices coming from the drawing room. One is clearly Phillip's and the other belongs to a lady, and it sounds vaguely familiar. It's definitely not Mrs Grist – I know she's gone to her sister-in-law's again today. I listen carefully as I hang up my hat and coat. The female voice has a West Country accent! It can't be Edie, surely? It does sound an awful lot like her.

The door is slightly ajar, so I peek in. It is Edie! She must have come to visit me! She's sitting on the edge of the settee, leaning slightly forward and talking to Phillip as if she's known him all her life.

I knock gently and walk into the room.

"Why Edie!" I exclaim. "What on earth are you doing here?"

"Oh, Aunt Bessie," she says, standing up. "I'm so pleased to see you! I hope you don't mind my calling on you like this. I'm sorry but I didn't have time to write to you beforehand. And I couldn't come all the way to London and not pay you a visit."

"I'm delighted to see you, my dear. But perhaps we should have met somewhere else. This is not my home and I don't want to take advantage..."

"Nonsense, Miss Hardwicke," Phillip says. "Of course it's your home. And my mother can hardly deny you the occasional visitor. I'm glad I was here today to receive Miss Bancroft. Sit down, why don't you? I'll leave you both to chat. I expect you have a lot to talk about."

"Are you sure? Edie can come up to my room. I don't want to disturb you."

"You're not disturbing me in the least. It was a pleasure talking to you, Miss Bancroft."

"Thank you," Edie says, blushing. "I enjoyed it too."

"He's so kind," she says once Phillip has left the room. "You're lucky to be employed by such a nice family, Aunt Bessie."

"Yes, I am," I say, not wanting to reveal my initial impressions, though perhaps Walter has already told her. "But tell me, Edie, what's brought you to London so suddenly?"

"Well, you might disapprove, but I'll tell you anyway. It was the women's march on Parliament that brought me here. I came with a friend from the nurses' training school – her uncle lives not far from here and we're staying there. We arrived on Thursday evening and we plan to catch an early train back home tomorrow morning."

"Oh, Edie, I can't believe you were at the march! That was surely a reckless thing to do! You could have been injured."

"Yes, I knew you wouldn't approve, Aunt Bessie. I know that not everyone agrees with the demands of the Suffragettes, and sometimes they can take things too far, but my friend Annie and I felt we should participate in such an important protest. When the foreign secretary, Sir Edward Grey, announced last week that there would be no further debate on the Conciliation Bill this year, the WSPU felt let down and wanted to make women's voices heard as loudly as possible. So they encouraged their many supporters to come to London to join the march."

"Well, I can't pretend I'm not shocked that you and your friend attended the protest. What did Walter have to say? Does he even know you're here?"

"No, Aunt, he doesn't. He wouldn't have wanted me to come and would've tried to stop me. He doesn't approve of my involvement with the Suffragette movement."

"It's only because he worries about you, Edie. In a way, I suppose it's a good thing you *didn't* tell him, as he'd have been worried sick about you, given the way things have turned out. It was reported that many women were injured or arrested. Thank goodness you're still in one piece!"

"Yes, I know, Walter would have been troubled. But I'll be back home tomorrow and will go to his uncle's house as soon as I can to see him. It was quite frightening in the end and perhaps we shouldn't have gone, but we kept as far away from the police with their truncheons as we could. We wanted to help those who were hurt – we are supposed to be nurses after all – but we couldn't get close to them without getting injured ourselves."

"I do admire your courage, my dear, and your

determination to do good, but I also understand Walter's concern. It's not that I'm against women's right to vote, but I wish it could be achieved in more peaceful ways. Anyway, I'm thankful you didn't come to any harm. Can I at least offer you a cup of tea since you've gone out of your way to come to see me?"

"Thank you, Aunt Bessie, but I really need to be getting back. Annie and her relatives are expecting me for dinner. I'm sorry we've had so little time to talk – I seem to have spent more time chatting with Mr Grist than with you. I should have let you know I was coming but, as I said, there was no time."

"But Edie, have you seen the weather outside? There's a thick fog and it's now dark. You're never going to be able to find your way back to where you're staying."

"I have no choice, Aunt. I have to get back there."

Despite my protests, Edie stands up and puts her coat on. But then Phillip enters the room and confirms what I've just told her.

"You can't walk alone in this weather," he says.

"Don't worry," she says. "I'll find my way. It's really not far from here."

"Then I must accompany you. I can navigate the streets around here with my eyes closed. Of course, that's if you'll consent to my walking with you, Miss Bancroft. But if you feel you'd like a chaperone, then perhaps Miss Hardwicke would care to come with us?"

"Yes, of course I will," I say. "I won't rest easy until I know you're safely back at your lodgings, Edie."

"No, there's really no need, Aunt," Edie says quickly. "It's getting late and you look so tired. If Mr Grist really doesn't mind accompanying me, then I'm happy to let him."

"Are you sure, Edie? I wouldn't want Walter to think…"

"I'm absolutely sure, Aunt Bessie. Please don't worry."

"Very well. Mr Grist has my full trust. I know you won't come to any harm in his safe hands."

"Then that's settled," Phillip says. "I won't be long, Miss Hardwicke. I know the area where Miss Bancroft is staying. It's barely fifteen minutes' walk away."

Edie and I hug each other and I see her to the door. The fog is growing denser by the minute. I do hope Phillip really does know the way. Walter will never forgive me if anything happens to his sweetheart. But I'm sure there's no need to worry. Phillip grew up in this neighbourhood so must be as familiar with the local streets as I am with the country lanes back home.

Edie looked so pretty today, I reflect, once she and Phillip have left the house. It's no wonder Walter is so much in love with her. Her golden curls were falling around her flushed, heart-shaped face and her blue eyes sparkled when she spoke of Friday's adventure. I hope Walter won't be too angry when he learns about her escapade. I don't approve of it either, but young women these days are determined to see changes in their lives, and are no longer content to play second fiddle to men who don't always treat them with the respect and consideration they deserve. I know that Walter just wants to protect Edie, not restrict her freedom, but Edie is so independent that she's never going to accept being wrapped in cotton wool, not even by as fine a man as my nephew.

I'm still sitting in the drawing room pondering the afternoon's events when Phillip returns. I've been so engrossed in my thoughts that it surprises me when I look at the clock and see that an hour has already passed.

"What a charming young lady your niece is," Phillip says as he enters the room, rubbing his hands together to warm them up.

"She's not really my niece," I say. "She's the betrothed – or soon to be betrothed – of my nephew Walter. Thank you so much for ensuring her safe return to where she's staying."

"It was a pleasure. We had an interesting talk. She told me about her involvement with the Suffragette movement and how she's travelled some distance to take part in the march. I was impressed by her courage and resolve."

"Yes, she's a brave and determined lass. But I don't think Walter will be pleased when he finds out where she's been. Apparently, she didn't tell him. He worries about her recklessness."

"Oh, I think she's well able to look after herself. And she didn't come alone, did she? She also told me that she's training to be a nurse. That's a commendable profession for a young woman."

"Yes. It's good for her to learn such valuable skills, but whether she'll be able to make a career out of nursing is doubtful."

"You mean she'll have to give it up when she gets married?"

"Exactly."

"Well, who knows, such antiquated rules may soon change. Let's hope so. In any case, it's a worthy calling and I admire her strength of character."

I nod my agreement and get up from the settee, bidding Phillip good night. I'm happy Edie's made such a favourable impression on him, but begin to wonder at my judgement in letting such an eligible young man walk alone with Walter's sweetheart on a dark and foggy night.

It's mid-morning when Mrs Grist arrives back at the house the next day. She looks tired and is irritable, as is often the case when she spends a night away from home.

I tell her that Harriet was delighted with the clothes and that both she and Patty send their sincere thanks. She makes no comment and leaves me wondering whether she now regrets her kindness in parting with so many good quality clothes and accessories.

"Did you see Phillip this morning?" she asks.

"Yes, I did" I say. "We passed on the stairs at about a quarter to eight. He was just leaving for work."

"So he came back yesterday?"

"Yes. He was here when I returned from Clapham."

"Hmm. He didn't want to come to his aunt's house, even though he was invited, so I wondered… Well, never mind. He's not a child. I can't spend my days worrying about his shifting moods."

I say nothing. If anyone has shifting moods, it's Mrs Grist herself. I don't want to tell her about Edie coming to the house, although if Phillip mentions it, she'll wonder why I didn't say anything and may be cross with me. But somehow, I don't think he'll tell his mother about our surprise visitor.

My thoughts are interrupted when she asks me to go to the pharmacy to buy some Beecham's pills for her indigestion.

"Doris employs the worst cook in the world," she says. "Every time I have a meal there, I come away with indigestion. How she and her family can stomach that heavy food every day, I have no idea."

She gives me a few coins and, once again, tells me not to waste time.

"No, of course I won't waste time," I say. "But I've noticed that on Mondays there's usually a queue at the pharmacy. A lot of people tend to feel poorly after the weekend."

I've never answered Mrs Grist back like that before, but the thought of her watching the clock makes me feel anxious and that's something that Mr Fielding notices right away.

"Well, be as quick as you can," she responds brusquely.

When I tell Mr Fielding about Mrs Grist's indigestion following her stay at her sister-in-law's, he laughs.

"Doris' cook is French," he says. "Fanny Grist has a strong dislike of anything 'foreign'. I'm sure the food is excellent, but perhaps a bit on the rich side. My belief is that Fanny is a little in awe of that cook, though she'd never admit it to anybody."

"I've heard that French food is the best in the world," I say, remembering what Lady Sophia Radcliffe told me after she visited Paris a couple of years ago.

"Hmm, I don't know if it's the best in the world, but it's certainly very good, and much more refined than English cuisine. I was once fortunate enough to be invited to the Café Royal in Piccadilly. The rack of lamb was excellent, as was the sauce it came with. I think the English generally consider the sauces to be too heavy, but of course that's a matter of taste.

"So you say Fanny has an upset stomach? How is she otherwise? And Phillip? How is he? You see, Bessie, I rely on you for news of the Grist family, especially since Fanny so rarely sets foot outside the house apart from her visits to Doris' home."

"I think she's still worried about Phillip, but to be honest I don't see that there's anything wrong with him. He appears to be in fairly good spirits, and he behaves like a gentleman. But I think the unpleasant business with Mr Hornby isn't yet resolved, according to a conversation that I overheard. He said Hornby recently cornered him in an attempt to sell him spirits – apparently, he's always on the lookout for him – and that he tried to force him to enter his house for… for other reasons. Phillip couldn't get away quickly enough. Mrs Grist mentioned an old feud between their fathers and told her son that she refuses to submit to Hornby's threats any longer. She also said you had promised to help put an end to his intimidation."

"Ah, yes. Let me tell you a secret, Bessie. It will help you understand the Grist family a bit better. Mr Frank Grist was a wealthy man some thirty years ago. His family owned property all over London. But his father cut him out of his will because he insisted on marrying beneath him. You looked shocked. It's true, Fanny's family were not rich, but she was a great beauty and Frank fell head over heels in love with her. Unfortunately, once the honeymoon years were over, their married life was always a bit of a struggle. He was a lawyer by profession, so even without an inheritance, he should have been able to make ends meet. But he was used to living well and wanted to continue in the same fashion. He would go to his club and drink and play cards until the late hours, and – as so often happens – he ended up in debt.

"Basil Hornby's father was a money-lender – the family's skulduggery stretches back at least a century – and Frank Grist became indebted to him. When Frank died of a heart attack two years ago, he still owed him money, and that's why there's all this talk of threats and blackmail. Hornby's father has now also passed away, but the son is determined to keep the feud alive. And he's worse than his father in many ways. Everything he touches has the stamp of corruption, be it the money lending, the sale of black market liquor, or the brothel he so flagrantly operates in our neighbourhood. From what Fanny has told me, she pays him a small sum every month even though the debt was paid in full a long time ago. She claims he's still charging her interest and making her purchase his illegal spirits as well. She's not poor by any means, but she no longer has an income, so her wealth is not inexhaustible. She has the house and her two elder sons make sure her needs are met – they both married well and have good jobs. Frank left her another property, which she sold – in part to pay off the debt – so she's not without funds in the bank, but obviously the fact that someone like Basil Hornby is continually breathing down her neck, insisting that she still owes him money, is making her both anxious and angry."

"My goodness – poor Mrs Grist. I had no idea she has such worries. I wish there was something I could do to help."

"You *are* helping her, Bessie. A friendly face does her a power of good."

"I don't know that I'm always such a friendly face. I tend to frown deeply whenever she utters a harsh word. Now that I know she may not always be mad at *me*, I'll try not to take offence so easily."

"Just be yourself, Bessie. That's all any of us can do. Being false does more harm than good."

"Thank you, Mr Fielding. I'll try to remember that."

"Mr Fielding?"

"Sorry, I mean Lionel. I have to be getting back now. How much are the pills?"

"Compliments of the house, Bessie. Give Fanny my regards."

I want to tell him about Harriet, and about Edie – so much news! – but his revelations regarding Mrs Grist have left no time left to talk about anything else. When another customer enters the shop, greeting Mr Fielding like an old friend, our conversation comes to an end.

On my walk back to the house, I think about what he told me about the Grist family. The fact that Mrs Grist is originally from a less well-to-do family surprises me most of all. She must have had a lot to endure when she was first married. She would have been looked down upon not only by her husband's family, but by his friends as well. I can't help but admire her. She's managed to become a sophisticated lady, and a formidable one at that. And she's clever too. She has acquired a wealth of general knowledge, is extremely well read and, moreover, has raised three sons who are a credit to her. It makes me wonder yet again why she chose someone as dull and ignorant as myself to be her companion.

But the more I think about it, the more it finally makes sense. Mrs Grist did not choose me for reasons of finance – as Mrs Evans implied – and certainly not because of my 'education' as she herself stated. Given her own past, she would not have wanted too highbrow a companion. She wouldn't have opted for someone who might suspect that she had climbed the social ladder from one of the lower rungs. No, she probably concluded that she would feel much more comfortable with someone whose origins were as humble as her own, regardless of the fact that *her* fortunes in life have turned out rather differently from those of yours truly.

17

As I've said before, it's become a habit for me to pick up the post in the mornings, since I'm the first one to come downstairs. This task, however, has now been taken over by Phillip. He usually leaves for work at the time I go down to the kitchen to make my breakfast, so I often bump into him in the hallway. Today, to my surprise, he hands me two letters, one that has clearly been hand-delivered since the envelope bears no stamp. I can see that the other one is from Walter.

"Is your nephew writing to you again?" he says good-naturedly. "You're the most popular aunt I've ever met. My mother has a number of nieces and nephews, but they never take the trouble to write to her."

"Oh, I have several others whom I never hear from. It's only Walter who writes to me. You see, his mother – my sister – died young and I helped to raise him. I suppose you could say I was like a substitute mother, except that I couldn't spend as much time with him as I would have liked."

"I'm sure you did the best you could. I think you told me that your nephew is Miss Bancroft's beau. Am I correct?"

"Yes, that's right. They make a lovely couple."

"Well, if his taste in women is anything to go by, you seem to have done a fine job in raising him, Miss Hardwicke."

I'm a bit shocked at Phillip's casual talk of taste in women, but put it down to his youth and modern ways.

"He has good taste in most things," I say, "and he has a wonderful character. Even as a small boy, he was kind and considerate, and he hasn't changed at all."

"Then he's a credit to you. I'd be much obliged, Miss

Hardwicke, if you could please tell my mother that I'll be a little late this evening. I'll probably be home by suppertime, but she shouldn't wait for me."

"Yes, of course, I'll let her know. Have a good day at work."

Before preparing my breakfast, I open the hand-delivered letter, wondering if the sender has made a mistake in addressing it to me. But I might have guessed – it's from Mr Fielding! I feel myself reddening, even though there's no one else present, and wonder if Phillip was able to recognise his handwriting. It was quite daring of Mr Fielding to put such a letter through Mrs Grist's letterbox. Mrs Grist herself could have picked up the post, and I'm sure she'd know immediately whose writing was on the envelope. He writes:

'Dearest Bessie,

Would you do me the honour of taking tea with me on Sunday afternoon, if you are not otherwise engaged? It would give me the greatest pleasure to receive you in my humble abode, which I hasten to add is somewhat more comfortable than the pharmacy's back parlour.

If you are inclined to accept my rather late invitation, please meet me outside my shop at four o'clock. There is no need to respond, Bessie. I shall wait for ten minutes and will not be offended if you fail to turn up. I shall, however, insist on inviting you again in the coming weeks.

Your sincere friend,
Lionel Fielding'

I stare at the letter in astonishment. What does this mean? Is it customary for a gentleman like Mr Fielding to invite someone who's been in service for most of her life to tea on a Sunday? I am flattered, certainly, but cannot escape the feeling that I may be getting myself into something that could later cause me a great deal of grief. But how can I refuse? He says that if I don't turn up, he'll keep inviting me, and I know how insistent he can be. And do I even want to refuse? No, I'm keen to find out the meaning of this unexpected friendship. But even though he's made it clear that he does regard me as a friend, what type of man befriends a middle-aged woman of a class well below his own? I find it hard to believe that he finds me attractive, or in any way interesting, despite all his compliments. Is it too fanciful to wonder if he has romance in mind? Even the thought mortifies me, despite my fantasies at bedtime. Imagination is one thing, but reality is something entirely different, and to entertain such notions in broad daylight leaves me flustered and embarrassed.

Well, since I won't be going to Patty and Robert's this Sunday, I'll go and take tea with Mr Fielding and find out what he wants from me. It's not appropriate, I know, and I would probably drop dead on the spot if Mrs Grist found out, but I suppose our respective ages make it far less scandalous than if we were both twenty-year-olds.

Let me not think about this invitation until the evening when I'm alone in my room. If I dwell on it too much during the day, Mrs Grist will notice that something is amiss and become inquisitive. It's hard for me to keep secrets from her – she notices immediately if there's something that's bothering me. I need to put this invitation right out of my mind if I'm to behave normally.

I prepare my breakfast – tea and toast – though my appetite has all but disappeared, and then open Walter's letter, intent on enjoying his news. But for once his words do not make me feel any less troubled. He tells me how shocked he was to discover that Edie had gone to London without discussing it first with him.

"She's so reckless," he writes. "She could have been injured and I would have known nothing about it. Her friend Annie is even worse. I think she must have persuaded Edie to go with her – I can't imagine that it was Edie's idea. The girls at the nurses' training school are much more worldly than Edie, and I fear that their views are affecting her judgement. I'm so sorry that she arrived on your doorstep unexpectedly – she would never have done that sort of thing in the past. She should have sent you a message about her planned visit and asked you to name a meeting place. Thank you for being so kind to her, Aunt Bessie. I'm sure you were as shocked as I was to hear that she had participated in the women's march." He goes on to say that Edie was not at all remorseful and they parted on unhappy terms.

This news makes me very sad and I hope and pray that they soon reconcile their differences. I do wonder what Edie told Walter. She had a much longer conversation with Phillip than with me, and he walked her back to her friend's relatives' house. I hope she didn't tell Walter about that. He'd be even more upset if he knew that a strange man had accompanied his sweetheart through the streets of London in a dense fog. And I have only myself to blame for that.

It's Sunday morning and I've just returned from church. My mind is much more at ease. The Reverend Thomas Wilson spoke about friendship and quoted Proverbs 13:20, 'He that walketh with wise men shall be wise: but a companion of fools shall be destroyed'. I think I can say with utmost confidence that Mr Fielding is a wise man and I should thus have no hesitation in walking with him, or taking tea with him for that matter. So I'm not going to worry about it. He's respectable in every way and is a friend of Mrs Grist and Phillip. Nothing disagreeable or inappropriate is going to happen to me. I shall spend a pleasant hour or so in his company and then come home.

So I knelt and prayed to God that he would protect me from harm. And I prayed for Walter and Edie, for Patty and Robert, for Michael and Harriet, for Edward and his sons, for Harold and his family, for dear, dear Ethel in Heaven, and last but not least, for my darling Arthur, 'my Arthur, whom I shall not see, till all my widow'd race be run'.

I had my bath and washed my hair yesterday evening. Since there's no lock on the kitchen door, I wedged the top of a heavy wooden chair under the handle so as to bar anyone – Phillip in particular – from entering. He'd gone to his brother's house with his mother and I didn't expect them home early, but one can never be too careful. So today my hair is clean and shiny, though so flyaway that it refuses to stay in place, and I am wearing a little rouge and lipstick. This is the first time I've worn cosmetics since coming to London. Lady Sophia gave me a bag of items she no longer had use for, but I've had no cause or desire to prettify myself… until now. It's a cold day with sudden gusts of wind, but my blue woollen cloak keeps me warm and I always feel elegant when I wear it. Underneath the cloak, however, my clothes are quite ordinary. I'm wearing a grey woollen dress, which is of good quality but very plain, complimented with a blue silk scarf that was a gift last Christmas from Sophia's mother, Lady Marguerite Radcliffe.

I take my umbrella with me, as there were showers earlier and the pavements are still full of puddles. It's hard to avoid getting my cloak splashed with muddy water when an automobile or horse-drawn carriage passes by, but I try to steer clear of the ever-present horse manure that somehow always seems to end up on the pavements. Still, it's not far to walk and, up ahead, already waiting for me, is Mr Fielding.

"Good afternoon, Bessie," he says cheerfully. I feel self-conscious and awkward, and wish I hadn't worn cosmetics. "You look wonderful," he continues. "Not that you don't always look wonderful, but today even more so."

"Thank you," I say, blushing. I wish I didn't always redden like a young girl when someone pays me a compliment, but I can't stop myself. I don't know what else to say – I'm not skilled in witty rejoinders – so I leave the conversation to my companion.

"My home is close by," he says. "In fact, it's close to Mr Basil Hornby's house. But, as you might guess, he's not a neighbour I choose to associate with."

He takes my arm and we walk in the direction of Mr Hornby's house. I'm secretly praying that we don't meet anyone. I'm not well known in the neighbourhood, but Mr Fielding is known to all and sundry. I can't believe that he would knowingly take the risk of walking arm-in-arm with me in broad daylight on a Sunday afternoon. He makes light conversation and I answer in monosyllables. He must already be wishing he hadn't invited me!

We finally reach his home, which to my relief is not in the same road as Mr Hornby's. It's a handsome red brick Victorian terraced house, not dissimilar to Mrs Grist's. In the hallway he takes my cloak, complimenting me on its flattering style and adding that the colour blue matches my eyes. I turn away so as not to reveal my reddening face.

In the drawing room he invites me to sit on the settee at the end closest to the fire. The settee and two armchairs are upholstered in an attractive blue and cream floral fabric that matches the blue velvet curtains, which he draws before taking a seat opposite me. The good quality furniture is arranged so as to give a feeling of cosiness, and the walls are decorated with paintings of pastoral scenes that remind me of the West Country. The room looks as though it has benefited from a woman's touch. I can't help wondering if the tasteful décor is thanks to the loving touch of Mr Fielding's late wife, or whether Mathilda has had a hand in its arrangement.

"Mathilda's maid has come to serve us tea," Mr Fielding says and, as if on cue, a young woman enters with a tray laden with the tea things.

"Thank you, Alice," he says. "Just place the tray on the tea table, if you please. I can pour the tea, while you bring in the sandwiches and cakes."

"Can I help in any way?" I ask.

"No, Bessie. You just sit there and relax."

I do as I am told, though not without wishing I could be useful. Once tea is under way, I begin to feel a bit more at ease.

"Don't you usually go to Mathilda's on a Sunday?" I ask my host.

"I do," he says. "But once in a while I like a change. And I thought you could do with one too."

"Well, as you know, I visit my friends in Clapham every other week. And remember I told you about the children, Michael and Harriet, who lost their parents in a fire? Well, thankfully, Harriet is now living with Patty and Robert, and was reunited with her brother last Sunday. It was wonderful to see them together at long last."

"Oh, I am pleased. Your friends sound like good, decent people. Am I right in thinking they don't have children of their own?"

"Yes, that's right. It's a shame that Patty couldn't have children. She would've loved a child of her own. Robert, however, is surrounded by youngsters all day long at the school where he works, so the lack of children at home doesn't bother him so much."

"And what work do you think the girl is capable of doing?"

"Well, she's a bright girl and I think she would be good at all sorts of things. For now, Patty's mother Celia is teaching her to use a sewing machine – just as I'd hoped she would – so she could possibly become a seamstress if she demonstrates the required skill. I believe she could also work with children, perhaps as a governess. Apparently, her reading and writing skills are excellent, so she could easily teach small children. But we'll have to wait and see. In the end, it'll be her decision, but Patty and Robert will try to guide her."

"And her brother? How is he finding school life? Is he now feeling more settled?"

"Yes, I think so. He hated his new school to begin with, but is happier now that he knows that Harriet is close by. He was so concerned about her that he couldn't attend to his lessons properly or make friends. I'm sure he'll quickly show improvement now that he doesn't have to worry about his sister's whereabouts."

"I really admire you for taking such an interest in these children, Bessie. Most people would choose to ignore their plight, believing nothing could be done to help them."

"Well, Patty and Robert are doing much more than I am. I would never have known about their misfortune if Robert hadn't asked me to read with Michael. Once the boy told me about the disaster that had struck his family, I couldn't really close my eyes to his sorrow."

"It's thanks to you that they've been reunited with each other. That's no small achievement. Now, Miss Bessie Hardwicke, you need to eat something. You've hardly touched that tongue sandwich. Is it not to your liking?"

"It's very much to my liking. It's delicious. Sorry, Lionel."

"There's no need to apologise. It's my fault for plying you with questions."

The fact is, I'm so used to eating alone that I feel embarrassed eating even a simple sandwich in the presence of others, except of course Patty and Robert. I've learnt good table manners – Lady Radcliffe taught me everything I needed to know – but I haven't had many occasions to practise my skills, and I'm scared I'll do something that's considered impolite, like talking with my mouth full or chewing too loudly.

"The other thing I wanted to tell you," I say, helping myself to another sandwich, "is that Walter's sweetheart Edie showed up at Mrs Grist's last Sunday afternoon. She'd come to London on Friday with a friend from the nurses' training school to attend the women's march on Parliament."

"My goodness!" Mr Fielding exclaims. "I hope she didn't come to any harm."

"No, she said they were at some distance from the more violent incidents. Still, they took a tremendous risk just by being there. Walter didn't know anything about it – he would've tried to stop her – and he's none too pleased that she didn't tell him beforehand."

"I can imagine he was upset that she felt she couldn't confide in him."

"Yes. I find it a bit worrying that they have such different views on quite important issues."

"Sometimes that can be a good thing, but in this case, I'm not so sure. I think he needs to try to see her side of things. I think I told you that Mathilda also supports the Suffragette movement. Fortunately, Ronald agrees with her views. He also believes that women should be given the vote and that they should receive higher education and more career opportunities. If he hadn't supported these goals, I don't think Mathilda would have married him."

"Oh dear. I hope Walter's opposition won't deter Edie from marrying *him*. I think it's hard for him to understand this sort of thing. As you know, he works as a stonemason – a hard, manual job where he associates mainly with menfolk. It doesn't enter their heads that women might want to have careers of their own. And to be fair, most of the women he knows don't. It's different in the countryside – things take a long time to change."

"You might find that changes will begin to happen a lot quicker than you'd expect, Bessie. The railway has made a huge difference to life in our country. And now we have the motorcar. Only the wealthy own one at the moment, but that will change. Prices will drop and the middle classes will soon be driving all over the country in their noisy automobiles. News will reach the remote areas much faster than it's done in the past and change will be inevitable. Even those of us who like to stick to our old-fashioned ways will find our opinions changing without our even realising it. I wouldn't be surprised if Walter's views soon become similar to those of Edie, especially if he's intent on sharing his life with her. I don't think it'll be the other way round."

"You're right, of course, and I hope Walter's views do change. I'd hate it if he and Edie drifted apart. She arrived at the house unexpectedly before I returned from Patty and Robert's, and Phillip was there to let her in. He was impressed that she'd travelled to London to support the Suffragettes. He said he admired her pluck. There was a terrible fog that evening – you must have experienced it too – and he offered to walk her back to her friend's relatives' house. I should have gone with them, but I was so exhausted from my walk back from Clapham and Edie said it wasn't necessary. Do you think I was wrong to let them walk together?"

"No, Bessie, I don't. Here is another example of change in our society. During Victorian times, young ladies were always chaperoned, but nowadays it's perfectly acceptable for a young man to accompany a young lady in the street – no one is going to look askance, especially in a big city like London. I'm glad Phillip made sure she got back to her lodgings safely. That fog was the worst we've had for some time. I almost lost my bearings myself!"

Before I can respond, the maid knocks at the drawing room door, asking if we'd like fresh tea. Mr Fielding refers the question to me and I decline. He tells her she can leave, thanking her for her assistance.

"She's a good girl," he says of the maid, once she's left the room. "I wish Fanny Grist had a young girl like her. Those two women she employs are not loyal, as you yourself have observed. I wouldn't be surprised if the cook came to her courtesy of Basil Hornby – I think she may be related to that shameful family. The other one was hired by Frank Grist and stopped being respectful towards Fanny the moment his funeral was over. I've advised her to get rid of them both, but she appears reluctant to take any action on that score."

"I wish she would," I say, folding up my serviette. "In any case, I think she only needs to employ one person. There's not that much to do. As you know, she rarely receives guests and the housework can be done in no time at all. Mrs Hopper and Mrs Evans spend most of their time gossiping in the kitchen."

"Do you think Phillip could persuade her to dismiss them? Shall I speak to him?"

"I'm sure he'd be happy to see the back of them both, especially Mrs Hopper. He doesn't get along well with her – you should have heard him telling her off for the mess she left in the kitchen the night you came to dinner. I suppose Mrs Grist would be more likely to agree to their departure if an immediate replacement could be found. She wouldn't like to be left with no one, though I'd happily do the work."

"No, Bessie, you're a lady's companion, not a cook or a housekeeper. Don't forget that. Don't ever undermine your position. I know it's your wont to put yourself down and underestimate your worth, but you're not to do that. Do you understand?"

"Yes, but I know I'd do a better job as a housekeeper than as a lady's companion."

"You're doing a fine job. You just need to have more confidence in your abilities."

"I'm not sure I'm doing such a fine job, Lionel, but thank you for your kind words."

Refusing to take no for an answer, I clear away the tea things and quickly wash them up while Mr Fielding dries. It seems the most natural thing in the world, but of course it isn't. He says I shouldn't feel I have to rush away, but I don't want to outstay my welcome so I tell him I need to get back to write some letters in time for the morning post. He helps me on with my cloak and walks with me as far as his shop. I refuse to let him come the rest of the way and, though he chides me for my fears, he doesn't insist. He takes my gloved hand and kisses it before we part ways. I walk a few yards and then turn around to wave goodbye. He, in turn, waves a handkerchief at me.

"You didn't ask for this back," he calls out, "so I'm going to keep it!"

18

I do enjoy Mr Fielding's compliments – though more so after the fact – but his attentiveness worries me as much as it pleases me. I am not his equal and my friendship with him, if I let it continue, can only lead to sorrow. If Mrs Grist found out that I'd taken tea in his home, it's quite possible she'd dismiss me. He's *her* friend, not mine, and it doesn't seem right that he's showing interest in me, her employee. The fact that I now know about her humble background makes no difference. She's risen to his social class both through marriage and her own competence, and she has every right to rebuke me if she finds out that I've been fraternising – her word, not mine – with her long-time friend. And there's a real likelihood that she *will* find out. Any number of prying eyes could have spotted us walking to and from his home on Sunday afternoon. Every time I accept an invitation, the risk will increase.

There's really nothing for it but to put an end to this budding friendship, however hard that may be. I haven't enjoyed such attentiveness from a man since my courtship with Arthur. If only I could confide in someone! The one person to whom I can open my heart is Patty, but it's increasingly difficult to find a moment alone with her. I suppose I could send her a letter, but I shy away from doing so. I've never expressed my private feelings in writing to anyone, so it would be a difficult letter to compose, even to as close a friend as Patty.

Mrs Grist says Phillip is now much better and will return to his lodgings at the end of the week. I shall miss his presence in the house, even though he's at work most days. He still seems to believe that he came to stay because his mother was unwell, not the other way around. I do hope that his mental state has now improved, though I haven't witnessed any signs of it being less than stable. It's probable that living alone isn't good for his nerves, but he clearly needs to feel independent and, as his mother is at pains to point out, the room he rents is near his workplace, which is convenient for him.

But Mrs Grist is not happy about the prospect of his leaving, which his late return the other evening seems to have precipitated. She was upset that she had to dine alone and an argument ensued the next morning. Later today I overhear yet another tense conversation between mother and son. Again, I don't want to give the impression that I'm always listening behind doors, but I have to pass the open door of the drawing room when going from my room down to the kitchen – often just to use the outhouse – or vice-versa, and if voices are raised, it's hard not to catch the gist of a conversation.

"Do you really have to go so soon?" she asks him. "You've only just begun to get your appetite back and gain a bit of weight."

"Mother, when will you accept that I'm not sick?" Phillip says. "I came here because I thought *you* needed *me*, not because I felt in any way under the weather."

"I do need you, Phillip. I don't feel safe without a man in the house. Basil Hornby lives just a couple of streets away and you know how threatening he can be."

"I know, but you're not alone, are you? Miss Hardwicke is here day and night. Besides, hasn't Lionel Fielding promised to do something about that man? Have you heard from him at all?"

"No, not yet. I'll send him a note tomorrow."

"I can go and talk to him if you like."

"Perhaps you can deliver the note. It might help. I can't keep sending Elizabeth."

"As you wish, Mama."

I wonder how Mr Fielding is planning to solve their problem. He's a man of his word, so if he says he's going to do something about it, then no doubt he will. What a loyal friend he is! Who else would willingly become involved in such an unpleasant affair?

Mid-week, I receive a letter from Walter. This time I retrieve it myself from the doormat since Phillip left for work before the post arrived. Walter tells me he is now in Salisbury; he's enclosed a postcard of the magnificent cathedral whose spire, I've heard, is the tallest in the country. He writes:

'Dear Aunt,

You will see from the enclosed card that I am now in Salisbury, working alongside a team of stonemasons hired to replace some decayed stone on the west front of the cathedral. It's difficult work but I'm enjoying the company of these skilled men, the master mason in particular, and learning from them as well.

Aunt, I'm pleased to tell you that Edie and I had a long talk before I left and we are no longer at odds. She promises not to travel to London again with her friend Annie without telling me first. I hope my previous letter didn't worry you.

How strange for me to mention Mr Henry Goode when we had tea together – I'm sorry to tell you that he died on Sunday evening after a brief illness. It came as such a shock to his wife and daughters, and to his many friends. I shall attend his funeral, as will my uncles who are as sad about his passing as I am.

Dear Aunt Bessie, I hope this will find you well, as it leaves me. I will write more in the next week or so. Love from all at home, especially Edie and myself.

Your affectionate nephew,
Walter'

Oh, I am glad to hear that Walter and Edie have patched up their differences – I was so worried about them. And I'm happy and proud to learn that Walter is working on such a celebrated cathedral – a national treasure, no less – where he can gain valuable experience. But I'm desperately sorry to hear that Mr Henry Goode is no longer with us. He was such a close friend of brothers Edward and Harold, and always had a kind word to say whenever I met him in the village. He's been a good friend to Walter too and has taught him a number of skills, including the basics of bookkeeping. He could only have been in his early forties, as I remember he was at school with Edward. Such a kind, honest man. His devoted wife and three lovely daughters will miss him sorely.

Mrs Hopper arrives while I'm washing up my breakfast dishes. I spent too long reading and rereading Walter's letter and thinking about poor Mr Goode that I hadn't realised the time. She looks annoyed to see me still in the kitchen and just gives a grunt in response to my polite "Good morning, Mrs Hopper."

But after a minute or two, she says, "You're friendly with that pharmacist, aren't you?" My heart sinks. What did she see and what does she know?

"You mean Mr Fielding?" I say. "Not really. But I know he's been kind to Mrs Grist and her son. He takes an interest in their welfare."

"Kind? Huh, in my opinion, he's nothing more than an interfering busybody. It's none of his business where they buy their spirits. He says Basil Hornby's brandy's not pure, but I ask myself, are his tonics pure? No one knows what he puts in them and they don't seem to do anyone any good."

I can breathe again; I don't think she's seen us together. She just wants to malign Mr Fielding and perhaps hopes that I'll take her side in defending Mr Hornby. Her act of confiding in me would be encouraging in any other circumstance, but I'm certainly not going to agree with her on this topic.

"Well, he is a respected pharmacist," I say, "so I'm sure his tonics are wholesome. I don't think he would knowingly do harm to anyone in the community."

"These pharmacists think they can get away with murder," she snaps, putting on her apron. "I wouldn't swallow even a tiny drop of the concoctions he forces on his customers. And he has the cheek to speak ill of my cousin for selling a few bottles of brandy!"

"I'm sure he acted in good faith," I say as I turn to leave the kitchen. "He probably just believes that alcohol of any kind is bad for the health. I don't doubt that he witnesses its ill effects on a daily basis."

Mrs Hopper stares at me in astonishment. She obviously didn't think I'd have the courage to stand up for Mr Fielding. And she's confirmed what he already suspected – that she and Hornby are related. In light of that, I need to be careful what I say to her, though I doubt she'll speak to me again after my having dared to contradict her!

I walk at a brisk pace to Patty and Robert's. It's now December and it's bitterly cold. In fact, there are occasional snow flurries, though I don't think they will amount to much. But how magnificent it would be to have a white Christmas in London! If one could wake up on Christmas morning to a pristine white blanket covering the city's dirty streets, it would be truly magical. Such thoughts remind me that I need to buy Christmas cards for my relatives and friends in the village. I've seen some coloured cards that picture bustling city streets carpeted with snow and lined with welcoming shops, their frosted windows illuminated by gas lamps. Warmly clad shoppers, laden with parcels for loved ones, appear oblivious to the cold as they greet one another with happy smiles. Is it too fanciful for me to hope that this year I might partake in such a pleasing scene?

I've been yearning to have some time alone with Patty and today is my lucky day. Robert has taken Michael and Harriet to the London Zoo as a pre-Christmas treat, and Celia is having her afternoon rest in the bedroom. Patty said Robert thought I would enjoy the zoo too – and indeed I would – but it was a last minute decision and he had no means of contacting me. But I'm glad to be alone with Patty and it's a real treat for us to sit down with a cup of tea and have a heart-to-heart conversation with no one else around.

"You've heard me mention Mr Fielding, the local pharmacist," I begin.

"I have indeed," Patty says with a twinkle in her eye.

"Well, Patty, I really don't know what to do. Mrs Grist is always sending me to the pharmacy for this, that and the other, and Mr Fielding's become a friend. I won't say it doesn't please me – it does, as I don't meet many friendly faces. Anyway, last Sunday, he invited me to his home for tea. I should tell you right away that he's a widower and lives alone. He's a kind, generous man and I'm fond of him, but Patty, he's of a different social class from you and me. And I honestly don't know what he sees in me. He knows that I come from a small country village, that I'm not worldly in any sense of the word, and that I used to be in service, but it doesn't seem to bother him. He's a close friend of the Grist family and I'm scared Mrs Grist will find out about our friendship and dismiss me for attempting to rise above my station. I should never have accepted his invitation, but he's not one to take no for an answer and, to be honest, I didn't want to decline."

"Oh, Bessie, what on earth is it that you're afraid of? If he's a friend of the Grist family, he's hardly likely to let you come to harm because of *his* actions, is he? And I'm sure Mrs Grist will think nothing of it if she does find out. It's wonderful that this gentleman is taking an interest in you. Do you think he has serious intentions?"

"I really don't know. On the one hand, I believe him to be honourable in every way, but on the other, he must know that I'm risking my good reputation by walking out with him. I don't think he would deliberately cause me shame, but then again, I could be mistaken. It's all my fault – I should have refused his invitation."

"Don't be silly, Bessie. Of course it's not your fault, and neither is it his. He's obviously fond of you. You shouldn't doubt him – it sounds to me as if he might be in earnest."

"But Patty, I just can't believe that he finds me the least bit attractive or in any way interesting. It's so confusing. I never know how to respond to the things he says, and I always feel awkward in his presence, though he pretends not to notice. And I'm so afraid people will spot us together and tongues will begin to wag."

"From what I've seen so far, Bessie, social life here in London is very different from what you and I are used to. Back home, as you know, if you walked out with someone new, it would be the talk of the town – or village in our case – in minutes, but here they don't seem to care as much. So I don't think you should worry. Just try to enjoy his company, be your usual charming self, and don't give any thought to what might happen next. He's probably as lonely as you are, so I don't see any harm in your spending time together."

"I don't think he's lonely. He attends to his customers all day long, most of whom he knows well. True, he lives alone, but his daughter is close by and he sees her almost every day. She's married and is expecting her first child in a few months. The other thing is, Patty, he's quite a bit older than me. I would say he's over fifty – perhaps mid-fifties – but he's in good health and is quite handsome in a mature sort of way. He should really be showing an interest in Mrs Grist, not me!"

"Oh come on, Bessie. He's attracted to you, not Mrs Grist. You need to have more confidence in yourself. You always used to tell me that. I can't believe I'm now the one saying it to you!"

What Patty has just said is true. She used to be so lacking in confidence that it was natural for me to try to give her a boost whenever she needed one. The fact that I was the one who tried to help her overcome *her* self-doubt, masked the fact that I was equally insecure myself. I don't think anyone ever perceived that on the day Father died, my sense of self-worth died also. Arthur was the one who helped me to start believing in myself again, but sadly that newfound belief was too fragile to survive his death.

"I know, Patty," I sigh. "It's true. Mr Fielding – or Lionel, I should say – tells me that too. It's just that since Arthur… Well, you know how it is. I haven't looked at another man for almost twenty years. And I really don't want to be made to look a fool. Lionel seems sincere, but I don't really know him at all. I grew up with Arthur – we both did – so it was easy to trust him. We knew each other so well and our backgrounds were the same, but this time…"

"Well, I didn't grow up with Robert, did I? I didn't really get to know him until well after we were married and our backgrounds couldn't have been more different. But I trusted him from the start. I think it's instinctive, Bessie. Don't question whether or not you trust him when your heart tells you he's an honest man. Sometimes you have to take risks, especially if it's long-term happiness you're after."

"Yes, you're right, as usual. I'll try to keep that in mind if he invites me again. It's just that I feel so... so inadequate."

"Look, if he didn't admire you, Bessie, he wouldn't be paying you so much attention. Why would he take the trouble to invite you for tea if he didn't wasn't attracted to both your appearance and your personality?"

"No, Patty. My appearance definitely doesn't come into it!"

"Really, Bessie. I don't know what you see when you look in the mirror, but it's clearly not what other people see. Now, I'd better make a fresh pot of tea and see what I can give those hungry children for their tea. They'll be back from the zoo any minute now."

"Let me help you, Patty. How is Harriet settling in? Does she like her new home?"

"I think so, though sometimes it's hard to know what's going on in her head. As Robert told you, she and Mother get along very well and she enjoys using the sewing machine, but she doesn't seem to be passionate about dressmaking the way Mother is. She asked if we had any books she could read, so Robert said he'd try to borrow a couple from the school library. We don't have many suitable books here, as Robert only reads the newspaper, or journals about gardening and suchlike, and I'm not like you, Bessie, I don't read a lot of fiction.

"But she helps me with the housework and is useful in the kitchen, so I've no complaints there. Still, I can't help feeling she's hiding something. She asked Robert if she could keep the coins he gave her at the orphanage, as she said she wanted to post a letter to a friend. He'd forgotten all about the money he'd given her for stamps, so it was honest of her to remind him, and of course he said yes. She didn't tell us any more but the next morning she asked for directions to the nearest post box. Robert offered to post a letter for her, but she said she'd like to go for a bit of a walk and so off she went."

"I suppose she wants to feel independent. Thirteen is a difficult age, no longer a child and not an adult either. Perhaps she's writing to Mrs Radford's daughter – they were good friends, according to Michael."

"Yes, it's possible, but if that were the case, why wouldn't she let Robert post her letter? In fact, Robert was the one who told her she should make sure she stayed in touch with the Radfords. I just have the impression she's being secretive about something, but I may be imagining it. And of course it's not a sin for her to have secrets. I have to admit, Bessie, I'm feeling a bit like a duck out of water. Having a young person in the house is a new experience for me. Not having had children, or even younger brothers or sisters, I feel unprepared in so many ways. But, don't get me wrong, Bessie, I'm not regretting our decision to give the girl a temporary home and, as I said, she's doing her best to be useful. It's my own attitude towards her that I'm questioning. Listen, I think that's Robert and the two of them coming in, so we'd better change the subject. They're back just in time for tea."

Throughout the meal, Michael and Harriet chatter excitedly about their visit to the zoo, commenting on and laughing about all the exotic animals they've seen. And as soon as we finish our tea, Michael – a completely different boy from the pale, anxious youngster I met a few months ago – takes a sketchpad out of his satchel and draws a picture of the tiger in its cage. He presents the sketch to Celia, who greatly admires it and says she'll treasure it always. Harriet tells us that Michael has always been good at drawing.

"Father said it was a girl's activity, not a boy's," Michael murmurs, "but I did it anyway."

"Well, Mother always liked your pictures," Harriet says, "and so did I. I've never been able to draw. You were the only artist in the Turnbull family."

The boy then proceeds to draw an elephant with one leg· raised and its trunk in the air, and gives that picture to Patty. Finally, he makes a sketch of two monkeys playing in their enclosure, which he hands to me. It really is the best of the lot. The way he has captured the comical expressions of the monkeys and used pencil pressure and shading for their fur is most effective. I'll put it with the collection of drawings that Walter has given me over the years. He too had a way with a pencil that was often referred to – by his Aunt Mabel at least – as 'wasting time'.

19

It's mid-December and Christmas is just around the corner. I have yet to finish buying and making presents for my nearest and dearest. Mrs Grist says I can have this coming Saturday free, as she'll be spending the entire weekend with her sister-in-law. Phillip has now returned to his lodgings and it's clear from her general downheartedness that she misses him terribly.

Yesterday, she asked me if I would be staying in London for Christmas. She said that if I wanted to go to my relatives in the village, she'd be happy to give me three days off work. I thanked her, but said that I planned to stay in London and would go to my friends in Clapham for dinner on the twenty-fifth. I added that I would prefer to go home at Easter when it's springtime and one can enjoy the blossoming trees and budding flowers. She just nodded and said, "We'll see, Elizabeth."

I haven't been sent to the pharmacy for some days now, so I've not seen Mr Fielding since our afternoon tea and he's made no attempt to contact me. This is both a regret and a relief. On the one hand, I'd be delighted to receive another invitation from him, yet on the other, I dread such a prospect. Does that make sense? I do have feelings for him, but they scare me to death. If he were to kiss me properly, I honestly believe I would die from embarrassment. And yet I long for it. If this is middle-age love, then I think I'm probably better off without it.

Free for the whole weekend, I decide to spend Saturday morning shopping for gifts. A second-hand bookshop is just a short walk away and I hope to find reading material there for both Michael and Harriet. An elderly man with long grey hair is rearranging the bookshelves when I enter the shop. It's dark, dusty and disordered inside, with dozens of books piled high on the floor. The light is so dim that it seems the poor man is having difficulty in deciphering the titles of the books he's putting back on the shelves. He's squinting through pince-nez and appears neither to have seen nor heard me enter.

"Good morning, sir," I say, raising my voice a little.

"Oh hello," he says, as he struggles to stand up straight, almost knocking over a pile of books in the process. He grimaces, places a hand on his lower back and then asks, "How may I help you, madam?"

"I'm looking for children's books," I say. "Well, I say that, but the boy is eleven and the girl almost fourteen. They're both strong readers, so I wouldn't want to give them anything too childish."

"See that shelf over there?" He points towards the back of the shop where the light is even fainter. "You might find something there. Have a browse and see if you find any of the titles suitable."

"Thank you. I'll take a look."

Glancing at the books strewn across the shelf in no particular order, I almost wish that Michael and Harriet were younger. How I would love to buy one or more of the Beatrix Potter editions with their exquisite drawings. I've read *The Tale of Peter Rabbit*, as Harold's youngest son acquired a copy, but I've yet to enjoy Miss Potter's later stories. Oh, and here is a copy of *The Wind in the Willows* – how can that be second hand? It was only published a couple of years ago and the book looks brand new. Another story for children that I long to read! But let me not waste time regretting what I can't buy today. I don't have enough money for more than one book per child, so after a long spell of indecision, I choose *Little Women* for Harriet and *The Swiss Family Robinson* for Michael. Both copies are in good condition. But then I see a well-thumbed copy of my favourite *David Copperfield*, which is only thruppence three-farthings, so I decide to buy that as well and give it to the two of them to share. Michael and I never did finish reading it together, so he can pick up where we left off.

"I think I saw you peeking at that Kenneth Grahame book," the shopkeeper says to me, as I count out my coins. "What's it called? Oh yes, *The Wind in the Willows*. It was brought in only yesterday. If you're interested, I can sell it to you for tuppence ha'penny. I don't get many customers wanting to buy children's books."

"Oh, thank you, that's so kind of you," I say, wondering if I can afford yet another purchase. But I don't like to refuse after he's offered me such a bargain, and I do so want to read about Rat and Mole's adventures on the riverbank that will surely remind me of my own ramblings at the water's edge with my dear nephew. So I find a few more coins and place them on the counter.

"Tuppence will do," the shopkeeper says, handing me back a halfpenny, "'Tis nearly Christmas, after all."

He wraps up my books in brown paper, chattering all the while, and then bids me good morning. A few yards up the road is a leather workshop, with some newly crafted goods displayed on a bench outside. A leather wallet catches my eye and I immediately think of Walter. A new wallet would be the perfect gift and I know it's something he needs. Again, it costs more than I was planning to spend, but having plucked up enough courage to enter the shop, I feel I can't leave empty-handed. Still, I think it's worth the price; the leather is as smooth as silk and the workmanship is excellent. I suppose I can save money on Edward's present. He doesn't care whether I give him a present or not, and I'm sure he'd rather Christmas didn't exist since it takes him away from his precious workshop. Still, despite him being such a Scrooge, I buy him a tin of pipe tobacco. I think that will please him more than anything else. Aside from work, smoking his pipe is my brother's greatest pleasure in life.

Before returning to the house, I pop into the haberdashery whose proprietress, Mrs Browning, is always welcoming despite my low-cost purchases. I buy two skeins of yarn, a bit of green felt, and a darning needle with a large eye. I tell her I'm in the process of making gifts for Christmas and she says she's doing the same thing. "In fact, this is a matinée coat for my newest granddaughter," she says, holding up a pink garment that she's almost finished knitting. "I have two more to make. Maria's just had twins, a boy and a girl, and Veronica's due to give birth in a couple of weeks." I congratulate her on her excellent work, and on her growing family, and tell her I'm sure to be back for more items before she closes for the Christmas break.

I have yet to buy a present for Mrs Grist. I decide to wait until my next visit to the pharmacy. She is sure to need some more tonic before the end of the week; only yesterday she announced that she was running low. While I'm there, I can buy her a small gift. I know Mr Fielding sells tins of scented talcum powder that are fairly inexpensive, and that's something I think she'll appreciate.

Back in my room, I make a list of everything I plan to accomplish this weekend. I've already finished knitting Celia's mittens, but I need to finish Robert's socks and start on the handkerchief case for Patty. I also want to do a bit of embroidery on a plain white handkerchief to enclose in the case. And, if I have time, I'd like to knit her a new tea cosy. Well, it's good that I have no engagement for tomorrow, except church of course. If I begin tonight, with any luck, I might finish all the handmade gifts before Mrs Grist's return on Monday morning.

After church on Sunday, I make a cheese and piccalilli sandwich for lunch and then settle down contentedly in the drawing room, planning to knit and sew for the rest of the day. Around four o'clock, however, the doorbell rings. I put down my knitting, wondering who on earth it can be, and make my way quietly to the front door, half inclined not to open it. But I'd hate for Mrs Grist to miss a delivery or an important message. Imagine my shock when I open the door and find Mr Fielding standing on the doorstep right in front of me!

"Oh, Lionel," I exclaim. "What a surprise. I'm afraid Mrs Grist isn't here – she's gone to her sister-in-law's for the whole weekend, and Phillip's already returned to his lodgings."

"It's you I came to see, Bessie," he says. "I know Fanny isn't here. May I come in?"

"Yes, of course. Let me take your hat and coat."

I follow him through to the drawing room, where he sits down on the settee. I feel a bit uneasy. I really shouldn't be receiving visitors in this house, despite what Phillip told me when Edie showed up unexpectedly. If Mrs Grist decides to come home early, she'll be shocked to find me entertaining Mr Fielding, of all people. Still, the least I can do is to offer him a cup of tea, otherwise he'll think me exceedingly rude.

He accepts my offer and is about to follow me down to the kitchen, but I tell him to remain seated. "Let me bring up a tray," I say. "I'll be back in a jiffy." I know it'll make me nervous to have him watch me make tea, simple task though it is, and I'll be unable to concentrate on whatever it is he wants to talk to me about.

"So what brings you here, Lionel?" I ask a few minutes later, pouring him a cup of tea and proffering a plate of the shortbread rounds I bought yesterday.

"Well," he begins, "Fanny wrote to me during the week and asked me to try to resolve a problem that's been bothering her for some time. I've just come from carrying out a task that I hope will settle the matter. As a result, I feel rather low in spirits and hoped you'd be here so we could talk about it. I knew that seeing your friendly face would cheer me up."

"What on earth was the task, Lionel?"

"Let me start from the beginning. I promised Fanny some time ago that I'd 'take care' of Basil Hornby for her, although I had no idea at the time how I'd accomplish that. She told me in her letter that she could no longer tolerate the hold he has over Phillip and herself, and begged me to go to see him to try to reach some understanding. As I told you before, she's more than paid off her late husband's debt, yet Hornby continues to torment them both, mother and son, what with demanding extra interest payments, forcing Fanny to buy his adulterated spirits, and trying to coerce Phillip into paying for favours with his loose women."

"So what did you do?"

"Oh, Bessie, I did a terrible thing. I threatened to reveal to the world something that's not been spoken about for two decades. I told him that if he persists in intimidating Fanny and Phillip Grist on account of a debt that was fully paid months ago, then I would make public a Hornby family secret that's been kept hidden all this time."

"But surely your threat is not as terrible as the way Mr Hornby's been treating Mrs Grist and Phillip. They both live in fear of that man."

"That's true, but I've never had to threaten anyone in

my life. I feel dreadful, even though I know what I did was justified."

"Do you want to tell me what the threat was?"

"I do, Bessie. I know I can trust you to keep a secret. I can't stress enough how confidential this is, but I have to tell someone. Will you be my one and only confidante?"

"Of course. I won't breathe a word of what you tell me to anyone."

"Well, Basil Hornby has a younger brother, who was disowned by his father. But Basil and Bertie were close as boys and, scoundrel that he is, I believe Basil still has a soft spot for his brother. Few people know why Bertie was disinherited, but I guessed the reason. As a pharmacist, I get to know a lot of things about people that they'd like to keep secret, and of course, I respect their privacy one hundred per cent. Bertie was sent away, banished you could say, when he was barely twenty, the reason being that he was engaging in homosexual acts. Do you know the meaning of homosexual acts, Bessie?"

"Yes, I do, though I've rarely heard it mentioned in conversation. Isn't such behaviour illegal?"

"It is. I'm sorry if I shock you, Bessie. The law stipulates that homosexuality is a punishable crime, though imprisonment arguably makes matters worse. Some people believe that it's an illness and can be cured by our worthy doctors. Others, and I count myself among this group, believe that same-sex attraction is something one is born with and that punishment and quack remedies can do no good whatsoever, and often lead to mental illness and suicide. Anyway, I told Basil Hornby that I would make public his brother's secret if he continued to harass Fanny Grist and her son. I made this threat, even though I continue to believe that it's not a crime for a man to love a man, or a woman to love a woman. Do you find that shocking, Bessie?"

"No, not when you explain it like that, Lionel. And if it is love, then surely it can't be wrong? Alfred Lord Tennyson wrote a poem in memory of his close friend, Arthur Hallam, who died at the age of twenty-two. The words are so beautiful – you'd think he was writing about a lover, and perhaps he was. We often don't have a choice over whom we fall in love with. Tennyson loved his friend so much that he penned an epic poem in which he expresses his profound grief at his passing. He makes no apologies for the fact than he loved a man."

"And why should he, indeed?"

"But regarding the more physical aspects of homosexuality," I say, blushing, "I've never really given much thought as to why some people engage in that sort of thing. I suppose I'm just naïve. I've always believed it to be morally wrong since the Bible says it's an abomination. But if what you say is true, that people are born that way, then no, I don't find it shocking at all."

"You're not naïve, Bessie, just refreshingly innocent, which is one of your attractions, I might add. I agree wholeheartedly that love can be as strong between friends as between lovers. Yes, you're right, the Christian faith shows no compassion at all on this matter and looks on homosexuality as a sin. Even though I call myself a Christian, as a man of science, I often find I'm in conflict with what the Bible tells us. I can tell that I've shocked you Bessie, so I'll say no more about religion."

"No, please, I like to hear your views. It does me good to think about things in a different way. How did Mr Hornby react to your threat?"

"I think he was astonished at first to learn that I knew about Bertie's secret. It took him a while to respond, but then he said he didn't know what I was talking about. I told him not to worry, that I had never told a soul what I knew to be true about his brother, but I repeated that if he continued to intimidate my friends, then all *his* friends and neighbours would get to hear of it. I asked him if he understood what I was saying. He refused to answer me, but I think he realised that I was being serious. I went on to say that I have a high opinion of Bertie and that it would be painful for me to have to reveal his secret. But I was emphatic in stating that if it did become necessary for me to make it public, then it would be his, Basil's, fault entirely. With that, I turned and left him to stew over my words."

"Do you mean what you say about having a high opinion of Bertie?"

"Oh yes, I do. I like Bertie very much. He was always polite and I think he was embarrassed by the coarse behaviour of his father and brother. Perhaps he took after his mother – I don't know. She died young and I never met her. All I know is that Basil followed in the footsteps of his father, while Bertie took a different path."

"Where is Bertie now? Do you know?"

"No, I don't. He left London when his father threw him out of the house. There was a rumour he'd gone abroad, but I don't know if that's true."

"Do you really think Basil Hornby will stop hounding Mrs Grist and Phillip now that you've spoken to him?"

"I think so. I hope so. The thing is, Bessie, even though I made that threat, I have no intention of letting Bertie's secret be known to anyone. I couldn't do that. Some people around here think of me as a doctor – an inadequate one, I know – but I have to respect people's privacy and I cannot intentionally injure any human being. I could never make public the knowledge I gleaned through Bertie's purchase of certain medications and one or two feminine traits I observed in him. I just hope that Basil doesn't see through my threat and realise that it's an empty one.

"Anyway, thank you for listening to me, my dear. I hated myself for what I said to Basil and needed to talk to someone. I'll be going to Mathilda's tonight for dinner, but obviously I can't say anything to her. Even if she vowed to keep it a secret, she wouldn't be able to stop herself from telling Ronald. After a drink or two, confidences are often betrayed. But I know I can trust you, dear Bessie."

"Of course you can, Lionel. What are you going to tell Mrs Grist?"

"I'll just say I've taken care of the matter, as I promised. I won't give her any details, but I'll tell her to let me know if Hornby threatens her again. Now I really must be on my way, so I'll leave you in peace. Is that a pair of socks you're knitting for me, Bessie?"

He's looking at the socks I'm knitting for Robert. I hesitate, not quite knowing how to respond.

"Don't worry," he says, smiling. "I know they're not for me. I was only joking. But you do knit beautifully."

I resolve then and there to knit Lionel a pair of socks, even if I have to work through the night to finish all my handicrafts. I accompany him to the front door and this time I receive a peck on the cheek. "You are my truest friend," he says. "I will not forget your kindness in letting me share with you my doubts and fears."

20

Mr Fielding is as good as his word. Mrs Grist receives his letter on Tuesday morning. I recognise his handwriting on the envelope when I pick it up from the mat. I hand my employer three or four letters, but she makes no attempt to open any of them. She places the small pile on her side table and resumes her needlework.

"Did you visit your friend on Sunday?" she asks.

"You mean Patty?" I say. "No, I didn't. I usually only visit every other Sunday and I was there last week. I did some Christmas shopping on Saturday and most of yesterday I spent knitting. I still have to finish these socks for Patty's husband Robert."

In fact, I've finished Robert's socks; the ones I'm working on now are for Mr Fielding, but I'm not going to tell Mrs Grist that.

"Did you visit the Selfridges department store in Oxford Street? Mr Harry Selfridge opened it last year with a great deal of publicity."

"Oh no, I didn't go there. I'm sure it's full of beautiful things, but probably far too expensive for me."

"I've shopped there a couple of times. In fact I went shortly after it opened. There's no obligation to buy. You can just go in and wander around to your heart's content, looking at all the latest fashions. But if you do have something particular in mind, the floorwalkers will tell you where to find it. It's quite a novel experience."

"Really? Then perhaps I'll go there some time, just to have a look."

"You should. You'll be amazed at the choice available. Do you always knit socks without a pattern, Elizabeth?"

"Yes. I've knitted many pairs over the years and don't

need to follow a pattern anymore."

"I used to knit when the boys were small, but my fingers have become arthritic now and I find it's painful to use the needles. In fact, that reminds me, I'd like you go to the pharmacy sometime today and ask Lionel Fielding if he has any suggestions for easing the pain. He usually has some remedy of his own that he'll swear by, though I have my doubts as to whether any of his treatments do any good. But I suppose they're better than nothing. And you can pick up another bottle of my tonic while you're there."

"Yes, of course. Do you want to open your letters first in case you need to respond to any of them? I pass by the post box on my way to the pharmacy, as you know."

"I'm sure none of them need an urgent response, but if you'll kindly pass me the letter opener, I'll take a quick look."

Mr Fielding's envelope is on the top of the pile, but she opens it last. She reads its content but her expression doesn't change. After a moment's thought, however, she says she needs to write to a short note to Phillip. Seated at her writing table, she scribbles a few lines on half a sheet of paper and encloses that, together with Mr Fielding's letter, in an envelope addressed to her son. She affixes a stamp and hands it to me.

"Perhaps you could kindly post this, Elizabeth," she says. "And remember to tell Mr Fielding that I have pain only in my fingers and not in my head. He always tries to tell me I'm imagining these aches and pains – I swear he thinks I'm a mad person."

"I'm sure he doesn't think that," I say, smiling. "I'll go there right away."

Fortunately, the shop is empty. Mr Fielding is rearranging some bottles on the shelf behind the counter. He turns as soon as he hears the jangling of the doorbell.

"Ah, Bessie," he says, "you're a sight for sore eyes. Are you bringing me a message from Fanny Grist?"

"No, I'm sorry, no message," I say. "She's sent me to buy her usual tonic and something for the arthritis in her fingers. Have you anything you could recommend?"

"Yes, of course, but for relief only. It's not a cure."

He selects two bottles from one of his drawers and places both on the counter. "Do you know if Fanny received my letter, Bessie?" he asks.

"Yes, she did. She read it and then enclosed it in a letter to Phillip, which I've just posted. I'm sure she'll respond to you very soon."

"She will, eventually. She doesn't like to feel indebted to me, so will probably make me wait a few days. Or she may be waiting to see if my mission was a success. For obvious reasons, I didn't elaborate on it, so she may have her doubts."

"It's possible she's waiting for Phillip's reaction before she responds to you. But I'm sure she appreciates your efforts to help her."

"I don't need her appreciation, Bessie. I just want her to feel she has someone she can trust. As I've said before, life hasn't been easy for her these last couple of years. Now, for her arthritis – which I know isn't as bad as she'd have us believe – I would recommend this oil." He points to the larger of the two bottles. "She should rub it into her finger joints. It may bring some relief. If she asks, tell her it consists of distilled oil from eucalyptus leaves mixed with almond oil. It's probably best that she apply it before going to bed so that the oil can be better absorbed. If she has some cotton gloves to wear during the night, then that will stop it from staining the bedclothes."

"Thank you, I'll tell her that. It sounds like a good remedy. I'd also like to purchase something, which I'll pay for separately. I haven't yet finished my Christmas shopping and time is getting short. I'd like a tin of the hyacinth-scented talcum powder you have in the glass cabinet by the door. Oh, and perhaps I could also buy a bottle of that oil – my friend Patty's mother suffers from arthritis in the finger joints as well, and it affects her ability to sew."

"And I suppose you want me to charge you for these items, Bessie?"

"Yes, of course."

"Very well. I'll take your coins this time, but only for the Christmas gift, not for the oil. Now, there's something I want to discuss with you and I can't do it in a public setting like this. When would you be free to meet with me?"

"Well, I'm only free on Sundays, and this Sunday afternoon I'll be going to my friends in Clapham. But wait a minute. I think Mrs Grist said she and Phillip were going to her eldest son's house for dinner on Friday. If she does go – and she didn't seem to be too enthusiastic about it – then I'll be free on Friday evening."

"That would be perfect. Why don't you come here as soon as you can on Friday? The shop will be closed but I'll still be here. Just knock on the door when you arrive. If you can't make it, I'll understand."

"Do you want to tell me what you want to discuss with me?"

"No, Bessie, not now. It'll have to wait until Friday. Now, have you got all your packages? Let me know how Fanny Grist gets on with the eucalyptus oil, and I hope it helps your friend's mother too. Goodbye, my dear."

The week passes slowly. Mrs Grist's mood deteriorates and she snaps at everyone, including me. I can bear the brunt of her criticisms, but Mrs Evans and Mrs Hopper, who've suffered more from her biting tongue than I have, are full of malice towards her.

"She's like this every December," I hear Mrs Hopper saying. "If I mention Christmas, she bites my head off. It's no season of goodwill for her ladyship. She hates Christmas and all that it stands for."

Well, I think that comment is a bit unfair and I'm not sure Mrs Hopper is qualified to talk about goodwill. She's certainly never shown me any! Besides, I don't believe that Mrs Grist hates what Christmas stands for; she just dislikes the obligation to socialise and be jolly. After all, not everyone enjoys one festive event after another, and some would say there's a hint of falsehood in the way people behave differently towards each other over Christmas. Even I sometimes ponder over the real meaning of Christmas and question whether we're really meant to be attending parties and putting so much emphasis on the giving and receiving of presents.

On Friday morning, things come to a head. Mrs Grist dismisses Mrs Hopper! She tells her in no uncertain terms that she has no need of a cook, as she eats very little these days. Miss Hardwicke, she says, can make her own meals. Besides, she points out, Mrs Evans' workload is minimal, so she'll expect her to work in the kitchen as needed. If she objects to this, she can leave too and another, more willing, housekeeper will be hired. She goes on to say she'll pay her a month's wages to tide her over a period of unemployment and will give her a reference if necessary, but she will not be needed after today and can leave now if she wishes.

Mrs Hopper is so flabbergasted by this sudden announcement that I almost feel sorry for her. When she fully digests what she's been told, she tries to change Mrs Grist's mind by saying that Mrs Evans doesn't even know how to boil an egg and that she'll regret her decision within days. Mrs Grist is unmoved; she says her mind is made up, and she instructs Mrs Hopper to leave the room forthwith. At this point the cook turns red in the face and blurts out a string of abuse, which I would be too ashamed to repeat. "Please leave now!" Mrs Grist commands.

Mrs Hopper makes her exit, visibly seething and muttering under her breath. Mrs Grist then calls in Mrs Evans, tells her about her new duties and asks if she's prepared to accept such an arrangement. To my surprise, Mrs Evans is wholly submissive – quite unlike her usual self – and accepts her new role without complaint. I find myself wishing she would refuse; such insincerity sickens me.

"So, Elizabeth," Mrs Grist says, once we are alone. "Is this new arrangement to your liking?"

"As long as it's to your liking," I say, "it's all right with me. I always make my own meals anyway. Mrs Hopper has never considered it her duty to feed *me*."

"Really? I know you eat in the kitchen, but always I thought your meals were the same as mine."

"No, not as a rule. Sometimes there are leftovers from which I might make a meal in the evenings. But for lunch I usually just make myself a sandwich."

"Then that's all the more reason for my terminating Enid Hopper's employment. I wish I'd known that before. Goodness knows what the woman did all day long with only one person to cook for."

I suspect that Mrs Grist's decision to fire Mrs Hopper is partly due to Phillip's dislike of her, and may also have something to do with Mr Fielding's letter to her about Mr Hornby. If she's no longer tormented by his menacing threats, then it's likely that she feels no further obligation to employ his cousin. I can't wait for this evening to tell Mr Fielding this latest piece of news.

This evening! How quickly the time has flown when earlier this week it seemed to pass so slowly. I haven't even decided what I'm going to wear. I don't want to look as if I've made an effort, but I should change into something other than my usual drab attire. In the end, I decide to wear my sky blue silk blouse – yet another welcome hand-me-down from the Radcliffes – and my navy blue flared skirt, which is no longer fashionable but is the only good one I have. I'm undecided about whether to wear my blue cloak, which I normally keep for Sundays and special occasions. At the last minute, I decide to wear it. For me, it is a special occasion and, besides, my old grey coat is splashed with mud and needs a good brushing.

Mr Fielding is looking out for me and is at the door before I even have a chance to knock. He ushers me inside.

"Good evening, Bessie," he says. "Come on through to the back parlour. It's warm in there and I have the kettle boiling."

It is indeed warm and cosy. A Victoria sponge has pride of place on the small table, sitting regally on a decorative cake stand.

"Mathilda brought this round a short while ago," he explains. "I told her earlier that I was expecting you, and she said I should offer you something more appetising than a couple of dry biscuits."

"That's kind of her," I say, surprised that he's told his daughter about our rendezvous. "Is she still in good health?"

"Oh yes. She's thriving. Less than four months to go now."

"That's so soon! What a blessing the baby will be for the proud parents, and for you of course."

"Yes, it's sure to be a joyful occasion. In fact, I wanted to talk to you about something that concerns Mathilda as well. Let me take care of the tea and then I'll tell you about the idea I've had."

Refusing my offer of help once again, he takes two teaspoonfuls of tea leaves from a caddy and drops them into the teapot. He adds boiling water, stirs, then lets it sit for a few minutes.

"I think you like your tea strong, Bessie," he says, cutting me a thick slice of cake. "Am I right?"

"Yes, I do prefer it strong. That's far too much cake for me, Lionel. Why don't you take that slice?"

"Nonsense. You need fattening up. No, actually you're just right. But I think you'll find the cake is quite light."

"Very well, if you say so. Thank you."

"The girl who left the orphanage," he says, once we are both sipping our tea. "How old did you say she was? Almost fourteen?"

"Yes. I believe she turns fourteen in March."

"Well, Mathilda will be in need of a nanny for her baby at around that exact time. I was wondering if the situation might suit the girl. Has she any experience with babies or young children?"

"I'm not sure. I can find out. But she's a capable girl, I'm certain of that. She cared for her sick mother and looked after her younger brother for years. But looking after a tiny baby is a big responsibility, Lionel. Would Mathilda really be willing to entrust her baby's care to a fourteen year old?"

"She wouldn't have sole responsibility. The housekeeper and the maidservant will help if necessary. And if I know Mathilda, she's not going to be the type of mother who leaves her baby in the nursery all day long. I'm sure she'll want to spend as much time as possible with the child."

"Well, in that case, I think Harriet would be an excellent choice of nanny."

"Do you think she'd be willing to be interviewed by Mathilda?"

"I'm sure she would. It might be a solution to her problems. Harriet hates the thought of being a burden on anyone and wants to be independent. Patty's mother is teaching her dressmaking, but she's not shown a strong desire to become a seamstress, partly because it could take years before she's skilled enough to earn a living that way. I think she feels she needs to start paying her own way in life as soon as possible. She might welcome the idea of being employed as a nanny."

"Then perhaps you could check with her the next time you see her. Didn't you tell me you're going to visit your friends on Sunday?"

"Yes. I'll certainly talk to her about it. I'll be going there on the twenty-fifth as well. It's going to be strange spending Christmas away from home."

"Well, you'll be with friends, so I'm sure you'll enjoy yourself. How did you used to spend Christmas?"

"Oh, on Christmas Day I'd go to my brother Edward's and Walter would be there too. I'd cook a goose or, more lately, a turkey for dinner. It was quiet but we enjoyed it, or at least Walter and I did. I'm not sure about Edward. He hates sitting around doing nothing, and he's not very sociable. But in the run up to Christmas at Farringdale House, there was a great deal of festive cheer. The Radcliffes would hold lavish parties and encourage the downstairs staff to have their own celebration. They'd give away a lot of food and drink, so no one went without. They were always very generous.

"What about you, Lionel? What will you do for Christmas?"

"I'll go to Mathilda's for dinner on the twenty-fifth. I

have a brother and two sisters I could visit if I wanted to, but they all live on the Sussex coast and have their own large families. Ronald, Mathilda's husband, will invite his parents and two of his sisters. I'll try to sneak away early, if Mathilda will let me. I'm not someone who's happy to eat, drink and be merry for more than a couple of hours at a time."

"I'm the same. I'm not as bad as Edward, but I'd much rather curl up with a good book than join in festivities that go on all night. But I suppose one has to make an effort sometimes. By the way, I have some surprising news from Mrs Grist's. She's terminated Mrs Hopper's employment! She told her she doesn't need to employ a cook any longer, as she eats so little these days, and that Mrs Evans can do a bit of extra work in the kitchen. I'm so relieved. I'd be even happier if Mrs Evans were to leave as well, but that would be too much to hope for."

"Well, for your sake, I'm happy Enid Hopper is leaving, but I hope Fanny doesn't end up regretting her decision. Enid will be making a report to Basil Hornby, and we can't yet be entirely sure that his threats will cease now that I've 'had a word' with him."

"Oh, I do hope she hasn't made a mistake in dismissing the woman too quickly. I think Phillip may have had a hand in it – he really couldn't stand her."

"Yes, well, there's some history there too. Her daughter Louisa was sweet on Phillip some years back, but he was enamoured with Mathilda at that time and didn't have eyes for anyone else. Enid considered it a slight, believing that Phillip wouldn't look at Louisa because he felt himself a class – or several classes – above her. She may have been right – even if he hadn't been in love with Mathilda, he probably wouldn't have encouraged Enid Hopper's daughter's attentions, pretty little thing though she is."

"Well, I hope Mrs Hopper finds another job easily. As much as I dislike her, I wouldn't want to think that she's in financial difficulties. I think I heard that she has six children."

"Oh, don't worry about her, Bessie. She can take care of herself and, if she can't, the Hornbys will make sure she has enough to tide her over until she finds a new job. These Cockney families are very close-knit and they look after their own."

"Well, one thing is sure. She wouldn't be worried about me if I were the one dismissed! I hope Mrs Grist will be in a better mood now. She's been downcast all week. It's as if she dreads the approach of Christmas."

"Hmm, I think I know the reason for that. Another piece of confidential information, Bessie. Fanny lost a daughter on Christmas Day some twenty-five years ago. Baby Emily lived for two days, then took her final breath. Fanny was beside herself with grief and it took her months to recover from the blow. She wanted a daughter more than anything in the world. Two years later she gave birth to Phillip and, while that was of course a blessing, it didn't make up for her loss of a daughter. I believe she felt guilty about wishing he'd been born a girl and she gave him more attention than she might otherwise have done; some say she even spoilt him. It's possible he guessed that his mother had hoped for a girl, or his brothers may have told him. He's not as emotionally stable as the other two boys, but I do hope he finds happiness eventually."

"Oh, that's so tragic! Poor Mrs Grist. I had no idea she'd lost a child. And on Christmas Day! No wonder she feels downhearted at this time of year. Christmas will always be a sad occasion for her."

"Yes, indeed. But let's talk about more cheerful

topics. What are you doing on Christmas Eve, Bessie? Has Fanny given you some days off?"

"Yes. She says she'll go to her sister-in-law's on the twenty-fourth for three days, until the twenty-seventh, I think. She thought I might want to go back to the village, but I told her I'd prefer to stay in London for Christmas and go back home at Easter."

"And what will you do on Christmas Eve?"

"I have no plans for the twenty-fourth."

"Then perhaps you'd like to accompany me to see *A Christmas Carol* in the evening? It's being performed at a local church hall by a group of amateur actors – they may not be very good, but I think it'll be enjoyable, nonetheless. I remember you told me you were a Dickens fan."

"Oh, Lionel, I can't think of anything I'd like more! Thank you so much. Yes, I've read most of Mr Dickens' novels and *A Christmas Carol* is one of my favourites."

"Then it's a date. I'll expect you here again at six o'clock next Saturday, Bessie. Who knows, 'the Ghost of Christmas Yet to Come' may have some surprises in store for both of us."

21

The Catholic boys' school will be breaking up for the Christmas break in a few days' time, yet Michael is miserable. He doesn't want to spend Christmas with his uncle unless Harriet can join them. Robert thinks that's out of the question. The uncle has already made it clear that he has no intention of welcoming Harriet into his home.

"Your uncle is paying for your education," Robert says to Michael, who's sitting on the floor playing with Romeo, trying to hold back his tears. "You have to show some appreciation. I'm sure he's looking forward to your company over Christmas."

"I doubt it," Michael says. "He sent me to boarding school to get rid of me. He doesn't want me around. I'd rather stay at school than spend Christmas with him."

"The school doesn't allow boarders to stay during the break. You know that, Michael. If you like, I can write to your uncle and ask him if you can spend Christmas Day with us, but I don't know how he'll react. He might think you're ungrateful and decide to stop paying your tuition."

"If he did that, then I'd have to live with him, wouldn't I? He's my guardian. That's the last thing he'd want, so I don't think he'll stop paying my school fees."

"On second thoughts," Robert says, ignoring Michael's remark, "I think it would be best if you wrote to your Uncle Gordon yourself. You can say you've been reunited with Harriet, who's now living close to the school, and that – if he doesn't mind – you'd like to spend at least one day over Christmas with her and the family she's staying with. If I get involved, he may think I'm interfering. Why don't you write the letter now and Aunt Bessie can post it on her way home?"

"All right. Aunt Bessie, will you help me write the letter?"

"Yes, of course, Michael," I say. "Let's get it done before tea."

Michael doesn't really need my help, but I can tell he needs some encouragement. His writing is as good as his reading, and he has a fine penmanship. I give him Robert and Patty's address to print at the top of the page and suggest that he try to be as polite as possible. His uncle will be more inclined to agree to the request if he doesn't suspect that his nephew is reluctant to spend Christmas with him. Michael covers one side of a piece of paper, and signs off by thanking his uncle for paying for his education. The mention of the school fees sounds a little ill-mannered, but I say nothing; the boy is only eleven after all. After turning the letter over to blot it, he folds it neatly and encloses it in the envelope Robert has provided.

"You do have his address, don't you Michael?" I ask, momentarily alarmed that we might not know where to send it.

"I have it," Harriet says. "Here, let me write it on the envelope."

Letter writing complete, I go into the kitchen to help Patty with the tea. As I slice a fresh loaf of bread, I tell her about Mr Fielding's suggestion that Harriet consider working as a nanny to his daughter's baby, due in March.

"That's sounds like a wonderful idea," Patty says. "We'll discuss it with Harriet, but I'm sure she won't object. Why would she? She'll be gaining experience in childcare and earning a bit of money at the same time. I take it she's expected to live in?"

"Yes, I think so. But Celia's going to miss Harriet a lot, isn't she?"

"I daresay she will. But she knows that if Harriet finds

a live-in position, then that's the best outcome for all of us. Her stay here was always supposed to be temporary.

"Now tell me, Bessie, did your Mr Fielding invite you a second time? Are you and he still just good friends, or are you now on more familiar terms?"

"No, we're just good friends," I say emphatically. "I haven't been back to his house, but I did meet with him in the back parlour of his shop. But don't get any ideas, Patty. It's a friendship, nothing more. He wanted to tell me about his idea regarding Harriet. You see, he's a good person and always tries to help people, even those he doesn't know. He suggested that Harriet go to his daughter's house for an interview at some point, if she agrees."

"I'm sure she'll be willing to do that. Do you want to speak with her about it?"

"Yes, I will. Can you tell Robert so he doesn't feel he's being left in the dark?"

"Of course, Bessie. He'll be delighted as well."

After tea I find a moment to draw Harriet aside and tell her about Mr Fielding's proposition.

"Do you have any experience with babies or young children?" I ask.

"Yes, I do," she says. "A week after I turned nine, Mother gave birth to a baby girl, my sister Angela. But she died when she was just eight months old. After the birth Mother was very ill and I had to help take care of Angela. I used to spoon-feed her, wash and change her, and sing her to sleep. Mother said I was better at caring for babies than she was."

I'm shocked to hear that Harriet and Michael's misfortunes also include the loss of a young sibling, and wonder how she died. But now is not the time to ask questions.

"Oh, I'm sorry to hear that you lost a sister, Harriet," I

say. "That must have been heartbreaking. But it does sound as if the position of nanny will suit you very well. Mrs Mathilda Cavendish expects to give birth in March and by then you'll be fourteen, so the timing couldn't be better. Obviously, she'd like to meet you first – it'll just be a chat, nothing too formal. As soon as I know a time that suits her, we can make arrangements for you to visit her at home."

"Thank you, Aunt Bessie. I'd like that very much."

"Excellent. Then I'll let her father know. I'll see you again on the twenty-fifth. Mr and Mrs Cartwright have invited me for the whole day since I've no family here in London. Let's hope your uncle allows Michael to join us. It's going to be a different Christmas for all of us, but I'm sure we'll find plenty of ways to enjoy ourselves."

Mrs Grist is back at the house when I return from Clapham. I ask her if she'd like anything from the kitchen – perhaps a cup of tea, a sandwich or a slice of cake.

"No, thank you, Elizabeth," she says. "I had a big meal at Doris' house. The cook roasted a chicken, though she insisted on calling it *poulet roti* just to show off. I won't need anything else to eat for the rest of the day."

"Mrs Grist," I say, forgetting Mr Fielding's advice, "I'll be more than happy to help Mrs Evans in the kitchen now that Mrs Hopper's gone. I don't mind taking on extra duties."

"No, Elizabeth. You're employed as my companion. And a word of warning to you – people like Mrs Evans won't take kindly to your offering to help them in their tasks. They won't respect you at all. There's a pecking order among domestic staff, a social hierarchy – I'm sure you know this already – and a lady's companion is on a par with a governess. I know you mean well, but don't degrade yourself – it won't be to your advantage.

"Remember Jane Eyre? She was a governess to Céline. She doesn't ever help with the household chores, does she?"

"Well, she did when Mrs Fairfax had to prepare Thornfield Hall for Mr Rochester's house party at short notice. She said she helped, or hindered, the cook and learnt to make custards and cheese-cakes and French pastry, and to truss game and garnish dessert-dishes."

"Goodness me, Elizabeth! You seem to have memorised that unremarkable sentence in its entirety! Why on earth would that scene in the kitchen stick in your mind? Anyway, that was different. As you say, it was at short notice – they needed as many willing hands as possible."

"True, but even so, you can hardly compare me to Jane Eyre. She was originally from a wealthy family. I don't deny she had plenty of misfortunes growing up, but she'd never been in service in her life."

"Oh, Elizabeth. Why are you arguing with me? I'm telling you for your own good that you shouldn't volunteer to undertake tasks that are not your responsibility. Do you understand?"

"Yes, thank you, Mrs Grist. I won't do it again."

Well, that's put me in my place, but it was good of her to speak frankly. In fact, it's exactly what Mr Fielding told me, though not quite so bluntly. I'll just continue to avoid Mrs Evans, as I've done in the past. I was hoping that we might become friends – no, that's going too far, not friends, but certainly not enemies – now that Mrs Hopper is no longer around, but I can't see that happening if she believes that I'm above her in the 'social hierarchy' of the household.

To my surprise, Mrs Evans doesn't seem at all bothered by Mrs Hopper's absence. In fact, I heard her singing as she went about her duties! Perhaps she had never really liked the cook at all, but considered it her duty, as a fellow servant, to take her side in denouncing everyone else in the house. I overheard Mrs Grist telling her that she shouldn't feel obliged to cook a hot meal if she had more pressing chores. But Mrs Evans said she'd already put a joint in the oven and peeled the carrots and potatoes. Cooking, she said, wasn't a chore at all as far as she was concerned; in fact, she found it enjoyable.

Mrs Grist still isn't in the best of moods, but the atmosphere in the house is noticeably less tense. I can only attribute this to Mrs Hopper not being around, viciously intent, as she was, on imposing her strategy of divide and rule. I hope and pray that this new sense of harmony will continue for some time to come.

In the middle of the week, Mrs Grist announces that she's going Christmas shopping in London's West End. Phillip, she says, has taken time off work to accompany her. He arrives at the house just as I'm coming down the stairs and gathers the letters from the doormat. Quite like old times!

"Good morning, Miss Hardwicke," he says. "Let me take this opportunity to wish you a happy Christmas, in case I don't see you again before the twenty-fifth."

"Thank you, Phillip," I say. "I wish you the same and a happy New Year as well."

"Many thanks. By the way, I received a letter from Miss Bancroft shortly after she left London. I'd given her the address of my lodgings and asked her to write to let me know she'd arrived home safely. You see, Miss Hardwicke, even though I'm prepared to give my support to the goals of the Suffragettes, I still feel nervous about young women travelling long distances without a male escort."

"Oh, that was thoughtful of you. But Edie was

travelling with her friend, so I don't think she was in any danger. And even though it was the first time she'd journeyed so far from home, I think she found the experience exciting rather than frightening."

"Have you heard from her lately?"

"No, but she isn't in the habit of writing to me herself. My nephew Walter writes to me regularly – as you know – and usually passes on her good wishes, though he doesn't see her as often as he'd like to. She's at the nurses' training school all week, and he works away from home a good deal. But hopefully they'll be able to spend some time together over Christmas."

"Have they set a date for their nuptials yet?"

"Oh no. Neither one is in a hurry to settle down, despite pressure from family and friends."

"I see. Well, I won't keep you any longer. I have to accompany Mother to the Selfridges department store in Oxford Street. Not a task to be envied I can assure you."

He gives me a sad smile and goes into the drawing room to wait for his mother. Why do I always feel so extremely sorry for this young man? He seems to wear his heart on his sleeve, ready to be broken at any moment. And his latest crush on Edie does not escape me. Why else would he be questioning me about her courtship with Walter? He was unlucky in love once before and it's a shame to think that he'll be disappointed yet again. But I wouldn't want it any other way. Edie's heart belongs to Walter and it's Walter's happiness I'm most concerned about. Phillip will have to bear the pain of unrequited love as best he can.

It's Christmas Eve already and I've been on tenterhooks all day waiting for Mrs Grist to leave for her sister-in-law's, since I don't want to explain to her where I'm going. She finally takes a Hansom cab at about five o'clock, laden with gifts. Just as she's leaving, she hands me a small package. "Don't open it until tomorrow," she instructs. I have a present for her too, but I'll give it to her when she returns. Hopefully, she'll be less agitated then.

I finished knitting Mr Fielding's socks yesterday afternoon and have wrapped them in tissue paper. I incorporated a Fair Isle design, which greatly impressed Mrs Grist. I just hope she doesn't see him wearing them!

I quickly change into my grey woollen dress. It's not very festive, I know, but I'm sure the church hall will be cold – such places usually are. Of course, I plan to wear my blue cloak and my leather gloves, and for the first time, a hat that's a bit more elaborate than the one I usually wear. It's navy blue, with a large floppy brim, a light blue ribbon around the crown and a bunch of imitation forget-me-nots on one side. Needless to say, it was a gift from Lady Sophia Radcliffe and I've been saving it for an extra-special occasion. I think I'm justified in wearing it tonight, though I have to admit that I feel over-dressed and self-conscious.

My boots, however, do not match the rest of my smart attire. I have only one pair and they're rather the worse for wear. They were new when I left Farringdale House, but with the amount of walking I've been doing and the state of the roads, the toes are scuffed and the heels are worn down on one side. I've polished them excessively, but they still look shabby. Goodness knows when I'll be able to afford a new pair. I don't have a penny to spare after all my Christmas shopping.

Mr Fielding invites me into his back parlour before we set off for the church hall. I hand him his present, wishing him a happy Christmas. He is surprised by my gesture, thanks me graciously, and opens the package right away.

"I hope you knew I was joking when I asked if the

socks you were knitting were for me, Bessie," he says with a smile.

"Yes, I did," I say, "and they weren't for you. They were for Robert. But then I thought I'd knit you a pair too, and in fact these are much nicer. I feel a bit guilty about that."

"I'm sure Robert's socks were knitted with just as much skill and, more importantly, affection. If he's half as pleased with his pair as I am with mine, then he's a lucky man. Now, Bessie, it's my turn to give you a present. I hope you will like it as much as I like the socks you've just given me."

He hands me a box, which I open tentatively. I gasp when I reveal a bottle of Guerlain's *Après l'Ondée* perfume. For a moment I'm lost for words at the extravagance of the gift, especially when compared with my humble offering of a pair of socks.

"This is magnificent," I exclaim. "But it's too much. You really shouldn't have, Lionel. I've never received such a precious gift in my whole life."

"Come on now, Bessie. Don't exaggerate. Do you want to open the bottle and smell the scent? I'm well aware that perfume is a risky gift to give, as each lady has her own preference, but I'm told this one is very popular."

"I'm sure I'll love it," I say, cradling the weighty crystal bottle and admiring the colour of the perfume, which is golden like liquid honey. I don't want to tell him that I've never actually owned a bottle of expensive perfume in my life, so have no particular preference. Lady Sophia often said I could sample any of the many fragrances that lined her dressing table, but I never did.

I cautiously remove the stopper. The intensity of the scent almost takes my breath away.

"It's wonderful, Lionel. It smells like a garden of

blossoming flowers after a rain shower in the month of May. I shall be reminded of the countryside each time I wear it."

"You've actually hit the nail on the head, Bessie. The shop assistant told me that this perfume is *supposed* to smell like flowers after the rain. How remarkable that you recognised that fragrance. In fact, *Après l'Ondée* translates as 'after the downpour'. Why don't you dab a little on your wrists and behind your ears before we go out?"

"Since it's Christmas Eve, I think I will. Really, I can't thank you enough for this exquisite present. I'll treasure it always."

"There you go again, Bessie, making a song and dance about a simple gift. Now, since we've finished opening our presents, shall we have a glass of sherry before braving the chilly night air?"

It's past ten o'clock by the time I arrive home. It was such a special evening – I shall remember it with pleasure and gratitude all my life. On our way to the church hall, Mr Fielding and I came upon a group of young carol singers and stopped to listen. They were singing 'The Holly and the Ivy', which is one of my favourites. My escort gave them a few coins and they asked which carol we'd like to hear next. I suggested 'Once in Royal David's City' and we all sang it together. It was a lovely experience.

Mr Fielding called the performance of *A Christmas Carol* amateurish, but I thought it was wonderful. I'm ashamed to admit it, but it's the first 'grown-up' play that I've ever been to see. What a sheltered life I've led! I've been to many nativity plays at the village school, which are always touching, but this was altogether different. As might have been expected, tears sprang to my eyes at the sight of Tiny Tim with his crutch and Mr Fielding handed me *my* handkerchief, which he says he always keeps in his coat pocket. When the play was over and the actors came onto the stage, I clapped so hard my palms ached. Afterwards, we walked back arm in arm like a proper couple and Lionel – I really should stop calling him Mr Fielding – gave me a hug, holding me for longer than might be considered proper, and a lingering kiss on the cheek. And as if the pleasures of this evening aren't enough to last me for months, if not years, I have something else to look forward to. He's invited me to his house for dinner on the thirty-first! What a fitting end to a year that's seen so many changes for me personally.

I want to be up early in the morning to go to church, so no more time for musing. This is the first time since childhood that I've not gone to church on Christmas Eve, and I feel rather guilty about the fact. It's an occasion that I always look forward to; I especially enjoy the carols and the festive camaraderie among the parishioners. So even though it means forgoing a lie in, I resolve to attend the early morning Christmas Day service. I need to give thanks for the blessings that have come my way just lately, and of course to celebrate in prayer and song the birth of Our Lord Jesus Christ.

But before going to bed, I open my bottle of perfume and dab a little of the precious scent on my pillow. The fragrance is heady and I fall asleep dreaming of warm summer nights in the countryside with Lionel. Somehow, in my dreams, Lionel becomes Arthur and we're together in the snow in London, both young and carefree. The contrariness is a bit unsettling, but I'm not going to read anything foreboding into it. I need to live life one day at a time and concentrate on making the most of the present and the future, uncertain though the latter may be. I've been living in the past for far too long.

22

My walk to Clapham – there are no motorbuses today – is a bit of a struggle as I'm carrying not only gifts but also a box of Tom Smith crackers and two packets of sugared almonds. I'm feeling very tired as I slept poorly and forced myself to get up early for church. But when I arrive at Patty and Robert's, my fatigue vanishes. Michael and Harriet are there at the door to greet me, and their excitement is contagious.

"Happy Christmas, Aunt Bessie!" they cry in unison, each presenting me with a gift. I'm so touched by their gesture – and so happy that Michael's uncle has agreed to let him join us – that I'm unable to stop my eyes from misting over.

"Oh, thank you so much, both of you," I exclaim. "Happy Christmas to you too! This is a lovely surprise. I'm so glad we're all spending Christmas Day together!"

"Come away from the door, you two," Patty says, "and let Aunt Bessie come in so she can put down her parcels and take off her coat. Welcome, dear Bessie. It's a bit chaotic here, as you can see for yourself."

In the corner of the room stands a small fir tree, decorated with candles and paper chains. At the top of the tree is an angel, made from cardboard with lace wings attached. Harriet tells me she made the angel herself and has named her Angela in memory of her baby sister, who she's sure is now a heavenly angel. I tell her I'm certain of it too. My eyes are misting over again!

"You see, Bessie," Robert says when he comes in from the garden, where he's been smoking his pipe, "for the first time we're following in the tradition of our German friends and bringing a fir tree into the home. As you're no doubt aware, Prince Albert introduced the

Christmas tree to this country by installing one at Windsor Castle in the 1840s, but this is the first time we've made the effort to decorate one ourselves. Having you and the children here on Christmas Day has made all the difference."

"It looks beautiful, Robert," I say, "and I think it's a tradition you should continue. I've always loved the smell of pine. Will you be lighting the candles?"

"Yes, we'll light them after dinner when it starts to get dark and when we exchange gifts." He takes my arm and says quietly, "Perhaps candles weren't such a good idea. The children's home was burnt down through an accident with a candle. We'll have to be very careful, especially with Romeo in the house."

I'm reminded of the large tree the Radcliffes used to decorate every Christmas in their main drawing room. It was covered in candles, each in its own holder, clipped onto the tree, and they were frequently lit. Thankfully, the children's nanny used to make sure the little ones didn't get too near, and we all kept a close eye on the dogs.

The dining table has already been laid with Patty's best damask tablecloth and her finest china. I feel guilty for not having arrived earlier as there is little for me to help with in the kitchen. The turkey is resting on the draining board, and the boiled ham is already sliced. Celia is busy mashing the potatoes and Patty is stirring the gravy. She says the peas, carrots and cabbage are ready to serve.

"We usually have a goose," Patty says, "but decided on a turkey this year. Robert's youngest brother has a farm in Surrey and does a good business fattening up the birds in time for Christmas. Harriet has been a godsend – she made both the bread sauce and the chestnut stuffing. I wouldn't be surprised if the stuffing is tastier than the turkey."

"Good for Harriet," I say. "The turkey smells wonderful, and I sure it tastes even better. But what can I do to help?"

"Don't you worry, Bessie. Everything's taken care of. You're our guest, so go and sit down. It's much too hot in the kitchen, even with the window open. The range fire's been burning since early morning. I know that Robert wants to give you a glass of mulled wine so that he can have one himself. Do go and join him."

"All right, but at least let me take a few of the dishes through if they're ready. You and Celia must have been up since before dawn. I wish I'd come earlier to help you."

"We're three women in the house, if you count Harriet, and you know the proverb 'too many cooks spoil the broth'. So please, go and sit yourself down. That's an order."

It is hot in the kitchen and I'm probably making it hotter, so I do as Patty says and join Robert and the children in the parlour. Harriet is wearing a dress of emerald green – one of Mrs Grist's discarded garments – and it fits her perfectly. The red trimming around the neck, wrists and hem complements her dark hair, which is tied back with a crimson bow. She looks the most festive of us all.

"Harriet," I say, after admiring her dress, "I spoke to Mrs Cavendish's father this week and told him you'd be interested in the position of nanny to her baby when he or she arrives. He says he'll tell his daughter and will let us know when she's ready to meet you. If all goes well, you'll probably start work once she begins her confinement – so perhaps the end of February or the beginning of March."

"Thank you, Aunt Bessie," Harriet says. "I do hope she likes me. I want to start earning some money so I can pay Mr and Mrs Cartwright back for letting me stay here. I'll always be grateful that they took me into their home when I had nowhere else to go, but I hate to be a burden on anyone."

"You're not a burden, Harriet," Robert says, having overheard the conversation. "Not at all. And there's nothing whatsoever to pay back. You're doing a lot of work in the kitchen and helping Patty and Celia with their mending and laundry. You've more than earned your keep. We'll miss you when you leave, that's for sure."

"Will I still be able to see Harriet when she goes to work at that place?" Michael asks worriedly. "Is it far away?"

"I'll still be London," Harriet says quickly. "And if I'm free on Sundays, I'll see you at least once a week, like I do now. Don't worry, little brother, I'll be keeping a close eye on you. So make sure you do well in your lessons. Please don't disappoint me."

"I'll try not to, but I'm not as clever as you, Harriet. What will happen to Romeo?"

"Romeo can stay here," Robert says. "He a member of the Cartwright family now."

The sumptuous turkey is consumed in a fraction of the time it took to prepare, and is followed by a fruit-packed plum pudding. The grown-ups feel quite drowsy after ingesting so much food and drinking many more glasses of mulled wine than intended. But both Michael and Harriet are anxious to open their presents, so we make an effort to stay awake.

They are delighted with the books I chose and Harriet says she'll keep *David Copperfield* safely in her possession while she's staying with the Cartwrights. My friends are also pleased with their presents and compliment me on my handiwork. As for me, I can hardly believe my eyes when they present me with a far more extravagant gift than the ones I've given them. And it's just what I need – a pair of boots!

"This is too much," I exclaim, embarrassed by such an expensive present. "These boots must have cost a fortune – the leather is so beautifully soft. You really shouldn't have spent so much on me."

"I knew you'd react in this way, Bessie," Patty says. "But it's a gift from all three of us, so it's not the extravagance you're making it out to be. And they're not new – they're second-hand, but in a good condition. So they didn't cost a fortune, not at all. I think we picked the right size, but do you want to try them on just to be sure?"

They fit perfectly and are comfortable too. Given the sorry state of the ones I'm wearing, they couldn't have come at a better time. It's now Michael and Harriet's turn to present me with gifts. Michael gives me a drawing of Romeo, which he's framed with some stiff cardboard. It's a charcoal sketch this time and he's managed to capture the black cat's likeness remarkably well. Harriet's present is just as thoughtful – she used Celia's sewing machine to fashion a book cover from a piece of blue velvet, on which she embroidered my initials. I'm quite overcome with emotion, yet again. If I have to spend Christmas Day away from Walter, I couldn't wish to be in the company of better friends.

By the time we finish exchanging presents, everyone is wide awake. We'd forgotten about the crackers so have great fun pulling them – though poor Romeo is not amused – chuckling at the jokes and donning the paper hats. Then Harriet insists that we play charades – based on well-known nursery rhymes – and a game called pass the parcel. I've seen the latter played at Farringdale House, but it's always been to the accompaniment of someone playing the piano. Since the Cartwrights don't own a piano, Harriet instructs Robert to turn away from us and sing a selection of carols while the rest of us pass the parcel.

The parcel loses a layer of wrapping each time Robert stops singing mid-carol. Whoever is lucky enough to tear off the last piece of wrapping paper will claim the hidden treasure. I'd quite forgotten what a melodious voice Robert has, and I find myself paying far more attention to his singing than to the game itself. Thankfully, I am not a winner. Michael wins the first game; he excitedly, with fumbling fingers, unwraps a sugar mouse. His little face beams with pure delight. And the second winner is Celia; she uncovers a tangerine that, to everyone's amusement, perfectly matches her paper hat.

Despite my objections, Robert says he'll walk me home as it's getting late and is pitch dark outside. He claims that he needs some exercise after being in the house all day. As soon as we step outside, however, the soot and smoke particles in the air catch in my throat and make me cough.

"Cover your nose and mouth with your scarf, Bessie," Robert says. "It's not good to breathe in this polluted air. And it leaves such an unpleasant metallic taste in your mouth. Are you sure you don't want to stay the night? We could make up a bed for you in the parlour."

"No, thank you, Robert," I say. "I do need to get back. Besides, isn't Michael staying the night with you?"

"Yes, but young boys like Michael don't care where they sleep. A couple of pillows in the cupboard under the stairs will suit him just as well as a feather bed in a fine bedchamber."

"How did his uncle react to the letter?"

"Quite reasonably, I would say. He said Michael could spend Christmas Day and Boxing Day with us. But he insisted on taking him to church on the evening of the twenty-fourth; he said that was the only tradition he intended to follow. He brought Michael to the house this morning and said he'll collect him tomorrow evening. He was an austere fellow of very few words and clearly set in his ways. But I believe he intends to do right by the boy, even though guardianship of an eleven-year old is not an obligation he particularly relishes."

"Well, he may have done the right thing in taking Michael in, but he certainly had no qualms about rejecting poor Harriet."

"Yes, but in a way, I can sympathise with his not wanting to take her. I think my own reaction might have been similar. You see, he's a bachelor and I imagine he's had little experience in dealing with women. I was the same before I met Patty. My mother died young, I didn't have sisters – we were six brothers – and I never had female friends. Not only that, but I took a job at a boys' school so, even as a grown man, I had no female acquaintances whatsoever. I wouldn't have known how to handle a girl like Harriet. I've changed a lot since I married Patty. I now realise that women are not such frightening creatures after all."

"I'm not sure I can forgive the uncle so easily, Robert, and I don't think for one moment that you'd have reacted similarly. He should at least have made sure Harriet had somewhere else to go. If Mrs Radford hadn't sent her to the convent, she could well have ended up on the streets."

"Yes, you're right. Mrs Radford is a good woman. By the way, Patty and I have now discovered the name of Harriet's correspondent. She started receiving letters through the post, so Patty asked her to whom she'd given our address. Apparently, it's a young man she met when she ran away from the orphanage. He helped her find her way to the Radfords in the middle of the night. She says his name is Alec. He's seventeen and works for his father, who's a blacksmith. I asked her what he was doing out of doors at that time of night, and she claims he's employed as a night watchman two nights a week. He should by rights have returned her to the orphanage, but I suppose she persuaded him not to. I wouldn't be surprised if Harriet made him feel like a hero. Anyway, they struck up a friendship; he gave her his address and they're now exchanging letters."

"Well, that seems innocent enough, wouldn't you say?"

"I suppose so. But don't forget, Harriet is still only thirteen. And we don't know anything about this young man. But, as I keep telling Patty, we're not the girl's guardians. We can try to help her and give her advice, but what she decides to do with her life is ultimately up to her. I'm glad you've found her a position with a good family, though I know it's not confirmed yet. But if they do accept her, then thankfully she'll be safe and out of trouble."

"Yes, indeed. I think she'll be happy there. Mrs Mathilda Cavendish is a lovely lady, so kind and considerate. And young enough to become a confidante and friend to Harriet, rather than an authoritative figure. It strikes me that Harriet is not terribly respectful of authority, having had to take on so much responsibility at far too young an age."

"You're right. Harriet is a law unto herself, to be sure. But she has a good heart and is hard-working. What she needs most of all is a sense of stability. Well, let's pray that both children find their purpose in life. At least they know they can always turn to us if ever they're in need of guidance or a shoulder to lean on."

I remember Mrs Grist's present just as I'm about to slip beneath the warm covers of my bed. She's wrapped a cardboard box neatly in brown paper and tied it with a red ribbon. Inside the box is a black lacquered jewellery case, with mother of pearl inlay in the shape of a tulip. I open the case to reveal a silver link bracelet resting on a lining of red silk. I can count on the fingers of one hand the pieces of jewellery I own – none of them valuable – so the bracelet comes as a lovely surprise. But it's the beautiful lacquered case that pleases me the most. I certainly didn't expect anything at all from Mrs Grist, so the fact that she's given me such a fine and costly gift comes as quite a shock. The tin of talcum powder I've yet to give her is so modest in comparison! I just hope she realises that the thought is there, and it's that which counts.

It occurs to me that I've received much more precious gifts this Christmas than the ones I've given. This is contrary to my long-held belief that it's better to give more and receive less. But I'll not spoil the day by feeling remorse at not having been in a position to be more generous. Instead, I'll take pleasure in my good fortune while praying that my kind-hearted friends will be forever blessed with God's bounty.

My Boxing Day is spent alone in the house, but I'm glad for the peace and quiet. Patty insisted on giving me some slices of cold turkey yesterday evening, so I have those for lunch with bubble and squeak, a favourite of mine. I make myself a cup of Camp coffee and am about to retreat to my room to lie on the bed and read one of Mrs Grist's novels when I hear someone knocking loudly on the front door. Who could it be, other than Lionel, and surely he wouldn't risk another visit? When I open the door, however, I find myself face to face with Mr Basil Hornby! So aghast am I to see him standing there on the doorstep with a smirk on his face that I take a couple of steps backwards, ready to slam the door shut if necessary. I'm sure my expression is one of horror, but he continues to look amused.

"Fanny not here?" he asks.

"No, Mrs Grist is away for a couple of days," I say before it strikes me that I should not be sharing this information. He'll know now that I'm alone in the house.

"Well, give her this," he says. "And tell her all is forgiven and forgotten. It's Christmas – the season of goodwill toward all men. Let bygones be bygones is what I say."

He thrusts a bottle of his illegal brandy into my hands. I'm about to give it back to him, but on second thoughts I place it on the console table. It's not my place to decline his gift for Mrs Grist, though I'm sure she wouldn't have hesitated in refusing it.

"Thank you," I say. "I'll give her the bottle as soon as she returns. I bid you good afternoon, sir."

"Haven't I seen you before?" he asks, making no effort to move away from the doorstep, even though I've half closed the door.

"No, I don't think so."

I'm desperate to shut and lock the door, especially since it's evident to me from his flushed face that he's been drinking.

"Hmm… Well, mind you give her the message. And make sure it's word for word. D'you remember what I said? Let bygones be bygones."

"I'll tell her that, I promise."

I shut the door and turn the key. My hand is trembling. I was so afraid he'd force his way in, but I may have misjudged him; perhaps he really does intend to bury the hatchet. Certainly, it'll be a weight off Mrs Grist's mind if he means what he says; that all is forgiven and forgotten. Not that it's Mr Hornby's place to forgive, but

I'm sure my employer will readily accept the offer of an olive branch if it truly means an end to his threatening behaviour.

23

Mrs Grist returns the next morning. She looks tired as she sinks into her easy chair. I thank her sincerely for the lovely present and give her my humble offering.

"Did you buy this at the pharmacy?" she asks.

"Yes," I say. "I'm sorry it's not a very original gift."

"It's more than I expected. You shouldn't spend your money on me, Elizabeth. But thank you. I've always liked the scent of hyacinth."

"Will you be going to your sister-in-law's for New Year's Eve?" I ask, hoping that the answer will be yes. I'd prefer to leave the house unnoticed for my evening with Lionel.

"Most likely. But to be honest, I'd rather not go. I'm tired of so much company. It's never-ending. No sooner does one guest leave then another arrives. I try to retire early, but the noise of their merriment keeps me awake for hours."

"Hopefully, we can look forward to a quieter time once we've welcomed in the New Year. I forgot to mention, Mrs Grist, on the hall table is a bottle of brandy. You may have noticed it when you came in. Mr Hornby called at the house yesterday and asked me to give it to you. He said to tell you that all is forgiven and forgotten and that you should both let bygones be bygones. Those were his exact words."

"Hmm, I wondered what that bottle was doing there. I thought perhaps Mrs Hopper had come by, hoping to get her job back. I can't imagine what Basil Hornby means by that. He always did have a strange way of expressing himself."

I realise that Mrs Grist doesn't know that I've been told about the bad blood between the Grists and the

Hornbys, so I say no more. But for her sake I hope that Mr Hornby's uncharacteristic gesture wasn't simply the result of his having taken one Christmas drink too many.

A letter from Walter reaches me on the Wednesday after Christmas. I open it with joyous anticipation, but its contents are enough to break my heart. He tells me that he and Edie are no longer courting and that they've parted ways. Walter writes:

'Dearest Aunt Bessie,

I hope you had an enjoyable Christmas with Aunt Patty and Mr Cartwright. Please give them both my best wishes for a happy and prosperous New Year.

Thank you so much, dear Aunt, for the beautiful wallet you sent me. It is the perfect choice of gift, especially since my old one was falling apart, as no doubt you noticed. It is the most thoughtful of presents and I can't thank you enough.

Aunt Bessie, I'm afraid I have something sad to tell you. I wanted to wait until the New Year before writing to you, but then I thought it would be better to get the bad news over with before 1911 begins. It's selfish of me, I know, but that way I can welcome in the New Year with a fresh state of mind, though the heartache will remain.

Edie told me yesterday that she is leaving me. She says she's transferring to a nurses' training college in London because she doesn't want to spend the rest of her life in the village where, she says, attitudes never change. Apparently, she's keen 'to move with the times'. Her words sadden me, but anger me too. I'm convinced that it was her trip to London and her involvement with the Suffragette movement that brought on this new way of thinking. I've tried to reason with her, but she says her mind is already made up. Sadly, we didn't part on a happy note, and that intensifies the hurt I feel.

To be honest, Aunt, it didn't come as a surprise. She's a village girl and attended the local school, but she was always a cut above her fellow students. I hoped she would learn to accept me and my backward ways, but once she started mixing with the daughters of townspeople, that seemed less and less likely. Perhaps it's for the best. I've learnt my lesson now. I'm not prepared to change my nature to please anyone, not even Edie. I'm a labourer, born and bred in the countryside, and proud of it. The woman I choose as my wife will have to accept that. I don't think that's too much to ask, do you, Aunt Bessie?

I'm sorry to burden you with this sad news. But please don't worry about me, dear Aunt. Life will go on and I shall get over it. Uncle Edward sends his love and thanks you for the tobacco. Thank you again for the splendid wallet.

Your ever-loving nephew, Walter'

I am deeply saddened by this news. My heart aches for my dear Walter. I never expected him to be thwarted in love, given his excellent character and his enviable looks. But if Edie's looking for someone with a more sophisticated background, then sadly, Walter doesn't fit the bill. I can't help but wonder if it's Phillip who's encouraged her to transfer to London. He was obviously taken with her and admitted that he's written to her. But I cannot dispel a nagging feeling that it's *me* who's to blame for this sudden turn of events. I am the one who allowed her to walk alone with Phillip in the fog that evening, and the easy familiarity between them may well have sowed the seeds of her dissatisfaction with village life.

I know it isn't his intention, but I feel as if Walter is

rebuking me for moving to London. He says he's a labourer, born and bred in the countryside, and isn't prepared to change for anyone, not even Edie. Well, I'm also from the countryside, yet I was prepared to leave our village, find a new occupation, and move to the city. Why couldn't I have been content to stay and look for another job in the village? Were I not living in London, Edie wouldn't have met Phillip Grist and been tempted by the idea of a more stylish way of life. And if she does begin a courtship with him, which is more than likely once she moves to London, Walter's bound to think that it's partly my fault, even if he's too loyal a nephew to tell me to my face.

But perhaps I'm jumping to conclusions. I don't know for sure that Phillip is the reason behind Edie's sudden decision to move to London. She's an intelligent young woman and she may have decided that there are more prospects for her in the big city. Still, the question remains: would she be making this move had she not met and begun a correspondence with Phillip? Somehow, I doubt it. Then there's Mrs Grist to consider. She'll be furious if she finds out that her favourite son is sweet on a girl from my village and will blame me for their meeting each other, regardless of the fact that the introductions happened in my absence.

I keep reading and re-reading Walter's letter and it's become stained with my tears. I think I've reached a decision, but it's one that makes me more upset than ever. I shall have to return to the village. I cannot let Walter grieve alone. And I cannot bear the thought of him thinking that I was not content with village life. I'll write to Edward and ask him if he'll take me in as housekeeper. I can earn a few shillings a month with my needlework and will transform his neglected garden into a thriving vegetable patch. Perhaps we can keep poultry and sell the eggs at the local market. It'll be a quiet, productive life and I can look after both Edward and Walter.

Common sense tells me that I shouldn't make such a life-changing decision while I'm this distraught. I'll wait until after New Year before I put pen to paper. I need to talk to someone before deciding on a course of action that I might regret, and the obvious person is Lionel. Of course, he's going to try to persuade me not to leave, but I'll put my foot down. I simply have to make amends for letting Walter down. And, if my suspicion about Edie and Phillip is correct, then I could not possibly continue working as a companion to Mrs Grist. It's better that I leave before I'm fired. I hope Lionel will understand that.

Mrs Grist *is* going to spend New Year's Eve with her sister-in-law, despite her stated reluctance. I imagine that she intended to go all along. She asked me if I had any plans and I told her another lie. I said I was going to Patty and Robert's, but would probably be back before midnight. I couldn't reveal that I actually intended to pass the evening with her long-time friend, Lionel Fielding.

My mood is sombre as I try to decide what to wear. It seems wrong for me to be celebrating the start of a new year with a special friend when Walter is most likely alone with Edward, grieving for Edie. As I've said before, Edward is the most silent of men and his company is hardly likely to cheer Walter up. I hope my dear nephew has the good sense to pass the evening with his Uncle Harold and his family, although seeing his cousin Joseph in the company of his betrothed, Miss Daisy Goode, will no doubt make him feel the pain of his loss more than ever.

Well, my brooding about Walter's heartache is not helping anyone. I should try to make an effort for Lionel. He's been so good to me and I feel undeserving of his attentions. I choose my sky blue silk blouse and long navy skirt. It's an outfit he's seen before, but I really don't have a lot of choice. I brush my hair into a roll on the top of my head – though I know it won't hold for long, however many pins I use – and dab some *Après l'Ondée* perfume on my wrists and behind my ears. I'm glad Mrs Grist isn't here to detect my expensive scent. She'd surely have questions to ask.

I'm to meet Lionel at his shop, as usual. He's there waiting for me, and his solid, cheerful presence lifts my mood slightly. He takes my arm as if it's the most commonplace of gestures, and we walk the short distance to his home. He apologises for not arranging something more exciting for the end of the year, but I assure him that excitement is not something I crave.

"Me neither," he says. "Mathilda's maid Alice has left us a cold supper. But there's some soup that I can heat up. We'll have a glass of sherry first. You look cold, Bessie. Sit closer to the fire."

He noticed me shivering when I took off my cloak. I do feel cold, but I soon start to feel warmer. The fire is blazing and Lionel draws the thick velvet curtains to keep out any draughts, though I don't think there are any. Unlike the sash windows in our old village cottages, the casement windows in these large London homes don't seem to have gaps that let in the cold air. It feels so cosy and intimate in Lionel's drawing room that I begin to feel nervous, whereas I should be feeling more relaxed.

"You don't seem quite yourself, my dear," Lionel says, handing me a glass of sherry. "Is anything wrong? Did you have an enjoyable Christmas with your friends?"

"Oh yes, I had a lovely time," I say. "Michael and Harriet were there and we all thoroughly enjoyed ourselves. My first Christmas in London couldn't have been nicer. And of course, our evening together at the theatre on Christmas Eve is now one of my most treasured memories. But since then I've received some sad news. You'll probably think it's nothing, but I feel so upset about it."

"What is it, Bessie dear?"

"I received a letter from Walter. He tells me that his sweetheart Edie has left him. She's going to transfer to a nurses' training college here in London. She says she doesn't want to spend the rest of her life in the village. But that's not all. Remember I told you she met Phillip when she was here for the Suffragettes' protest? Well, since then they've been corresponding – Phillip told me himself that he'd written to her. I have a feeling that she's left Walter for Phillip, and I can't help thinking that I'm to blame. And I know Mrs Grist won't approve of her son stepping out with a village girl like Edie. When she discovers my connection with her, I'm sure to lose my job."

"I do think you're over-reacting, Bessie my dear. They're both young and young people have a habit of falling in and out of love. Nothing that you, me, Fanny Grist or anyone else can say or do will change that fact. I'm sorry for Walter obviously, but he's certain to meet someone else sooner than you think. And truth be told, I'm rather pleased for Phillip, if what you say is true. A new love interest is just what he needs at this moment in his life. He'll treat Edie well, don't worry about that, and if she's anything like you, Bessie, I don't see how Fanny will be able to stop herself from liking her."

"Oh, Lionel, Edie is nothing like me. She's caring, intelligent and beautiful. It's so completely out of character for her to let Walter down in this way, but I suppose it's better that it's happened now, rather than later. But the worst of it is, I feel *I've* let Walter down. I can tell you off by heart what he said in his letter. He says he's not prepared to change his nature to please anyone, not even Edie. He's a labourer, born and bred in the countryside, and proud of it. The woman he chooses as his wife will have to accept that. Don't you see, Lionel, how disappointed he must be in me for leaving the village for a job in the city, forsaking my own countrymen and women and, even worse, not being there when he needs me most? I honestly feel that the right thing for me to do now is to return to the village, live with my brother Edward and make a home for the two of them. That's the least I can do under the circumstances."

"Now, now, Bessie, calm yourself and listen to me. Firstly, like Edie, you're caring, intelligent and, in my eyes, beautiful. Secondly, although I realise it may be less common in the countryside, here in London young people don't always stay with the first suitor they meet. My Mathilda is an example of that. And thirdly, Walter is now an adult. You were there for him throughout his childhood and you're still an important figure in his life, only now at a distance. He doesn't need you like he did when he was a child. You said yourself that he works away from home a lot of the time, so it's not as if you'd see him every day even if you did return to your village. And sooner or later, he'll marry and move into his own home. You have to think of your own life, Bessie. Do you *want* to live with your brother? Does Walter really need your company? I suspect that the answer to both those questions is no."

At this point, I'm unable to stop myself from weeping. All that Lionel has said is true, except, of course, the ridiculous remark that Edie and I are alike. But his words don't make me feel any better. How will I face Mrs Grist when she finds out about Phillip and Edie? The only solution I can think of is to run away, coward-like, back to the village.

"Come on now, Bessie, don't be upset," Lionel says, taking my hand. "Walter wouldn't want to be the cause of *your* suffering. We don't know for sure that Phillip is the only reason for Edie transferring to London. She may well have been influenced by her visit here, whether by the excitement of city life, her involvement with the Suffragettes, or her encounter with Phillip – who knows? Or she may simply be thinking of her own career. You are not to blame for her decision. Sooner or later she'd have left Walter, and you'd have been powerless to stop her. Remember when you told me that Phillip wasn't the first young man to be thwarted in love and that I shouldn't feel responsible for Mathilda breaking his heart? Well, now I'm saying the same thing to you. If what you tell me is true about Walter, and I'm sure it is, he'll have no trouble in finding love again. He's so young, Bessie. And as for Phillip, I think he deserves a little happiness, don't you?"

"You're right, as you always are, Lionel. But still, I don't think I can stay in London. How can I ever face Mrs Grist when she finds out what I'm sure is true – that Phillip and Edie are about to begin a courtship – and that it's because of me they met?"

"Fanny Grist is not as hard-hearted as you think she is. She wants Phillip to be happy and I don't think she's likely to look down on a girl from the countryside, given her own humble beginnings. Didn't you tell me that Edie grew up on a farm? Well, there's a lot to commend her in that. I'm sure she's a hard-working young woman, ready to take on responsibility and face whatever challenges life throws at her. Since Phillip has a tendency to be melancholic, he needs a strong woman in his life in a way I suspect Walter doesn't. Edie may be the making of him, Bessie."

I can't contradict Lionel. He's not wrong in what he

says. Phillip deserves happiness just as much as Walter. If Edie and Phillip do become sweethearts, then I'll wish them all the best. But I shan't ever forget that Edie was Walter's girl first.

"Now," he says after a slight pause that gives me time to pull myself together, "let's heat the soup over the fire, as the range hasn't been lit today. It's leek and potato – is that all right? There's cold beef and ham, and more than one type of cheese. We can toast some bread too, as I believe there's a dish of beef dripping in the pantry. I'm sorry that I'm only offering you left-overs, Bessie, but it's all good, tasty food."

"Everything sounds wonderful, Lionel. I've brought fruitcake for pudding. But we may be too full up to eat it, in which case you can save it for another day."

"I'll certainly make room for a slice, my dear. And I have a surprise. Champagne! I've put it out on the windowsill to cool. We'll have a glass with our fruitcake. Have you ever tasted Champagne before?"

"No, never. The Radcliffes often drank it on special occasions, but I haven't tried it myself."

"There's a first time for everything. You'll love it, I promise you."

I try to be a bit more cheerful as we eat our meal. Lionel has gone to such a great deal of trouble that it's ungrateful of me to be in such a downcast mood, especially since traditionally it's a night for celebration and he could, if he wished, be enjoying more animated company.

Once we've eaten our fill, he suggests that I sit on the settee and relax while he opens the bottle of Champagne, which he retrieves from the windowsill. He finds it a bit of a struggle to pull out the cork, but it finally emerges with a loud pop and flies across the room, giving me quite a fright. Thankfully, Lionel manages to avoid any spills by acting quickly with a tea towel.

"I don't often open bottles of Champagne," he admits. "And I have to tell you, Bessie, that I cannot take credit for its purchase. It was given to me by one of my oldest and wealthiest customers. I've been serving him for many years and he's now moving north to live with his son in Edinburgh. He wanted to thank me for all the homeopathic advice I've shared with him over three decades. He has a distrust of modern medicine, so would come to me for more natural remedies. Between you and me, that's where my own interest chiefly lies. Major Cunningham is quite a character – I'm going to miss him."

"I'm sure he'll miss you just as much. It was good of him to give you the Champagne, but shouldn't you be sharing it with your family, Lionel? I don't think I'll be able to manage more than one glass. The sherry has already made me a bit tipsy. Did you not want to spend New Year's Eve with Mathilda and Ronald?"

"No, I wanted to spend it with you, Miss Bessie Hardwicke. Besides, they've gone to Ronald's parents' house – or mansion I should say – in Hampstead and will stay overnight. I was invited, but I declined. The whole extended Cavendish family will be there and, as I've said before, I'm not a fan of such big social gatherings. Now, let's not speculate on how many glasses you will or will not drink. We'll start with half a glass and take it slowly – how does that sound?"

He pours me a half a glass of the bubbly celebratory drink, apologising for not having actual Champagne glasses. As if I would have known the difference! He then pours himself a full glass and sits down next to me on the settee. We each have a slice of fruitcake to nibble on between sips. It's the most delicious drink I've ever tasted and, although I can feel it making my head a little light, I don't feel as tipsy as when I drink more than one glass of sherry.

But, as usual, instead of just enjoying the moment, I'm already thinking about where this physical nearness is going to lead. Lionel is sitting alongside me and I'm starting to feel uneasy. He senses my discomfort.

"Relax, Bessie," he says. 'You have to trust me. I respect you too much to take advantage of you. All I want is for us to enjoy each other's company. How do you like the Champagne?"

"I like it very much indeed," I say, reddening at the thought that he's so easily able to read my mind. "And I've loved everything about this evening. I can't think of a New Year's Eve that I've enjoyed more."

"Now, my dear, you know that's not true. You're just being polite. You shed tears earlier on, remember?"

"Yes, but you made me see sense. If you hadn't invited me here, I'd probably already be packing my bags and preparing to leave London in the morning. It's thanks to you that I'm welcoming in the New Year with a smile on my face instead of a frown."

"I'm glad I've made you smile, Bessie. You know, there's an old wives' tale that whatever one is doing when the clock strikes twelve on Old Year's Night will influence how much happiness or otherwise one can expect to receive throughout the coming year. My faithful grandfather clock over there tells me that the time is a minute to midnight. Would you object to my embracing you at this moment so as to ensure that our friendship continues well into the New Year?"

It's too late to object. He puts his arms around me, pulls me close and at the stroke of midnight kisses me softly on the lips.

24

It was just the one kiss. I didn't exactly resist, but I didn't show much enthusiasm either and was the first to pull away. Again, Lionel sensed my unease and didn't attempt a second one. He continued to chat in his usual open and pleasant way; if he was offended, he didn't show it. Of course, now that I'm back in my room – at one o'clock in the morning – I regret not being more responsive. The fact is, I don't have much practice in kissing. Arthur and I would embrace when we were alone together in the woods, but he hadn't had much practice either and we were both just experimenting with kisses and caresses. I hope I haven't come across as cold and ungrateful, but it's all so new to me. It still hasn't really sunk in that he finds me attractive in a physical way – I cannot understand it at all. He has so many attributes and I have so few. I know I'm being self-deprecating again, but I can't help it. I'm thirty-nine, quite ordinary looking, lacking in self-confidence and uninformed about so many things. Yet he continues to act as if I'm the most desirable woman in the world. It doesn't make any sense.

I wake early, having slept poorly. The sherry and the Champagne – in the end I drank two full glasses – have given me a headache. Is this a hangover? If so, it's the first time I've suffered from one. I go down to the kitchen and make a cup of tea to take back to my room. I'll try to sleep for another hour before getting ready to go to church. It's the first of January, 1911. It seems only right to thank the Lord for giving us all a new beginning, and to assure him of our gratitude and everlasting faith. I will pray for Walter and Edie, and for Phillip too – that all three may find happiness in one way or another.

I'm invited to Patty and Robert's again this afternoon.

I enjoy the walk to Clapham; being out of doors clears my head of its fuzziness. The weather is mild for the time of year, almost spring-like, which is a welcome change from the bitter cold of the last couple of weeks.

Harriet greets me at the door, wishes me a happy New Year, and then resumes her seat on the couch alongside another young lady whose face looks familiar. She notices my puzzled expression and says, "Don't you remember Marie-Thérèse, Aunt Bessie?"

Of course! It's Harriet's friend from the orphanage. But what on earth is she doing here at the Cartwrights', dressed like a fashionable young lady rather than a sister of the Roman Catholic faith?

I tell her it's a pleasure to see her again and that she's looking well, although I almost didn't recognise her. She answers me politely, but looks embarrassed. Celia, who's sitting in her window seat darning a stocking, looks up, smiles and says, "Such a pretty young lady, isn't she?"

"She is indeed," I say, waiting in vain for some explanation. Robert is nowhere to be seen and Patty's in the kitchen, making tea. I excuse myself and escape to the kitchen; Patty will surely know the reason for Marie-Thérèse's surprising presence.

"She's left the order," Patty says. "The young man, Alec, egged on by Harriet of course, persuaded her to abscond. Robert is furious. He says Harriet had no right to interfere."

"But what's she going to do? She can't stay here, can she?"

"No, certainly not. Robert would never agree to it. But, apparently, Alec is going to take care of her. It turns out that he's not really Harriet's friend at all – it's Marie-Thérèse he's known since childhood. When Harriet was planning her own 'escape', as she calls it, Marie-Thérèse wrote to this young man and asked him to help her friend.

In turn, Harriet persuaded Alec to urge Marie-Thérèse also to leave the convent. He was only too happy to oblige. She'd been much too afraid and timid to make any such move of her own accord, but Harriet convinced her that there was a life outside the convent walls. I do feel sorry for her, Bessie. Her parents died when she was just a baby, and she was brought to London and raised by a French aunt. When the aunt became ill, her dying wish was that her niece should enter the convent. Marie-Thérèse was just twelve when she was taken in by the nuns – she had no other choice. Alec was keen to keep up their friendship and wrote to her every week until the Mother Superior began to suspect a secret liaison and confiscated his letters.

"Robert is also angry with Harriet for lying about her friendship with Alec. You'll remember that she told us she met him by chance when she was running away, but of course that wasn't true. He'd been waiting outside the orphanage the night she escaped and helped her scale the wall. Just imagine! It's like a tale in one of your storybooks, Bessie! Fortunately, Marie-Thérèse didn't face any such danger; she was simply able to walk out through the gates. Honestly, Harriet's such a headstrong girl that I'm beginning to wonder if we did the right thing in letting her live with us. Robert wants to take Marie-Thérèse back to the convent and negotiate her separation with the nuns. She's taken no vows, so they have no right to stop her from leaving, but Robert wants the thing done properly. The poor girl is terrified of returning. I think she may also have suffered some abuse when she was younger – she's so fearful of facing her superiors now that she's finally defied their authority."

"Where is Robert now, Patty?"

"He's gone to the school. He had a bit of work to do before the boys return next week. He shouldn't be working on a Sunday – he knows that – but he said he'd make a confession at church this evening."

"And Michael's not here?"

"No, his uncle wasn't able to bring him. I'm sorry you won't see him this afternoon, Bessie."

"That's all right. Listen, Patty. Why don't you suggest that Harriet accompany Marie-Thérèse back to wherever she's staying before Robert comes home. It's devious, I know, but the girl will be traumatised if Robert takes her back to the convent and she has to face the Mother Superior, who's bound to be angry with her for running away."

"Yes, you're right. Marie-Thérèse is staying with Alec's family. She came this afternoon because she wanted to thank Harriet for her friendship. She gave her a gift of a wooden crucifix, which I thought was a kind gesture and shows that she's not forgotten her faith. But it was a shock when she arrived because Harriet hadn't told us anything about her leaving the convent. It would probably have been better if it had been kept a secret, but once Marie-Thérèse showed up on our doorstep, Harriet had to tell us what had happened. Anyway, I'll do as you say and tell them both to leave before Robert returns. Marie-Thérèse knows the way back to Alec's house. He brought her here, but wouldn't come in. She told him she'd return by five o'clock."

"What's he like?"

"He seems a pleasant young man. A bit shabbily dressed and clearly London born and bred, but he spoke kindly and seemed trustworthy. He had the most extraordinary eyes from what I could see under the peak of his cap. They were the most beautiful shade of green."

"Is that right? The young man who helped me carry the carpetbag of clothes for Harriet had exquisite green eyes too, and he knew your street like the back of his hand."

"Hmm… it might have been Alec. He knew our address from their correspondence and I know Harriet's met him on more than one occasion."

"Well, I thought he was a nice lad. What did Robert think of him?"

"I don't know. He didn't say. He was too upset with Harriet. He didn't want to make a scene in front of company, so asked her to step outside with him. She admitted lying and apologised, saying she was only trying to help her friend. I did try to reason with him about taking Marie-Thérèse back to the convent – after all, it's none of our business really and she's Alec's responsibility now. Harriet may have encouraged her, but she was just a willing accomplice who happens to be staying with us. But Robert wasn't in any mood to listen."

"Does he not believe that Marie-Thérèse may also have been ill-treated when she was younger?"

"I think his idea of ill-treatment differs from ours, Bessie. He doesn't regard a slap on the hand with a ruler or a pinch on the upper arm to be harsh, just a means of discipline. I'm not saying that's all that the girl suffered, but he thinks that Harriet exaggerated her own punishments and may have made Marie-Thérèse believe she was maltreated too. He sees both the orphanage and the convent as sanctuaries that protect the young from greater suffering on the streets of London or in the workhouse. Don't forget, he's a Roman Catholic so we have to be careful what we say in front of him. He takes his faith seriously, even though he's married to a Protestant whose faith has lapsed quite a bit since moving to London.

"Anyway, let me go and tell Harriet and Marie-Thérèse to leave right away, as Robert said he'd be back by tea-time."

I remain in the kitchen while Patty talks to Harriet. I hate deceiving Robert, but my heart goes out to Marie-Thérèse. She's such a shy, softly spoken young woman that I'm sure the older sisters singled her out for intimidation. But if the alternative for an unskilled, kinless girl of twelve was the workhouse, then the convent was clearly the right choice.

Upon his return, Robert questions Harriet's absence and is cross when Patty explains that she's accompanying Marie-Thérèse back to Alec's family home.

"And where might that be?" he asks.

"I think she said Brixton," Patty says. "Not more than half an hour's walk away, but Marie-Thérèse didn't want to go alone."

"But Harriet has to come back alone, I presume?"

"Well, yes. But you know Harriet. She's not afraid of anything. Life is a constant adventure for her."

"Am I correct in understanding that the boy's family have willingly taken Sister Marie-Thérèse to live under their roof? Are they Roman Catholic themselves?"

"I don't know their religion, but it does seem as if they've welcomed her into their family, just as we've welcomed Harriet into ours. And don't continue to call her 'Sister', Robert. She's left the convent – it was her ardent wish to do so. It's regrettable that she didn't speak about it first with her superiors, but she's still so young. In fact, they're all young – Harriet, Marie-Thérèse, Alec. Don't be too harsh on them, Robert. You were young once and I'm sure you acted impulsively and made rash decisions too."

"I don't think I did, Patty. I think I was always the level-headed one. Though marrying you was pretty rash, wouldn't you say?"

Robert is now smiling at his wife. I think he'll forgive

Harriet once he's given her a lecture or two. He tells us later that he intends to make a donation to the convent's chapel as restitution for the time Marie-Thérèse spent in the sisters' care. Patty frowns; she doesn't think it necessary, but she says nothing. Robert is honourable in every sense of the word, but his faith appears to give him as much disquiet as comfort. He's not responsible for Marie-Thérèse's actions, but he won't rest easy until he's confessed his knowledge of her flight from the convent and taken steps to counter what he believes is an errant act – in no small way due to Harriet's wayward influence.

"Robert and I will never be rich," Patty says to me afterwards. "Just as well, I suppose. What was it Jesus said? 'It is easier for a camel to go through the eye of a needle than for someone who is rich to enter the kingdom of heaven'. Well, at least I'm able to take comfort in the knowledge that Robert and I are assured of our places in paradise!"

Last week I wrote a letter to Mrs Radford to let her know how Harriet was getting on and to thank her for her concern regarding the girl's welfare. To my surprise, she wrote back to me, asking if I'd like to take tea with her this Sunday. Of course, I've accepted her invitation, but am curious to know what prompted it.

I'm a bit more used to public transport now, so on Sunday afternoon I board a motorbus that takes me to Hammersmith and from there I manage to reach Greyhound Road, after asking a policeman for directions. Mrs Radford answers the door and invites me in. She tells me her daughter Rosamund is spending the day with her cousins, so we'll be alone.

"Let's go into the kitchen," she says. "It's warmer in there. I've had the range fire going all day. Roy is due back tomorrow and I've been baking non-stop. He does so enjoy home-cooked food after months away at sea. Pity he couldn't have been here for Christmas, but the weather was bad and his ship had to change course. Rosamund was terribly disappointed. He always brings her little keepsakes from his travels and it would have been nice if he could have given them to her on Christmas Day. Never mind, he should be here tomorrow, all being well. Sit yourself down at the table, Miss Hardwicke and I'll make a pot of tea."

She places a freshly-baked pound cake on the table and cuts me a generous slice. After pouring the tea, she says she'd like to tell me exactly what happened on the day of the fire at the Turnbulls' house.

"I've have been having nightmares about that day," she says. "I can't imagine how poor Harriet is managing to sleep at night after what she witnessed. Let me explain to you what happened."

"Are you saying the fire wasn't a result of a candle accidentally being knocked over?" I ask anxiously.

"Well, no one can be sure, but in my opinion, it wasn't an accident. Let me start from the beginning. That evening – it was late, about ten o'clock – Harriet came knocking at my door in a terrible state. She said her mother was unconscious and would I come over to see if I could resuscitate her. She'd tried herself but without success. When I asked her where her father was, she said he was out drinking and hadn't yet come home. Michael, she said, was asleep in his bed.

"Of course, I went there right away and I made an attempt to revive her dear mother, but I could tell it was too late. She had already passed away and looked more at peace than in all the years I've known her. Harriet was weeping uncontrollably, so I suggested we kneel down and say a prayer for her mother's safe passage to heaven where she would rest in eternal peace. No sooner had we done so than we heard a terrible hullabaloo coming from downstairs. Norman Turnbull had returned from the pub. I went down to speak with him – I needed to tell him what had happened – but he just wouldn't hear me out. He was determined to take out his anger on the girl, saying he knew she would kill her mother one day. Whether his fury was the result of grief or simply drunkenness, I don't know. I felt I had to get Harriet out of the house before he injured her physically. She'd gone to the room she shared with Michael, who was now awake but still unaware that his mother had died. I told them both to come with me quickly. The father was now in the bedroom shaking his dead wife and screaming that it was all Harriet's doing. It was a terrible scene to witness.

"So I brought Harriet and Michael over here and made them both some hot milk. Harriet had calmed down a bit, but Michael was starting to sob hysterically. He asked if he could see his mother's body, but of course that wasn't possible with a madman in the house. I said I'd try to take him to see her the next day, but that they'd both be spending the night with me. The noise of Michael's crying had awoken Rosamund, so I asked her to take her friends upstairs and make them comfortable in her room. She would be sleeping with me that night. Before turning in myself, I went to draw the curtains in the front room and that's when I saw a strange light coming from next door. I could hardly believe my eyes – the Turnbulls' house was ablaze! Some neighbours had already seen the flames and had run to fetch the fire brigade, but they arrived too late to save Norman Turnbull's life. He died in the fire.

"The police were soon on the scene and I should have explained exactly what had occurred, but it seemed easier to let everyone think that one of the parents had accidentally knocked a candle over and that *both* had lost their lives in the fire. My own belief is that Norman started it deliberately, intending to kill himself *and* the children. I'd heard him say, in his drunken state, that now that his wife had perished, they would all perish – or words to that effect. As far as I know, he wasn't aware that I'd brought Harriet and Michael over here. But, to protect the children, I didn't want my suspicion to become common knowledge. Such an act of evil on the part of their father would surely hang over their heads for the rest of their lives. How could they – the boy especially – live with the knowledge that their father intended to kill his own flesh and blood? So I insisted that he must have accidentally knocked over a candle. And, who knows, that may have been the truth.

"I told Harriet she should stick to the story that she and her brother were at my house that night and not speak of their mother's earlier death – it would raise too many questions. I'm certain no one saw me leave the house with the children, as we always used the back way. And it wasn't unusual for them to come over here when their mother had taken a heavy dose of laudanum and wouldn't be needing anything for several hours. But now I question whether my actions that night were the right ones. I felt the need to tell the truth to someone, and the only person I could think of was your good self, especially after the kind letter you wrote to me. I'm sorry to make you party to my own deceptive role in this sad affair."

"Well," I say, finally. "Whichever way you look at it, it *is* a sad affair. And what you've told me today doesn't change that fact. On the whole, I think you did the right thing. It goes without saying that I'm all in favour of protecting the children – I can't believe that Harriet's father tried to blame her for her mother's death. I'm certainly glad Mrs Turnbull *didn't* die in the fire – no one deserves that kind of a death."

"It's not the first time Norman Turnbull has tried to blame his daughter for a tragedy. Has Harriet told you about her baby sister, Angela? The child's death wasn't through natural causes. Her father killed her by shaking her when she wouldn't stop crying. The baby was unwell with colic, according to Harriet, who saw what he did. She loved Angela and it broke her heart when she died. To make matters worse, he told his wife that Harriet had smothered her to death. Not that Agnes Turnbull believed him of course. It's a terrible thing to say, but if you ask me, with Agnes now deceased, it's a blessing he's gone too. He would have made the children's lives a misery."

"Poor Harriet. What a lot of sadness she's suffered in her short life. I do appreciate your telling me all of this, Mrs Radford. I won't breathe a word to anyone. We'll let everyone continue to believe that it was an accident, that a knocked-over candle started the fire. As you say, that may indeed have been the case, though obviously it wasn't the mother's fault. But do the children believe that the fire wasn't caused deliberately?"

"Well, I'm sure Harriet has her doubts, but I don't believe Michael suspects foul play. It's better than way. He heard his father raging in the bedroom, but he was barely awake when Harriet and I got him out of bed and brought him over here. And to be honest, his father was so often drunk and out of control that the uproar wouldn't have seemed unusual to him. Harriet told him not to tell the police or anyone else that their mother had died before the fire started, or she might be blamed. He always listens to his sister and will never betray her. I'm so glad you've taken him under your wing, Miss Hardwicke. He's a vulnerable boy and it'll be a while before he can recover from the effects of his father's neglect."

"I'm happy to help Michael in any way I can. But I

think now that he knows his sister is safe and living close to his school, he's well on the way to recovering from the trauma, though it's going to be a slow process. I'll write to you again, Mrs Radford, when I have more news. I think Harriet also intends to write to you."

"I did receive a letter from her, though she didn't tell me much, just that she liked where she was staying and was learning to use a sewing machine. I truly hope she can put the events of the last few months behind her and start afresh. She's still young, so I don't think she'll be scarred for life by what has happened, though she'll certainly never forget the horrors of that night. Yes, I'd appreciate it if you'd let me know from time to time how both children are getting on. Rosamund misses them terribly and still hasn't forgiven me for not letting them stay with us for longer."

"Of course, Mrs Radford. We'll stay in touch. Thank you for inviting me here today."

"No, thank *you*, Miss Hardwicke. It's a weight off my mind, I can tell you, to have spoken the truth about what happened on that fateful night."

25

It's the first of April and I think we've seen the last of the rain showers that persisted throughout March. Folk are saying it's now spring, but it still feels decidedly chilly and the sun has yet to make an appearance, so it's possible we're being taken for April fools. Since I have an hour to myself – Mrs Grist is taking a nap – I'll try to record all that has happened in the last couple of months. For once, there's mostly good news all round.

Mathilda had her baby on the 20th of March – a beautiful, healthy boy. She and Ronald have named him Geoffrey Lionel. His grandfather is over the moon. Surprisingly, Harriet decided not to accept the post of nanny and suggested that Marie-Thérèse be considered for the position instead. Although there was initially some doubt as to her suitability, everyone now agrees that she's perfect for the job, given her gentle character and modest behaviour. She began working with the family three weeks ago. She and Alec are engaged to be married, but will not tie the knot until Alec finishes his blacksmithing apprenticeship, which won't be for another two years.

Harriet, it now appears, is more skilled in dressmaking than anyone could have imagined. Celia said she'd seen it all along, but Harriet needed to be convinced that her talents would be rewarding in a financial sense. Ever the one to take initiative, she wrote to her uncle and asked him to buy her the latest model of sewing machine, so as not to have to use Celia's, which admittedly is quite ancient. With a new machine, she claimed, she could make twice as many garments to sell at the weekly market, and take in more alteration work. She guessed that her uncle would agree, if only to lessen his guilt about abandoning her. She was right; a week later, a brand-new Singer machine arrived at the Cartwrights'. Harriet is now working all hours of the day and night in the bedroom she shares with Celia.

Patty and Robert are resigned to Harriet's continued presence in the house; she asked them if she could stay indefinitely and they didn't object. Celia, of course, is delighted. Now that Harriet has a vocation and a sense of stability, Patty says, she's less impulsive and secretive. When she's not busy dressmaking or out buying cloth, she assists in the kitchen and does the grocery shopping, which helps Patty enormously. And her contribution to the weekly housekeeping, however modest, is much appreciated. The rest of her earnings go straight into her piggybank, which is filling up quickly. Her savings, she says, will help support Michael's further education, should that be necessary. Thankfully, Michael is now an excellent student and has one or two good friends at school, but is still more than happy to spend Sunday afternoons with his sister at Patty and Robert's.

In the months ahead, Harriet's assistance in the Cartwright household will become even more vital. Patty astonished us all by announcing that, at the age of thirty-nine, she's expecting a baby! This news was greeted at first with disbelief, but then with great joy. No one could be more shocked than Patty herself, as she was convinced that she was unable to conceive a child. Robert, who'd always insisted that he didn't want children, is both ecstatic and fretful. He insists that Patty needs constant rest and won't let her lift a finger when he's there to keep an eye on her. She's not used to such pampering and breathes a sigh of relief when he leaves for work in the mornings. Her pregnancy certainly wasn't planned, but it's fortunate that Harriet will be under the same roof when the baby is born. Her experience in looking after her baby sister Angela will hold her in good stead to care for Patty's newborn when he or she arrives in September.

Edie came to my church one Sunday morning in February and we walked to the park together afterwards. She admitted that she's been keeping up a correspondence with Phillip, but insisted that he was not the reason for her move to London. Her passion, she said, lay with paediatric nursing, and she's been given the opportunity to finish her training at the Great Ormond Street Hospital, an important centre for educating nurses in children's healthcare. So for the moment she's concentrating on her studies and making friends with those nurses who, like her, support the Suffragettes and their dedication to women's rights.

Edie's desire to become a paediatric nurse was news to me; Walter hasn't mentioned it in any of his letters. If fact, he's barely mentioned his former sweetheart at all, except to say that he now sees their break-up as being inevitable, and is surprised that it didn't happen sooner. Edie told me that even though her heart still aches for Walter, she doesn't regret that they went their separate ways. She always had the feeling that their paths would diverge at some point. I still feel sad when I think of their parting company, but am glad both of them now accept that it was for the best.

I congratulated Edie on her career choice, told her that I was certain she would do well, and asked her if she'd seen Phillip in person since coming to London. This was quite an impertinent question, but I'm ashamed to say that curiosity got the better of me. She said they had taken tea together a couple of times, but denied having any designs on him. "You know perfectly well, Aunt Bessie," she said, "that he's not likely to consider a future with someone from a farming family. It's really just a friendship, nothing more." I didn't contradict her, but I think she may be underestimating her ability to attract men of all social classes, and may yet find herself in a courtship with Mr Phillip Grist.

She has become more keenly involved with the Suffragettes since coming to London, and spoke animatedly about their goals. I do hope she manages to stay out of trouble. Its supporters boycotted the national census earlier this month; they gave false information and didn't stay home as requested. The satirical magazine *Punch* joked, 'The suffragettes have definitely taken leave of their census', which made Mrs Grist smile. The women are also threatening to disrupt the coronation this summer, which will be a shameful thing to do and unlikely to help them in their cause.

I'm happy to report that my dear nephew is now stepping out with another lovely young lady. Blanche is the middle daughter of the late Mr Henry Goode, whom Walter has known all his life. In fact, he and Blanche were sweet on each other for a while before Edie captured his heart. Walter wrote to me saying that he will have to tread carefully; Blanche's heart was broken when he transferred his affections to Edie – understandably so – and he doesn't want her to think he's returning to her on the rebound. He said he's explained to her that his courtship with Edie was nothing more than a whirlwind romance, and he now realises that they could not have made each other happy in the long term. Blanche is still doubtful about Walter's intentions, but they're becoming closer by the day. Apparently, he's been helping Mrs Goode with some of the tasks her husband used to do, such as chopping wood and digging hard ground in the vegetable garden. And since his cousin Joseph is engaged to the eldest Goode daughter, Daisy, the four of them often take walks together and eat their meals under the same roof.

I remember Blanche quite well – she's a pretty, petite girl, with striking red hair. All the sisters are identical; it's always been difficult for me to tell them apart. Blanche has a sweet, obliging temperament and will one day make a man very happy. I have no objection whatsoever to that man being my Walter. If they should marry – though I'm getting ahead of myself here – I wonder how she'll react to being Mrs Blanche Blanch. I'm sure Mrs Grist would have something to say about that! When I mentioned this to Mathilda, she said that perhaps Blanche could keep her maiden name; apparently choosing to do so is not unknown in America. She saw how shocked I was by such an idea and told me not to worry, she was only joking. It would be many more years, she said, before such a feminist notion became commonplace in America, let alone England.

Now I must come to the most surprising news of all – at least as far as I'm concerned. A great change is soon to occur in my life. I'm going to be married to Mr Lionel Fielding! I still cannot quite believe it – I keep thinking it must be one of my fanciful dreams and I have to pinch myself to make sure I'm awake. Ever since that kiss on the stroke of midnight at the start of the New Year, he's become more intimate with me each time we've met. Well, to my shame, the more affectionate he became, the more I resisted his embraces. Finally, out of the blue, he asked me if I would become his wife. He didn't get down on bended knee or anything like that; on the contrary, he was quite matter of fact and even confessed that he had convinced himself that I would refuse his hand in marriage, but was determined to make the offer anyway. He said he's conscious of the gap in our ages – he's fifty-five, I'm thirty-nine – but he personally doesn't see that as a problem. Perhaps though, he added, it's the reason why I recoil each time he touches me.

Well, as you can imagine, I had quite a bit of explaining to do, but firstly I told him that I would be happy and honoured to become his wife. I confessed that I had not been the object of any man's affections since my courtship with Arthur, and it was therefore difficult for me to show my feelings in a physical way. And I honestly thought that he would never ask me to marry him, given our social differences, and I didn't want to become his 'bit on the side'. He looked quite shocked when I told him that, but said he understood. I insisted that the age gap didn't matter to me one little bit, but that it might take some time for me to become fully relaxed with him physically. I admitted that I had never lain with a man in my life, not even Arthur – we were planning to wait until we were married – so he might find I had some inadequacies in that department. I was so embarrassed to tell him such a thing, but it needed to be said. The dear man put his arm around me and smiled; he said we'd take that one step at a time and he would never force me to do anything I wasn't comfortable with.

Of course I said yes. I didn't have to think twice. I still can't quite believe that Lionel really wants to make me his wife. And the thing that makes me even happier – if that is actually possible – is that he proposes we move out of London and live in a small town on the Devonshire coast. He says a friend of his – a fellow pharmacist with whom he studied – is retiring due to ill health and has suggested that he replace him. "It'll be a slower pace of life," Lionel said, "but I think that will suit you, Bessie. Am I right?" He knows me so well already!

He's sure I will like the town, which is situated close to the seashore. When I told him I've yet to see the sea for the first time, he looked at me in disbelief. "Then you'll most certainly fall in love with it," he said. "But what about Mathilda and the new baby?" I asked him. "Do you really want to be so far from them?" He confessed that he would miss them terribly, but said that since Ronald now has a motorcar, they could easily come to Devon on holiday. And from time to time, he said, we could go to London on the train and stay in a fancy hotel. Now it was my turn to look at him in disbelief – the idea that I, Bessie Hardwicke, could ever be a guest at a fancy hotel was one that I struggled to take seriously.

Lionel spoke about his plan to sell his London house and buy a small thatched cottage. He noticed the smile disappear from my face and asked me what was the matter. I told him that I couldn't look at a thatch without recalling the tragedy of Arthur's death. He apologised and said he completely understood my abhorrence of thatches and promised that we'd find a cottage with a modern tiled roof. "Are you sure you haven't set your heart on a thatch?" I asked him. "Not at all," he said. "Come to think of it, thatched roofs need a lot of maintenance and are known to be a fire hazard. That's the last thing we want, especially after the Turnbull disaster. I promise you, Bessie, there won't be a thatch within a mile of where we live."

It's all a bit too much to take in. And, coward that I am, my first concern was how to tell Mrs Grist not only that I would be leaving her, but also that I planned to marry her friend, Lionel Fielding. Lionel offered to tell her himself, but I decided to face up to my fears and show some courage for once in my life. I was visibly shaking when I told her, and couldn't look her in the eye. She was so surprised, she said nothing for a few moments, but then feigned indifference and said that what I did with my life was no concern of hers. She claimed that she'd been planning to dismiss me anyway since her recently widowed cousin-in-law would be coming to live with her in a few months' time. A short while later, she must have recalled the look of hurt on my face and regretted her curtness. She then wished me future happiness, adding that Lionel was an honest man and she was sure I would make him a good wife. Of course, after I'd thanked her, she had to have the last word. She said, "I just hope you know what you're getting yourself into, Elizabeth!" But the remark was followed by a chuckle, so I don't think it was meant to be unkind.

I've told Walter my news and he is delighted. How could I ever have thought that he might begrudge me a life of my own? I can't wait to introduce him to Lionel – I'm sure they will get along splendidly. We're planning a small wedding in London with the minimum of fuss and just a few guests. Walter will be there, of course, as will Patty, Robert and Celia. Walter has asked me if I will allow him to give me away. As if I'd refuse! I'm sure there aren't many brides who are given away by their nephews, but I can't think of a better man than Walter to fill that role. Once the wedding is over, Lionel suggests spending a few days in my village, where he can meet my two brothers and their families, and familiarise himself with the place that will always be close to my heart. I feel a bit anxious about introducing him to my relatives, Edward especially, but thankfully, Walter will be there to ease the awkward moments.

And what about dear Arthur, have I stopped loving him? No, I'll always love my handsome young thatcher, but I'll no longer let the grief that's plagued me for the last two decades influence the way I live my life. Who knows, had we been able to make a life together, the reality might not have turned out to be the blissful existence that I've yearned for each night since his tragic death. Alfred Lord Tennyson expresses that sentiment perfectly:

> 'And is it that the haze of grief
> Makes former gladness loom so great?
> The lowness of the present state,
> That sets the past in this relief?
>
> Or that the past will always win
> A glory from its being far;
> And orb into the perfect star
> We saw not, when we moved therein?'

About the Author

Susan E Jones grew up in Stroud in Gloucestershire, but chose Penzance in Cornwall as her home when she returned to the UK after years of living and working abroad. She was then in a position to devote more of her free time to writing, which had long been her ambition. Long daily walks along the South West Coastal Path continue to give her both a sense of wellbeing and an opportunity to think about ideas for her next work of fiction.

After the Rain is Susan's first purely fictional novel and was inspired by the contents of her great-great aunt's postcard album. Many of the postcards are from her aunt's nephew, with whom she was evidently close, and they captured Susan's imagination. They gave her a fascinating glimpse into life in the early 1900s – a period of relative calm before years of calamitous change.

www.blossomspringpublishing.com

Printed in Great Britain
by Amazon

16991805R00171